Broken by Sin

Samantha Barrett

memento mori

Author Note

This book contains violence, explicit sexual acts, and language that may offend. Kidnapping and many other triggers such as torture, death and gruesome scenes.

If those are triggers for you then I recommend closing this book and moving on to another amazing read.

But, if you are down with the get down and want to get fucked hard and have your heart shattered and ripped out of your fucking chest then this is the book for you, babes.

Welcome to the *Next Generation* of Murdochs that fuck harder and play dirtier than the OG's.

Memento Mori

*(Latin for 'remember that you [have to] die') is **an artistic or symbolic trope acting as a reminder of the inevitability of death.***

Who Are They?

When the card is dropped, you are marked.
There is no escaping *them*, they come for their prey and will
hunt until your blood soaks the ground beneath your cold,
lifeless body. They are the new generation and they have
something to prove. They are hungry to show the OG's that
they are ready to lead, except, the princess was tired of waiting
to be seen. She showed them all that she alone can bring a
swift death to her enemies like no other.

The king of clubs belongs to the heir.
The princess owns the queen of hearts.
Jack of spades represents the coming Chaos.
Ace of diamonds is for the Havoc.

Chapter One

CHANEL

2 years ago...

I've never been the type to want to lay around, cuddle and watch a movie, while a guy twirls my hair between his fingers and randomly kisses my head every so often, but I've become that girl. I don't know how it happened or when it even started. Now I'm here and I don't hate it like I thought I would. Connor places a kiss on the top of my head and tightens his arm around my shoulders drawing me closer into his side, and like a pathetic, love-sick dog, I melt into him and soak up his warmth.

"How long before you have to leave?" he asks. I deflate slightly, hating that I have to sneak around but the twins and Royal would give me shit if they knew I was seeing someone. Connor Ryker isn't just someone though... he's more than that.

"I have twenty minutes." Connor has no idea who I really

am. He thinks I'm just a normal college student who has three best friends that are guys. He's never pushed me for information or even pried into my life, he's happy with the little things I tell him about myself, even though most of them are lies. He swivels on the sofa, forcing me to move so I can face him as he looks at me. His blue eyes shine with longing and I fight a groan from breaking free. Most college guys last a minute or two, but not Connor. He wouldn't know what a quickie was if it punched him in the dick. "Stop looking at me like that!"

A sexy smirk pulls at the corners of his mouth. He darts his tongue out to moisten his lips and I'm immediately captivated by the sight, knowing exactly what that tongue can do and how it can bring me to such a high that I feel like I am going to pass out. God, the memory of how he ate me out in the janitor's closet this morning between classes, has me squirming in my seat. The cunning look in his eyes tells me he knows exactly what I am thinking about.

He reaches out and glides the tips of his fingers down the exposed skin on my chest, sending a shiver down my spine. "I'm confident I could get you to change your mind and blow off your friends and spend the night with me." My breaths come in short pants as he circles my nipple through my tank top. I push my chest out, needing him to touch me. "I'm taking that as a yes?"

Words fail me, I smack his hand out of the way and launch myself at him, claiming his mouth with a kiss that's filled with need. He grips the sides of my thighs and shifts us slightly so I can straddle him. I can feel how hard he is already, groaning into his mouth as I grind down against him, relishing in the hiss that escapes him. I've never felt more powerful in my life until I had Connor beneath me, chanting my name as he came inside me. Knowing I brought him to such a mind-shattering release, filled me with a sense of power I never knew I had.

He breaks the kiss and yanks my top down, then laps at my nipples through the lace of my bra, forcing me to throw my head back and moan. "I love these fucking tits, Sin." I grind down harder on him, loving the way he growls his approval. Connor started calling me Sin when we met six months ago. He says the name fits because I am sinfully dreadful to any man trying to conceal a boner at the sight of me.

He yanks the cup of my bra down and bites my nipple, drawing a sharp cry from me. "Connor." He releases my nipple with a wet pop and stares up at me with a smirk.

"Yeah, Sin?" I groan. I need him inside me so fucking badly but I can't ditch Royal and the twins tonight. Havoc set his mark, dropped his card and we need to be there to fulfill his oath of ending the mayor's nephew.

"I have to go—" Before I can finish speaking, my cell phone rings. I slam my eyes closed and pray for mercy, because my pussy is throbbing and I know it won't be getting a release tonight. I climb off Connor and fix my top, as I grab my phone from the side table in the living room of Connor's apartment—he lives off campus.

I answer the call and grab my backpack off the ground, then motion to Connor that I'm going to the bathroom. He nods begrudgingly and tries to adjust his cock in his jeans. "Yeah?" I answer as I exit the room.

"Where are you?" Royal snaps.

"On my way. I got held up."

"Doing what?" I can hear the skepticism in his voice. I have been MIA a lot lately and I know the three of them have noticed, but I'm just not ready to tell them about Connor.

"I had shit to do. I'll be there in ten minutes." I end the call not wanting to hear more of his shit. I quickly use the restroom, grab my gun from my pack and shove it into the waistband of my jeans, then head back out to the living room but freeze when I hear Connor mention my name, my real fucking name! Royal, Havoc, Chaos and I have never used our actual last names. No one knows we are Murdochs or that I am a Murelo. As far as anyone here knows, I am Chanel Ricci.

"I can't, Quintin." I peek around the bookcase to see Connor pacing the length of the living room with his phone pressed against his ear. "Rico Vargas is here, he's the target, not Chanel Murelo." I tense and slink back flush against the wall as Connor darts his gaze toward the hallway making sure I'm still in the bathroom. My heart cracks inside my chest, I feel tears begin to prick the backs of my eyes. I told him three weeks ago that I loved him.

I let him in!

Anger rolls through me. I was a fucking fool.

"Q, I can't do that to her–" He stops speaking to hear whatever it is this Quintin is saying to him before he continues, "No, I agreed to go undercover to flip Emilio Vargas's son, not go after Chanel Murelo. How did you even know she was here?"

Pain explodes inside me—he's a fucking cop! I push off the wall and round the corner, at the sight of me Connor freezes. His face pales, he ends the call and tosses his phone on the sofa as he rounds it to come to me. I shake my head, urging him to stop but he ignores it so I pull my gun from my jeans and point it at him. He stills at the sight. I stare at him trying to figure out how I missed the signs of him being a cop.

"Sin–"

"Don't fucking call me that!" I scream. He recoils a step and nods. "Let me explain."

"Explain what, Connor? How you're a fucking cop?" He flinches.

"I'm not a cop."

I push all the pain that rages inside me away, feeling my heart hardening and it's all his fault. He forced me to lower the walls I had built around my heart and let him in. He made me believe that he actually cared about me, not who I am or where I came from. I thought he just saw me!

"I heard you on the phone–"

"I'm not a cop, Chanel, I'm FBI." Now I stagger back a step, shaking my head trying to deny what he is saying. He stands tall and unyielding, giving me time to wrap my head around this shit.

"You're a fucking fed?" I scream as I push the barrel of my gun into the center of his chest. He doesn't try to fight back, he just stands here in front of me with a remorseful look on his face. "Answer me!"

"Yes. I'm an undercover agent for the FBI. I was sent here to flip Rico Vargas." He doesn't look like a fed—blond hair, blue eyes and a killer smile. He gives off surfer vibes, kind of like how Paul Walker did.

"You were using me," I force out past the lump in my throat. At the watery tone of my voice, he pushes my arm away and steps into me cupping my face between his hands and tilting my head so I'm forced to look up at him. Pain radiates inside me.

"I never used you, Chanel. I swear to fucking God. I didn't even know who you were when we first met."

"When did you find out?" His brows draw in as guilty looks shadows his features. "When?" I snarl.

"Six weeks ago." A distraught scoff comes from me. He knew who I was when I told him I loved him. "Chanel, I love you–"

"Fuck you!" I scream as I tear out of his hold and head for the door. He grabs my arm and yanks me back. I spin around and knee him right in the dick. He drops to his knees before me, groaning in pain. I push my gun into the center of his forehead, a shuddering breath leaves him as the first tear falls from my eye. I have never felt pain like this before. It feels like my chest is being ripped open and having acid poured directly into my wound.

"I love you."

I scoff. "You never loved me. You fucking used me and faked everything—"

"I wasn't faking shit!"

"No, I'm the one that wasn't faking!" I scream so fucking loud, I know his neighbors would have heard. "I let you in, I let you fucking inside me and gave you something I have never given anyone. I... loved you." Tears fall on their own accord now. I let them run unchecked down my face as I stare down at the man who fucking destroyed me.

"Chanel–"

I cut him off as my phone begins to ring again, "I never want to see you again–"

"I have a job to do here–"

"I don't give a fuck, Connor! You pack your shit tonight and leave. If I ever see you again, I will put a fucking bullet between your eyes. You know who I am and where I come from... you know who my family is. I don't make empty threats."

"Don't do this," he begs.

Looking down at him as tears begin to fill his blue eyes, breaks something inside me. I hate that I can see and hear it in his words that he really does love me. No matter how I feel about him, he and I could never be together because he's a fucking fed and I am the daughter of The Bloodhound.

"Leave and never come back," I say as I turn and leave. Gripping the door, I yank it open but his words have me freezing on the spot.

"What if I don't? What if I come back for *you*?" I don't

turn around as I answer him, deciding to tell him the truth, hoping he'll heed my warning.

"Then I'll have no choice but to kill the first person I ever fell in love with. Don't make me do that because they will find out you are a fed and I'll be buried in the hole next to you."

Chapter Two

CHANEL

Present...

It's been over a week since my dad busted me meeting up with Connor. He flew back to New York the next day without saying a word to me. I've been on edge for days wondering what the fuck Dad is going to do. I've ignored all Connor's calls and texts, not giving a fuck about meeting him to check in and go over the details of the raid from last week. Havoc and Royal know there is something wrong with me but I refuse to tell them. If they found out I was working with the feds to keep us and our parents out of prison, they would kill me. Connor showed me photos. I know he has proof of the shit not only we have done but our fathers as well.

I've been trying to figure out a way to get out from under Connor's thumb and just take out whoever the fuck it is that wants to lock us up, but killing a federal agent isn't as easy as people think it is. I had the chance to end all of this two years ago. I should have killed him the night I found out he was a fed but... I couldn't pull the fucking trigger! I open a new tab on the browser of my laptop and search Chance's name. He is still classed as missing. The FBI not airing to the world that they have the governor's remains is sketchy as fuck. I do something I know I shouldn't, I look Connor up on social media.

"Bastard," I growl. Of course, being a fed, he has no social media presence. I slam the lid of my laptop down and stand from my chair in my bedroom. I gaze out the window and the second I spot Erika laying on the lawn on a blanket with a book in her hands, I clench my hands into fists at my sides. How she can just lay there in the sun and read a fucking book like nothing else is going on infuriates me. The fucking bitch does nothing except suck Royal's dick.

My phone begins to vibrate in my pocket. I debate on leaving it to ring out but when I check the caller ID and see it's my dad, I answer.

"Dad?" I breathe out, feeling slightly uncertain and worried he may force me to rat myself out to the others. He has to know doing that would mean certain death for me.

"We need to talk." His tone is clipped and curt. He's never spoken to me like this before and I can't say I'm a fan of it.

"So, talk," I grit out.

"Don't fucking start, Chanel. Meet me at the pier in an hour."

My eyes widened in surprise. "You're in Miami?"

"Yes. One hour. Don't keep me waiting, Chanel." He ends the call. I stare at the blank screen of my phone for a solid minute before I manage to shake myself out of my stupor and rush into action. I quickly change into a pair of jeans and an off the shoulder tee that has tears throughout it. Tying my hair into a messy bun I deem myself ready without even checking my reflection in the mirror. I don't care for looks like most girls, shit, I don't even wear makeup or a dress. The day you catch me in a dress, heels and makeup is the day you know the world is about to end.

Rushing downstairs, I swipe a set of keys off the counter and head for the front door. I pull my sunglasses off my head and secure them on my face as I round the corner to one of the Chevy pickups Royal has here but slam to a halt at the site of Erika leaning against the truck.

"The fuck are you doing?" I grit out.

The little bitch just rolls her eyes and pulls the door open. "Royal texted me and said to go with you." I brush the feeling of dread pooling inside me at her words and climb in on the other side. I caress the steering wheel for a second before starting this big bitch. The sound of her engine purring and the way she roars to life has me smiling—driving this beast gives me big dick energy. I say nothing to Erika as I drive along the coastal roads with the windows down and music up loud. She takes my silence as me not liking her. I don't correct her because the truth is, I am a fucking nervous wreck.

Not only is my father here in Miami but apparently he's already with Royal and that scares me. I know my dad likes to think that because we are family that snitching can be forgiven. He is out of his mind. Royal doesn't give second chances. If he were to find out what I have done he would kill me, there is no doubt in my mind about that. I try to find comfort in the fact that I know Royal won't drag out my death, because we are family he will make it swift and painless. Pulling up near the pier, I find a spot and take a second to gather my thoughts. I grip the handle ready to climb out but Erika's words have me pausing.

"You hate me, I get it. But, I can also see there is something that is weighing on you. I don't claim to know you or anything like that, Chanel, but I want you to know that if there is ever a moment you need someone and can't talk to Royal, I am here. You have my word that nothing you tell me will go any further, I would never betray you by telling him." I peer over my shoulder at her, her eyes are filled with unease as she waits for me to snap at her like I always do.

"I don't hate you, Erika." Her eyes widen. "I envy you." Her jaw unhinges. I leave her sitting there as I climb out of the truck and head across to the pier where I can see my dad, Royal and Havoc standing at the end. The three of them stand there with dark sunglasses covering their eyes. Both my cousins wear dark jeans and black tees while my dad stands there in shorts and a tank. I take a deep breath and stuff my hands into my pockets, cracking my neck from side to side as I make my way down to them. I'm halfway there when Erika finally catches up to me.

"I got your back," she whispers before racing ahead, her sundress billowing around her as she launches herself at Royal. He looks like a menacing bastard standing there stoically but the moment Erika throws herself at him, a broad smile stretches across his face and he catches her with ease, burying his face in the crook of her neck. I never thought I would see the day a woman managed to snag his attention for longer than an hour, yet here he is in love with a woman who was meant to be the demise of our family.

The moment I stand before them, Havoc nods in greeting. Royal may not see that he is struggling without his twin, but I do. Havoc relies on Chaos so much, he can't function without his brother by his side—the same can't be said for Chaos. He thrives on his own, relishes in the spotlight that is cast on him. Out of the four of us, he is the one who has struggled the most with having to keep a low profile. Since we came to Miami, we have had to work harder to conceal our identities. Royal being the Don and me as his underboss has pushed us into the spotlight of the underworld. I ignore Royal as he continues to whisper what I'm sure are disgusting promises in Erika's ear and look at my dad.

Vincent Murelo aka The Bloodhound is a formidable force. He stands there with his head tilted down at me and his lips set in a firm line. Him being here without my mom is a sure sign that I'm not going to like what he has to say as my dad is never away from my mom unless he absolutely has to be.

"Sin." I tear my gaze from my dad to look at Royal, who now has a blushing Erika tucked into his side. I say nothing as I wait for him to say whatever is on his mind. "Why didn't you tell me?"

Dread churns inside me, I keep my gaze on my cousin and force myself to remain calm. "I didn't have a—"

"She didn't know how to ask you for time off." I cut a glance to my dad and frown. "I filled Royal and Havoc in," he says.

"About?" I query.

"About you coming on a job with me to help hone your skill set, plus I need to train you in the art of reading people and certain situations better." That was a cheap shot and he knows it but I remain silent. "It will help you better serve your cousin as his second. I assured him that you would be much better at your job after this mission." I grind my teeth. This mission he speaks of is bullshit. My dad has never taken me on jobs even when I begged and pleaded. If I'm reading this right, then the job he speaks of is just a cover story so he can take me with him to kill Connor.

"I think Sin is perfectly capable of running shit as is," Royal says in my defense.

"That may be but as my only daughter, I would like you to humor me, nephew, and allow me this chance to assure myself that my daughter is well equipped and ready to move into this life with ease," Dad tactfully adds.

"She was born for this shit," Havoc says. Hearing both my cousins come to my defense and knowing they have faith in me, bolsters my sense of belonging but it also has guilt gnawing inside me.

"Sin is a badass. She's the best at what she does, Uncle Vin. I know Chanel better than anyone and I am telling you now, you should trust her and her abilities because I trust her with my life." I have a first class ticket to hell. I'm going to burn for all eternity. I drop my gaze to my shoes, feeling like utter shit.

"Of course she is, she is her mother's daughter after all," Dad says with a hint of pride in his voice. "Give me this time with her and I swear to you that I will never interfere in your business again." I remain silent not knowing what to say. I fucking hate this shit. I have never lied to Royal and it sickens me that I have no choice but to follow Connor's orders or risk my family ending up behind bars.

"It's Sin's choice," Royal finally says after a moment. I slowly lift my gaze to his and inhale a deep breath. I know without my dad needing to say it, if I don't go with him and do whatever it is he wants me to, then he will rat me out.

"I'll continue to run things remotely for you until I get back. Havoc can step up and take over the day to day shit until then." Royal nods stiffly. I can see in his demeanor that he knows something is up, but he won't call me on it in front of everyone.

"Very well." A whoosh of air escapes me at his agreement. "I want to be updated daily. You have four weeks to sort this shit before we make a move on the Albanians and I need you by my side when that shit happens, Chanel." I nod my head eagerly.

"I swear I'll be there, I always have your back."

"As I do yours, never forget that," he says with such conviction.

"See you soon, Sin. I got a mark to take out and a body to disembowel," Havoc says casually. I shake my head, he talks about murder like we are discussing the weather.

"I got a meeting in the city. Erika and I will stay at the penthouse for the night and be back in the morning," Royal says to Havoc before turning back to me. He pulls away from Erika so he can pull me to him and wrap me in a hug. I sigh and return his embrace. "Whatever it is that is troubling you, I'm here Sin, always." His whispered words have me slamming my eyes closed and willing the guilt to remain inside me and not leak out in the form of tears.

"I swear, everything I am doing is for the family," I force out past the lump in my throat. He nods and pulls away, then he, Havoc and Erika walk away. I stand here staring after them feeling a divide forming between me and Royal. We have never been divided before and I fucking hate that this is happening to us because of my mistake.

"Give me the keys," Dad says. I hand him the truck keys without argument and follow after him silently. He says nothing as we climb in the truck and he heads in the opposite direction from our house.

"Where are we going?" I ask as we hit the interstate.

"Your boyfriend is based in Fort Lauderdale. We're going to scope his spot out and then we strike." My eyes widen, I push my sunglasses to the top of my head and stare at my dad. He's gripping the steering wheel in a vice-like grip.

"He isn't my boyfriend and you can't just fucking kill him, Dad, he's FBI–"

"Yes, I can!" he roars. I jerk back into my seat. My father has never raised his voice to me like this, not even when I have pissed him off or when I disobeyed him and ran off with Royal. "You are going to end this shit before this fucking family tries to end you."

"I didn't have a choice," I mutter weakly as I turn to stare out the window.

"You always have a choice, Chanel. You just chose wrong.

He is the enemy and you let him..." He clamps his mouth closed and growls.

I turn back to face my father and scowl at the judgmental asshole. "Let him what, Daddy? Let him fuck me? Touch me? Eat me out–"

"Enough!" he roars.

"It'll never be enough, because you already believe me to be guilty. I am doing this to protect the fucking family."

"Your uncle and Royal would deal with it. They know the feds are always after them—"

I snap, unable to deal with his judgment. "They aren't coming after them! Connor's helping me to save—"

"He's a fucking fed–"

"I lied! They didn't find Chance's body." He swings his gaze to me for a second and frowns.

"You said he had proof, Chanel." Sighing, I pull my phone from my pocket and bring up the picture that was emailed to me from Connor's boss and show my dad. The second he sees it, he swerves and quickly rights the car before he sideswipes the car beside us. "How the fuck did you get that?" I stare down at the still shot of my seven year old mother tied to her bed while her father lays atop her. Bile rises in my throat and I fight to keep it down. "Answer me!"

"Connor's boss sent it to me. I'm not doing this for Royal or anyone else, I'm doing this to protect mom."

"They have nothing on her," he grits out.

"They are trying to pin her father's death on her. Apparently Chance supplied the FBI with video footage of mom being... of her dad... of that shit happening and they are trying to pin his murder on her."

"They can't prove shit. Bishop made sure of that. The FBI having those videos means there is some corrupt fucker inside their network. That is child pornography, Chanel, they cannot do anything with that."

I swipe across to the next picture and hold my phone out for him to see. He curses beneath his breath. "A street camera, you must have missed when covering your tracks, caught a video of Mom killing Dominic Savatella when you went to Brazil. They may not be able to use the videos Chance the sick fuck sent them, but they sure as fuck can post a video of Mom killing the Brazilian Prime Minister."

"Fuck," he grits out as he starts to hit the steering wheel.

"Now you can stop judging me. Connor is trying to help me get her out of this shit. He said if I gave him Chance's body, he might be able to persuade his boss to let it go…"

Dad bows his head. "You can't give him Chance."

My hope dwindles. "Why?"

"Because we put him through a stump grinder and then took the pieces of him out to the ocean to use as chum. We need to find another way to get these videos from the feds."

"What the fuck do you think I have been doing?" I snap angrily.

"Call your boyfriend and set up a meet. He can either help us or I'm going to kill him and every other mother fucker he works with, until I find every fucking thing they have against your mother. I won't let any cunt threaten my wife. You're about to get your wish, Daughter." He turns to meet my stare.

"What wish?"

"You're about to see why they call me The Bloodhound. I won't stop until I'm sure Carlina is free. I'll never let another motherfucker hurt my wife. I'll kill every single one of them, starting with your boyfriend if he doesn't agree."

"Not my boyfriend," I grit out. I can't deny that I am fucking excited to see my father in action, I have waited my whole life to see this shit in person. I may never admit it out loud but I have always aspired to be like my dad. He's my hero. He hates that I aspire to be like him, he wanted a different life for me but he doesn't get to choose the path I take in life.

Chapter Three

KACEY

There is a fucking traitor in here and I am going to find out who the fuck it is and burn the son of a bitch alive!

All my life, all I have ever wanted was to be an agent just like my dad and his dad before him. Being an agent is like a rite of passage in my family. My parents thought Marcus would be the first of their sons to be an agent as he's the oldest, but that sorry excuse for a human turned to drugs and sold his soul to the devil for his next hit. I'm the middle child, so of course the expectation to follow in my father's footsteps fell to me. Ashley got a free pass because he's the baby of the family. He's a pro baseball player and a damn good fucking pitcher at that.

My parents forgot all about me once Ash turned pro. Mom manages him and Dad's his agent, so they travel every-where he does. It doesn't bother me though, I know Marcus's bullshit took a toll on them and I understand why they had to get away from me. I had no choice but to arrest my own brother when we did a raid on the stash houses a couple years back and found him there. He's still in prison serving out an eight year sentence with the possibility of parole next year.

"Yo, Vaughn." I spin away from my desk and look over at Bentley. The fucker grins and wags his brows, earning a glare from me.

"What the fuck do you want? I got work to do," I snap. Bentley may be my partner but the asshole thinks everything is a joke. He's got a girl and kid at home but he'd still rather work overtime—by work, I mean sit across from me and toss a tennis ball into the air.

"Do you see Leonie?"

"Who?"

He rolls his eyes and points to where Owen's office is at the other end. Unlike our boss, our desks are right out in the middle and when it's office hours this place is bustling and you never get a minute of peace.

"Leonie is from the head office. Court reckons Owen is getting a verbal ass beating from head office because he failed to file the paperwork for the Jones case and didn't procure a warrant before we busted in his door." Now he has my attention, the Jones raid he is referring to is the same raid I was on when I arrested Marcus.

"If he didn't have a warrant then that means..."

Ben shoots me a pitying look and nods. "None of the arrests are going to stick, the cases will be thrown out and all those fuckers will go free."

The pencil in my hand snaps as anger courses through me. They found pictures of children and scared teenage girls chained in the basement of that house that's why they busted in the door and made an arrest. They were to be used as mules to traffic narcotics across the border.

"Motherfucker!" I snarl.

"Calm down. Leonie is going to try make this shit stick but—"

"He didn't have a fucking warrant! There is no way a judge is going to accept some bullshit ass excuse. All that evidence was obtained illegally and will be fucking thrown out. We have nothing," I roar as I pound my fist down on my desk. Ben looks around the office but it's only us in the open space. The sound of shouting can be heard coming from Owen's office, the sound of his voice peaks my anger. I shove back from my desk, grab my gun from the drawer and storm out of there, ignoring Bentley's shouts to come back. If I stay there, I know without a doubt, I'll wind up punching my boss and I don't fancy being put in a cell next to my brother.

I peel out of the underground car park and speed in the direction of my apartment. I need to get home and work out my frustration on the boxing bag. If Owen's fuck-up means that I arrested my brother for nothing, then all of the shit I have gone through for the past year is for nothing. I already have my suspicions about who the fucking mole is, but this just confirms it. I knew Chanel coming into my life wasn't a coincidence. That day we raided the airfield and I saw her on the roof. I did everything I could to keep her concealed from the others but it was no use. Owen wanted her brought in and flipped. He threatened to put Boston in charge of handling that situation. One call to Quintin and I had that idea nixed. She may hate me and think I am a fucking piece of shit but the truth is, I am the only one in that office she can trust to do the right thing by her.

I was sick to my stomach when I saw the pictures Owen had sent her. I called Quintin—he is the big boss of this operation and Owen answers to him—but even he said it was a necessary evil to use that still shot of her mother to flip her. We are no better than these thugs we take off the streets. Carlina Murelo was only seven or eight in that video and the fact that Owen and Q both refused to tell me who it came from, I knew then, they had received the clip illegally, which is why I did some digging and found out the thumb drive came from our *late* governor. The sun is setting and as darkness begins to descend, my mood grows darker. The sound of my phone ringing through my Camaro's car speakers pulls me from my wayward thoughts. I hit answer on the steering wheel without looking at the caller ID.

"Yeah?" When no reply comes, I frown and check the screen of my stereo to see who the caller is. My eyes widened at the sight of her name. "Sin?"

"Don't call me that." Her angry retort ricochets through the car.

"Why? I mean, I was the one to give you that nickname after all." I know I shouldn't push her, but the truth is, I'm in no state of mind to deal with her right now.

"You were also the first person to ever use me, but hey..." My grip on the steering wheel tightens.

"What do you want, Chanel?" I growl.

"You sound wound up, baby. I heard wrapping your car around a power pole helps with that. Or, I also heard a bottle of pills and a razor blade is even better." I know she is pissed and she has every right to be, but right now isn't the time for her to be fucking with me because it won't end well, for *her*.

"I also heard murdering people and dropping a queen of hearts on top of their corpses isn't exactly a great stress reliever, but hey, we all have our vices right?"

A growl fills the speakers. "Get fucked, Connor!"

"Is that an invitation?"

"I'll never let you touch me again."

"Been there, tasted that sweet-ass pussy and still craving more."

"You're disgusting." Try as she might to sound pissed off, the slight hitch in her voice alerts me to her thinking about the times I made her come all over my face.

"You loved it once."

"I also loved to piss in the bath as a toddler and I managed to grow out of that habit, just like I've outgrown any feelings I ever had for you."

Ouch.

"Golden showers aren't my thing, but I'm down to try it if you are?" I know mocking her and playing with her is starting to get on her nerves, but the truth is, the more pissed off she gets the calmer I become.

"I'd rather eat glass."

"You wound me, baby."

"I'm not your fucking—"

"What did you need, Chanel?" I cut in not wanting to hear her bullshit threats. I know I fucked up and I hurt her but I never meant to. Everything else may have been a lie but my feelings for her were all real.

"I want a meet."

That surprises me. "Why?"

"We need to talk."

"About?"

"Stop being a fucking dick!"

"You used to love my dick." I can't manage to stop myself from taunting her. This is the most she has spoken to me without threatening to murder me and then piss on my corpse before she burns my body. My girl has a bit of a temper problem.

My girl?

I push that thought away as she answers, "I also loved faking coming all over your undersized cock just to help inflate your ego, but hey, we all have our vices, right, baby?"

A humorless laugh escapes me at her throwing my own words back at me. "I'll meet you at VanVoorhis in an hour." I end the call without waiting for her reply as I pull up out front of my apartment.

Forty five minutes later, I'm showered, changed and sitting in a booth at the back of the local pub VanVoorhis waiting for the star of all my wet dreams to arrive. It's a Friday night so it's extra crowded in here. I took a gamble guessing she was in Fort Lauderdale so I told her to meet here just to gauge if I was right. She has never asked for a meet before and to be honest, I am worried that this is an ambush—but there is also another part of me that knows she won't kill me.

If Chanel Murelo wanted me dead, she would have murdered my sorry ass two years ago when she found out I was undercover at UNLV.

The moment she enters the crowded pub, my breath hitches. Her long hair is tied in a high ponytail atop her head. She wears a white shirt that clings to her ample chest, and the black leather jacket she wears is for style not warmth given it's one of those crop jackets. I run my gaze down her legs and groan, she's wearing skin-tight white jeans with black leather boots that reach her knees.

Jesus Christ, I'm rock fucking hard at the sight of her. When her brown eyes land on me, the easy look on her face vanishes and is replaced with loathing as she makes her way toward me, ignoring the stares of every male in this joint openly checking her out. I grit my teeth to keep myself from snapping at them to fucking look away and stop staring at her tits and ass. Chanel isn't like most women, she uses the assets God gave her to her advantage to get what she wants. She places her hand at the end of the diner-style table, cocks her hip to the side and peers down her nose at me.

"Loki." I recline back on the bench seat and quirk a brow at her.

"*Loki?*"

She shrugs and smirks deviously. "Well, he was the master prankster after all and I feel the name is fitting since you pulled off the best prank of all time."

"Which was?" She folds over the table and gets right in my face leaving a tiny sliver of space between us. If I pucker my lips I could kiss her.

"I'll tell you my secret if you tell me yours?"

I keep my face relaxed as I reach out and grip the back of her neck, grinning when a small moan comes from her. "How about I show you mine and you show me yours?" I taunt.

Her eyes glimmer with triumph which gives me pause. "Okay, me first." When I feel the distinct feeling of a knife pressed to my side, my eyes widen. I didn't even feel her shift to grab her knife. Wait, the better question is where the fuck did she manage to stash that thing on her body?

"You gonna stab me, baby?" For one split second her mask of bitchiness slips and I see the torment of emotions in her eyes before she quickly masks it.

"If you don't tell me what I want to know, yes." I open my mouth to answer but at that moment I spot Romeo and Xavier making their way over to us. I grip her wrist that holds the knife and use my hold on her neck and wrist to swing her tiny body around so she is on the bench seat next to me. She struggles for a second, but stills the moment the guys make it to our table, grinning like a couple college kids. The dirty minx beside me shifts. I feel her wrist brush my inner thigh and I throw my arm around her shoulders, then tense the second I feel the point of her blade press against my cock.

"Kacey, what's up, man." Chanel stiffens beside me. Fuck. Romeo flicks his gaze from me to stare at Chanel with a cunning smirk on his face. "And who might you be, darling?"

"His worst nightmare," she answers without missing a beat. Romeo and Xavier both laugh.

"Oh, I like you already!" X snarks as he wiggles his brows.

"I'm Xavier and this is Romeo. Don't let the name fool you, he is anything but a gentleman." Ro playfully punches X in the arm.

"I'm a ladies man. What can I say?" Chanel laughs and to my surprise, it isn't forced or faked. I didn't realize how much I missed the sound of her laughter until this moment. Ro and Xavier slide into the bench seat opposite us. I shift forward to tell them to fuck off but I clamp my mouth closed when Chanel speaks.

"So, how do you both know *Kacey*?" I tighten my hold on her in warning. The shithead pushes the blade harder against my cock, causing me to jump slightly.

"We've known him since high school. We both practically lived at his house. Mrs. Vaughn said we were her adopted sons."

Fuck!

Chapter Four

CHANEL

Kacey Vaughn.

That's his name, not Connor Ryker. I fell in love with a fucking lie and didn't even know his real goddamn name! I feel him attempt to shift closer to me, so I press the dagger harder against his erection. When a small hiss escapes him, I know without a doubt I cut through his jeans. I fight to keep the smile off my face as his two childhood friends reveal all the details about his family and where they all grew up. Con-Kacey tries to cut them off numerous times. Still, they ignore him and continue to tell embarrassing stories about their friend without knowing they are giving me all the ammo I need to take this fucker down.

"So, how do you two know each other?" Xavier asks. I smile viciously as I turn to the man at my side.

"Did you want to tell them or should I, *Kacey*?" His left eye twitches. I know that look and it used to send shivers down my spine because I knew he would punish me for it later. He is the only man I have ever let throw me around and bark orders at me—only in the bedroom of course.

"Sure thing, *Sin*." My nostrils flare at the use of the nickname that is no longer his, only Royal and the twins get to call me that. Not him, not anymore. The bastard has a death wish and clearly doesn't give a shit if I stab his dick because he leans in and places a quick peck on my lips before turning back to his friends. "We're dating." I nearly snap my neck as I reel back, ready to deny his claim. He uses my shock to his advantage, and pulls the dagger away from his dick, then kisses me...

For a second, one split second, I forget about the past and what he did to me. Nothing matters as he slips his tongue past my lips and I taste him for the first time in two years. I'm transported back to a time when I didn't hate everything in this world, I didn't thirst for the blood of those who wronged me. I remember how happy I used to be, how I thought life could be some big fairytale where a boy I fell in love with would be welcomed into my family.

But it was all a lie.

I bite down on his tongue and snap my eyes open to his blue ones shooting wide as a groan tears from him. I release his tongue and shove him back. His friends laugh at his expense as I stand from the booth and rush toward the back of the pub where I spotted the bathrooms on my way in. I head straight for the disabled one, needing a minute alone without the sounds of women bitching in the stall next to me. I grip the sink and take a deep breath trying to gather myself. After two fucking years of fighting to keep every ounce of emotion I have ever felt for him buried deep inside me, one single kiss and it all resurfaces.

I pull my phone from my pocket and dial the one person I know I can always rely on.

He answers on the third ring. "Sin, you good?"

A whoosh of air escapes me at the sound of Royal's voice.

Over the years he has become my crutch, the person I lean on when I need to be brought back from the brink when the need for destruction consumes me.

"If you made a mistake, a mistake so fucking huge that you knew that the people you loved most in this world would never forgive you for it, what would you do about it?" I know I'm making no sense but I can't tell him the truth. He can never know about Con-Kacey. He would want to kill him on sight, not only because he is a fed, but because Kacey Vaughn broke my heart, and is the reason I changed who the fuck I am, becoming this angry jaded bitch that trusts no one.

"I would come to you for advice and beg you to help me fix it." *Fuck!* "Sin, I know you better than anyone and I know for a fact your dad lied to me. This trip isn't about him needing to let you go or teach some shit, is it?"

"No," I breathe out.

"You gonna tell me what this is really about?"

I take a shuddering breath and shake my head even though I know he can't see it. "I want to tell you but..."

"You can't?"

"Yeah," I whisper.

I hear him exhale tiredly and hate myself a little more inside. I detest liars and the fact I am lying to the one person who has had my back my whole life, makes me hate Kacey just that little bit more.

"No matter what happens, I will always be here for you, Chanel. I know shit has changed since I met Erika. I'm trying to work out a balance—"

I cut him off before he can continue. "Royal, stop. Erika changes nothing between us."

"Then why the fuck are you pulling away, Chanel? I can feel it. I thought making you my underboss would help us get back to how things were back at UNLV, but it only seems to have made things worse. The twins even noticed that you've changed, and you know those idiots don't notice shit!"

"It isn't that simple!" I defend.

"It never is with you. I'm fucking trying here. I need you to help me out and explain what the fuck changed two years ago. Don't tell me I'm imagining shit either. Something happened back then and I can feel the same thing happening now. If you need my help, I won't ask questions, Sin. You know I will help you hide a body and never judge you for a single fucking thing." I know he would. I also know if I told him about my Kacey problem, he would take care of it. But that's the thing, Kacey seems to be the line I won't fucking cross. Knocking on the door of the restroom pulls me out of my mild breakdown.

"I have to go," I clip out. Royal tries to argue but it's too late, I end the call and shove my phone back into my pocket and unlock the door, only to pause. "What the fuck–" The words die in my throat as Kacey pushes me back inside and locks the door behind himself. This space felt bigger a second ago but with his hulking frame in here, I feel claustrophobic.

"You think this is a fucking game?" he snarls an inch from my face. I push in until my nose is pressed against his.

"Did you think it was a game when you were lying to me and fucking me at the same time, *Kacey*?" His bravado falters. Scoffing, I shake my head and shove him back a step. He tries to reach for me, so I grip his arm and spin so it's wrenched halfway up his back and shove him against the wall. "Don't ever fucking touch me again," I growl. The bastard does an elaborate move that has our positions reversed and me pressed flat against the wall with his pelvis flush against my ass.

"I took it easy on you before for obvious reasons, Chanel, but make no mistake, this time there are no secrets between us and I won't handle you with kid gloves." I try to push off the wall but he uses his body weight to pin me there.

"You have three fucking seconds to let me go or I will hurt you and feel not an ounce of guilt." He ignores my warning and leans down running his nose from the base of my neck up to my ear where he nibbles on my lobe.

"I call bullshit," he whispers huskily.

"You would have been right about that two years ago but things have changed. Your cock does nothing to inspire my submission." His hold on my arm drops but he quickly grips the back of my neck and continues to use his body to pin me flush against the wall, earning a growl of annoyance from me.

"My cock used to inspire so much more from you, baby."

I snort. "That was because I had no other experience but now, I am well equipped in that area and know exactly how useless your cock is. I also learned that I shouldn't have had to fake orgasms when there are real men out there that know exactly how to make a woman come."

He spins me around, grips both my wrists in one hand, and holds them above my head as he bends so we are eye level. The angry glint in his eyes fills me with satisfaction, knowing I'm getting under his skin.

"You let some other motherfucker touch what is *mine*?" he growls, making my nostrils flare in anger.

"You own nothing—"

"I own everything about you!" he roars right in my face. He stands before me vibrating with anger. "You want to stand here and bullshit about faking orgasms to make yourself feel better, go for it, Sin. You and I both know that you never faked shit, your pussy was squirting all over my cock daily. You can hate me all you want and hey, maybe in your head you really do hate me, but your body doesn't." To drive his point home he cups my pussy through my jeans, drawing a gasp from me. "Let me find out that you did let someone else touch this, baby, and I'll plant evidence on the fucker that will have him behind bars for life."

"Bullshit," I seethe.

"Fuck around and find out, Chanel." My chest rises and falls in quick succession as I try to tamper down my anger and think rationally, but that all goes out the window the moment he slips his hand inside my jeans.

"Kacey," I warn.

"Hmm, say my name like that again, baby girl," he purrs as he pushes my thong to the side and runs a finger through my slick folds, drawing a strangled moan from me. He buries his face in the crook of my neck as he continues to rub circles around my clit. Need coils deep in my belly as he sucks and nips at the tender flesh of my neck. The moment he pushes a finger inside my greedy little pussy, I cry out. "Outside that door you get to be the bad bitch that everyone expects you to be, but in here? You love that I take control and bend you to my will, so you don't have to think." I moan as he strokes that sweet spot deep inside my pussy. "Hate me all you want, Chanel, but you can't deny that I am the only one who you submit to willingly. You will let me do anything I want behind closed doors because you trust me to put you back together after I break you apart."

He sounds so far away. The only thing I can hear is the sound of my blood rushing in my ears and the beat of my heart skyrocketing as my body prepares itself for the orgasm we have been waiting years for. No matter how many times I have tried to get myself off, I never come as hard as he makes me. He has this ability to rip me apart, then slowly fuck me back together again.

My orgasm crests and my labored breathing starts to grow ragged as Kacey bites down on the tender flesh between my neck and shoulder. The pain mixed with the pleasure is the push I need to fall over the edge. I come all over his fingers, screaming out his name. When my knees give out, he drops his hold on my wrists and wraps his arm around my waist to hold me close as he slowly works me down from my high as I fold into him.

The moment I feel tears prick the backs of my eyes, I pull back. He stares at me in confusion, which just snaps the restraint of my anger and I lash out, punching him right in the nose.

"Fuck," he roars as he stumbles backward a step and pinches the bridge of his nose, to try stop the bleeding. "What the fuck, Sin?"

"Don't you ever fucking touch me. You have no fucking right–"

"You wanted me to touch you, I saw it in your eyes. You can lie to yourself as much as you want, Sin, try to make yourself hate me, but your eyes betray you. You want me as much as I want you."

"I don't want you," I shout.

"Your pussy would disagree with you."

I scoff. "Please, that thirsty bitch would be satisfied with one of your friends out there touching her." His eyes darken at my taunt.

"Do it. You think you are the only one with control issues? Think again, baby. Try and find some shmuck to go home with you and see what the fuck I do. I dare you." The threat is clear and I'll be damned if the possessive tone he uses doesn't have my greedy cunt clenching on air. I reach inside my jacket pocket and grip the card I had stashed there, then toss it to him. It lands on the ground in front of his boots. His eyes widen as he stares down at the queen of hearts. His shocked gaze flicks back to me, I've just confirmed his suspicions of who I really am by showing him my card.. "You're the *Memento Mori*," he mutters in disbelief.

"You've been marked." His brows raise to his hairline at my words. I leave him standing in that stall as I walk out, hating myself inside a little more for my momentary lapse in judgment and letting him touch me. I could have killed him if I wanted to, but the truth is, I don't want to hurt him. Now that the card has been dealt and he is marked, I have no choice but to end his life.

Why does that notion fill me with a sense of foreboding?

Chapter Five

KASEY

It's been three days since my little meet up with Chanel, I haven't been able to get the image of her coming all over my hand out of my head. I loath to admit that I couldn't help but suck her juices off my fingers that night, and fuck me, I can still taste her on my tongue. Instead of helping Bentley try to get a jump on everything we will need for the Jones case, I not only spent my weekend researching and going over old cases that had a card attached to them, but I have also been looking into why Owen wanted Chanel as a mole. My phone buzzes with a text.

UNKNOWN

NSU Art Museum one hour.

ME

Who the fuck is this?

Unknown

The one person you can't seem to find any information on.

ME

See you soon, Sin.

I pocket my phone, suddenly feeling excited at the prospect of bickering with her again. That's our form of foreplay it seems these days and I can't say I'm mad about it. I know I'm supposed to be gathering intel on her family, but since Owen has been so distracted with this Jones case I decided to leave her alone in the hopes she wouldn't hate me as much as she does, but I guess time doesn't heal all wounds. I spend the next twenty minutes trying to find anything from these cold cases that will link back to her but nothing does, Chanel and her cousins were ghosts until recently. I know who each of them are but I could never bring myself to point each of them out even when I got debriefed and they threatened to fire me. I couldn't hurt her like that.

Benny doesn't question me when I tell him that I'm heading out to meet with an informant, he's too lost in trying to find a loophole to save Owen's ass. I've chosen to keep my mind off that shit, what's the point when we all know that without a warrant legally obtained that they will all go free— Marcus included. I haven't had the gumption to call my parents and tell them what is happening. Ever since I arrested my brother, my parents haven't looked at me the same. They knew Marcus was spiraling and into some shady shit but they never tried to help him, they channeled everything into Ashley.

I thought my dad would understand that I did what I had to do, but I was wrong, he took it the hardest. He hated that his son who followed in his footsteps like he wanted/forced me to do, had arrested the son he had pinned all his hopes and dreams on, only for Marcus to snort them away.

Pulling up out front of NSU, I park my car, then head inside. I look at the exhibits and shake my head, who the fuck has a spare fifty grand to spend on a painting that looks like a toddler painted it? One painting captures my attention, not because it's the most expensive or because it's bright and bold, it draws me in because of how simple it is. Every other painting is loud with colors but this one is just a painting of a single person. So many different shades of brown make up the image of the weeping woman. Something about the pain in her features resonates with me.

"The weeping woman," Chanel says as she comes to stand by my side. I say nothing for a while as I continue to gaze at the woman. "The artist painted this for his mother. It's his representation of her grief after her husband passed."

"You're suddenly into art now?" I ask as I turn to face her. She keeps her gaze on the painting as I drink in the sight of her. Fuck, she looks stunning in a pair of leather pants, knee high boots and a plain red shirt. Her brown hair is piled on top of her head in a messy bun with stray strands loose across her face. Her face is free of makeup but she doesn't need it. Chanel's beauty is radiant and consuming without that shit.

"We're not here to talk about me."

"What are we doing here then, Sin?" I ask as I reach for her, but she side steps me at the last moment. Her eyes are cold and guarded as she looks up at me.

"Don't touch me," she grits out,

Not wanting to argue with her, I shove my hands into the pockets of my jeans and ask, "What do you need?"

"What is the cost of my freedom from this little deal?" She spits the word deal at me like it burnt her tongue. From the moment I made contact with her after the airfield, I told her there was a price for her freedom. Thing is, I lied to her.

"You don't want to pay that price, Chanel."

"Tell me what the price is," she grits out.

"Your cousin... Give me everything you have on him and his operation and I will make sure you get immunity." It's a reach, I know, but I also can't have her knowing that there is no out for her. She is too much of an asset to the Bureau to give up. She is the daughter of Carlina Murdoch, niece to the Don of the biggest mafia family in existence and if the word on the street is right, she is also the underboss to the *Memento Mori*. The fact she gave me a card three days ago confirms the latter.

"You give me all the evidence you have against my mother and you can have *me*." My brows draw in as I study her.

"You would spend the rest of your life behind bars?"

She shrugs as if it's no big deal. "I'll do whatever I have to, but just so we are clear, if you don't hand over the evidence you have on my mother or give me an out, we won't help you save your family." I turn ridged as a cruel smirk graces her beautiful face.

"You touch my family and—"

"And you'll what?" she forces out through clenched teeth. Darting forward, I grip her arms and pull her into me, my hold punishing but she doesn't squirm. "Careful, Kacey. I would hate for these onlookers to report you." I dart my gaze around and find that no one is paying us any attention, except for the guy across the room with a baseball cap slung low over his eyes and a phone in hand pointed at us.

"You trying to blackmail me, Sin?"

"I learned from the best didn't I?" she snaps back.

"Leave my family out of this, Chanel."

Her brown eyes harden as she glares up at me. "Fuck you. You were the one who came after my family first-"

"Don't you touch them." I'm almost pleading now.

"Who said I was the one that was going to hurt them?"

I'm going to kill Romeo and Xavier for giving this ammo against me, she didn't even know my real name until three days ago.

"Don't make me arrest you."

"Do it," she taunts. "You can't, can you?" I release her with a shove and pace a small circle, tugging at the strands of my hair. I know without a doubt the guy recording us is her father. I spent many years studying the Murdochs and their significant others. Thanks to them being hotel, club and other establishment owners, they have been in the public eye for years. Unlike their children, who have kept a low profile their whole lives and make it fucking hard to track them. "Now you know what it feels like to be backed into a corner."

"Chanel, my family had nothing to do with any of this. You want to hurt someone then hurt me but not them, please," I beg her to understand. I know I sound like a hypocrite right now after asking her to hand her cousin up on a silver platter, but this is different. My family has never done anything illegal. My parents and Ash haven't done anything remotely in the gray, unlike me or even Marcus, who straight up jumped into the black when he decided to help the Albanians with distribution.

"I am not the one coming after your family, Kacey. I marked *you, not* them." Cocking my head to the side, I stare down at her confused and slightly baffled by her meaning.

"But you said–"

"It was a warning. Give me my freedom and I will help you save your family from the threat that is now after them."

"What the fuck are you saying, Sin?" She pushes into me until her full tits brush against me, her eyes cold and unforgiving as she stares up at me.

"Did you really think I wouldn't go snooping around after your friends gave up information on you so freely?" She doesn't give me a chance to answer. "The Albanians are after your family, Kacey. There is a bounty on your parents and your brother. Your other brother needs to be moved out of gen pop now, because they think he is the one that snitched."

I shake my head denying her claim. "I–no... Marcus–how do you know about him?" No one knew Marcus was my brother aside from Owen, Q, and Bentley. We kept that shit under wraps so he wouldn't be a target in prison.

"If I told you how I knew about your brother working for the Albanians, I'd have to kill you."

"Who put the hit out?" I ask in a tone devoid of all emotion. I'm an undercover agent, my job is to be a ghost and become whoever I need to be in order to infiltrate a gang, enterprise or even become a college student if it's needed. I am the best there is and that is why I am afforded so much leeway and able to call the shots in some instances, like being Chanel's handler.

"Halil Kozma." I frown, I've never heard of that name before. "You know him as *Jones*." My eyes widen. We have been searching for over a year to find any information we can on Jones, it's the only name we have had for the ringleader of the Albanian Cartel here in Miami. "We'll help you take out your enemy."

"What's the catch?" I've been doing this job since I was nineteen and know without a doubt everything comes with a price.

"After your problem is solved, I want my freedom. You are to never contact me, disclose my identity or ever come for my family."

"I thought I was marked?" I snark.

"If you decline my offer, I'll bury you next to your parents and brothers. You have twenty four hours, Loki." She turns to leave but pauses a couple feet away and peers back at me over her shoulder. "I'd call your pal Benny and have him move Marcus before they get to him." I keep the shock from my face. She spent the past three days doing exactly the same thing as I did, gathering intel on me and my family. I watch her walk away with the guy in the baseball cap tailing after her. The moment they disappear out of sight, I jump into action and head in the opposite direction to them and dial Benny doing exactly as she said—getting him to put in a call to have Marcus moved into solitary.

Benny, Romeo, Xavier and I are all sitting in my living room with files upon files scattered over the small table between us. Romeo and Xavier aren't FBI, they are local beat cops but we have been friends since grade school and I trust them with my life. Benny and I met in Quantico and he has become one of my best friends. I trust him as I do Ro and Xav.

"How the fuck do you know there is a price on Marlee, Jim and Ash's heads?" Ro asks.

"How did you know Marcus was going to get shanked?" Benny adds. I scrub a hand down my face, debating how much to tell them. They don't know about Chanel and I want to keep it that way if I can. Q and Owen are the only two inside the Bureau that know I am handling her.

"I was tipped off," I answer. Xav eyes me warily.

"You're hiding shit," Xavier accuses. "Now isn't the time for hiding shit, Kace. We were with the FBI on the raid, so if these fuckers are coming after arresting officers then we have a right to know." He has a valid point.

"Look, all I know for sure is that they somehow figured out who the fuck I am."

"How?" Benny asks. I shrug, I have no idea how they found out. My cover was airtight and wasn't blown the night of the arrest. I was masked up the night of the raid, we made sure to scatter all the fuckers across the country into different prisons so they would never be able to find which prison I was supposed to be in if they looked.

"I don't know, B. I have spent all afternoon trying to figure that shit out," I growl, annoyed as fuck that I can't figure this shit out. I know I could call Chanel and ask but I have a feeling she wouldn't tell me.

"Would Marcus rat you out?" Ro asks hesitantly, I can't say the thought hadn't crossed my mind.

"Marcus is a scummy piece of shit but he wouldn't do that because he knows it would mean the Albanians coming after me."

Ben snorts. "Dude, Marcus hates you."

The other two grunt their agreement. "He hates me but naming me and telling them the truth puts our parents and Ash in danger, he's a fuck up but not even he would risk them coming after our family."

"We need intel, who the fuck told you Jones's real name is Halil Kozma?" Ro asks me.

"My informant." I answer in a brisk tone that doesn't go unnoticed by my friends.

"Who is your informant, Kace?" Ro pushes. I grit my teeth and shake my head.

"No one."

"Kacey, who the fuck are you getting this intel from? The four of us have been busting our asses for over a year to find the head of this syndicate then suddenly you have this new informant and bam, you got a name?" I understand their need for information but I also know they would go off the deep end if they found out that my informant was Chanel Murelo. Fuck, if they found out I had a relationship with her while undercover they would lose their fucking minds.

Benny's phone rings and I sigh with relief, he answers the call and the three of us sit here and watch as his face morphs from surprise to unease then shock, before settling on disbelief as he ends the call and faces the three of us.

"What happened?" I ask. He opens and closes his mouth three times before he is able to finally answer.

"Kacey..." He shakes his head as he looks at me.

"Spit it the fuck out," I snarl.

A pitying look enters his eyes. "Kacey, I'm so sorry, brother."

I recoil into the sofa. "Sorry for what?" I snap.

"Kace, Marcus was found in his cell, unresponsive, forty minutes ago." My heart skips a beat as the blood slowly drains from my face. Tingles begin to spread throughout my body as his words slowly sink in.

My brother is dead.

Marcus is gone.

They killed him and she knew they were coming.

She knew what was about to happen and didn't tell me, now she will learn why they call me the *Draugur!*

Chapter Six

CHANEL

"They were too late. His brother was found murdered in his cell two hours ago." Regret blooms inside me at my father's words as I look up from my laptop. I tried to warn Kacey to have his brother moved from gen pop, that the Albanians were planning a move against him and the easiest target was his older brother who had no escape.

"The death of his brother changes nothing. He either accepts my offer or I kill him." Dad looks me up and down skeptically, causing my ire to rise further. "What?" I snap, tired of his silent judgment. Since arriving here, he has barely spoken to me and when he does, it is always curt and short. I know I fucked up but him constantly reminding me of my fuck up doesn't help me. Neither does avoiding Royal's calls but I can't talk to him right now without confessing everything to him.

"You may be able to fool your cousins into thinking you are some cold, fearless killer but you don't fool me, Chanel. I saw the way you looked at that fed today." I tense in my seat but keep the torment of emotions from my face. "The only bullet you would fire for him is to save his life, not end it. You are towing a fine line here, Daughter, so I urge you to choose, the fed or the family that raised and loved you, because you cannot have both." I say nothing as he turns and leaves the living room and heads down the hall to his bedroom. His door slams after a minute and I cringe. My father has never been this angry at me and I honestly don't know how to fix this rift between us.

Before I can dwell on it too much, an incoming Facetime call comes through on my laptop from my mom. I debate on if I should answer it or not, but I know if I don't, she will just call my dad and he will force me to speak to her.

"Hey, Mom," I say as I answer the call.

She beams at me through her camera. "Hi, baby. How is the bonding time with your father going?" My dad spun my mom the same story he did Havoc and Royal.

"Uh, yeah, it's going good I guess," I say with a shrug.

"You guess it's going good?" she says as she purses her lips to the side.

"What do you want me to say? He hates that I want to be like him and wants to train me for my new life in Miami, he is so...argh," I groan as I drop my head back and stare up at the ceiling.

"Oh, honey," she coos, drawing my focus back to her. "You're his baby. He just wants this time with you so he can bond with his daughter." I fight the scoff that wants to break free. If only she knew why her husband was really here, I don't think she would be looking at me with pity in her eyes.

"Yay for bonding time," I snark, earning a disapproving look from her.

"Have an open mind, Chanel. He's trying here." I know he is but I also know that he is so disappointed in me and honestly, I would take him being angry at me any day over disappointing him. I hate the look in his eyes each time he looks at me. I can see the judgment and that shit kills me inside.

It's after midnight and we're still perched on the rooftop across the road from Micha Vatoli's apartment. According to Dad's research, Micha is the one who was helping not only Chance but Halil Kozma with acquiring real estate in Miami. We don't have a direct line to Halil yet but Micha is a good stepping stone to get us the intel we need to go after his boss. I delivered his card to him yesterday and it gave me great satisfaction to see him snort and toss it. If only he knew what that card meant. Don't fret, he'll find out soon enough what happens to those that are marked by the *Memento Mori*.

"We're on," Dad clips out. We have been here for over an hour and the man hasn't fidgeted or taken his eye off the scope of his gun once. His discipline is unparallel to anything I have ever seen before. I look through the scope of my own rifle and note that he is right. Micha walks into his lavish apartment with his phone tucked between his ear and shoulder. I keep my eye on the door to see if anyone else walks in after him, but no one does. We wait another hour for the dirt bag to shower and prepare for bed. I nearly threw up in my mouth when he settled in bed and began to fondle himself. Dad snapped at me to close my eyes. I couldn't help the laughter that burst out of me.

"Dad, I have seen—"

"Close your fucking mouth now and do not finish that sentence, Chanel!" he orders. I roll my lips over my teeth to keep from laughing. I'm twenty years old, soon to be twenty-one in a couple months and my dad still thinks I have never seen a cock. Fuck, he would die of a stroke if he knew what I did in the restroom with Kacey while he was waiting in the car.

"You do realize how old I am, right?"

His eyes narrow. "In my mind, you are still the little girl that used to crawl into my bed in the middle of the night because she swore there was a monster hiding under her bed." I roll my eyes and shake my head.

"I haven't been that little girl in a long time," I say quietly. A whirl of emotions crosses through his eyes.

"Don't I know it," he mutters as he begins to pack his things up. I follow his lead, then follow him silently down the fire escape. We place our rifles in the trunk of the car before grabbing our handguns and screwing a silencer onto them. Dad hands me a bulletproof vest. I stare at the thing for a second before shaking my head, and continue to load my magazine. "Put it on now."

"No."

His eyes shine with indignation. "It wasn't a request."

"I don't care. You may view me as a little girl... Newsflash, old man, I'm not that kid anymore. I have tits and an ass now. Pretty sure I didn't have those things when I thought there was a monster under my bed." His face contorts in disgust as a shiver runs down his spine.

"Don't ever let me hear that shit come out of your mouth again!"

I scoff. "You say worse shit to Mom!' I defend.

"That's different, she's my wife. I'm allowed to say those things to her and she enjoys it." I screw my face up in disgust.

"That is so freaking gross!"

He smiles wide and wiggles his brows. "How do you think you were made?" I shudder and snag a baseball cap from the trunk, then spin away from him, storming toward Micha's building with his laughter following after me. I never, and I mean never, want to know about my parents *doing it*. A fresh wave of nausea rolls over me. I push those feelings away and get my head back in the game as we approach his building. We don't go through the front, we round the back and come in through the service entrance, where we know there are no cameras after a quick hack into their security system.

We act casually as we pass staff members. I play my part perfectly and stumble into one of the young cleaners and snag her keycard without her noticing, then head for the employee elevator. It's a quiet, tense ride up to Micah's floor. I pull my hat lower to shield my face from the cameras as Dad covers his face using the hood of his jacket. I insert the card into his door and push it open. The sound of his snoring can be heard all the way out here. My dad quietly shuts the door, then we both draw our guns as we make our way toward the back of the apartment, where we know his bedroom is. I press up against the wall as I peek around the corner to make sure he is actually sleeping. Dad tries to take the lead but I cut in front of him, needing to show him that I can do this.

He says nothing as I reach up and twist my cap around backward, then swiftly climb on the bed and straddle Micah's lap. He wakes instantly and tries to sit up, but the second I press the end of the silencer against his forehead he freezes. His eyes squint, trying to get a good look at me. Even with the curtains open, the moon doesn't illuminate my features enough.

"Who the fuck are you?" he snarls. I see my dad slink into the shadows of the room and remain out of sight, allowing me to handle the situation on my own.

"I ask the questions, you answer right and you get to keep breathing." He snarls and tries to reach for me. Shifting my gun, I shoot through his palm then press the hot barrel back to his forehead and relish in the pained cries that come from him. He thrashes beneath me. Gripping his throat in my other hand, I lean forward and snarl in his hideous face. "Tell me where the fuck Halil is." The fucker is so predictable, he strikes out with his other hand, earning another shot through that palm. For the next hour, we keep doing the same dance. Dad and I drag his sorry ass out of bed and tie him to a dining room chair in the bathroom, so it will be easier to clean up after we're finished.

"You fucking bitch!" Micha wails as I take out his other kneecap. So far I have put bullets through his hands, elbows, feet and now his kneecaps. Crouching down in front of him, I keep my gun dangling between my legs and shake my head.

"Micha, Micha, Micha." I taunt, tears continue to flow down his cheeks. "You were warned–"

"I never received no warning!" he shouts.

"Yes, you did."

"Swear to God, you said nothing to me about no warning."

"The queen of hearts you received yesterday from the doorman was your warning. You were marked from that moment." His eyes widen to the point of almost looking painful.

"The rumors are true then?" A look of fear overcomes his features, which confuses me. I have shot the man eight times and not once did this look cross his face, until I mentioned the calling cards.

"What rumors?" I hedge.

"Word on the street is there's a new crew in town. They call themselves the *Memento Mori*, bringers of death or some shit." I bristle but remain silent. "They say they hand out cards to people they plan to kill. Johnny heard they took out the KP of the Vargas Cartel, then made the Governor disappear."

"Who are they?" my dad asks, speaking for the first time since entering Micha's apartment. The waste of space is smart enough to keep his eyes on me and not look at my dad as he speaks.

"No one knows for sure. Some say the son of Bishop Murdoch is the Don of the crew but then some say it's some new guy on the scene." I make a mental note to call Royal and alert him to the fact people are looking into who we are.

"Well, let me tell you a secret," I say quietly and lean in. He does the same, well as far as his restraints will allow. "My name is Chanel Murelo and I am the underboss to the Don of the *Memento Mori*." He reels back and stares down at me with utter shock and fear in his eyes. That look right there is what I have been chasing my whole life. I want my name alone to inspire fear and from the look on Micha's face, I'm paving my way for that to be a thing.

"If I tell you, you gonna let me go, right?" He looks between me and my dad before settling his gaze on me.

I smile and nod. "Of course, Micha. I'm not a total savage, ya know?" A pained chuckle escapes him.

"I don't got a direct line on Halil, but his second, Omar, is in town taking care of a problem."

"What problem?" I push.

"Turns out one of Halil's stash houses got raided a while back and one of his distros is the brother to some fed."

"That so?" he nods his head eagerly.

"This ain't just some ordinary fed though, this fed has infiltrated a shit load of cartels and no one can find anything on the *Draugur*."

"Draugur?" I query.

"It means *ghost* in Icelandic. It's what everyone has been calling him, until now."

"You know who he is?" A vicious smile graces his pained face.

"Yes. Halil and Omar are going to make him pay for ruining everything they set into motion. They already killed one of his brothers and now they are going after anyone else he holds near. Omar is already tailing him–" I've heard enough, I lift the gun and put a bullet between his eyes.

"Chanel!" My dad chastises me. I ignore him as I pull my card from the pocket of my jeans, drop it on his lap, before rushing out of there with my dad hot on my heels. I need to warn Kacey. Call me crazy but not even me, the queen of being cold and unfeeling, can allow his innocent family to be murdered.

Chapter Seven

KACEY

Standing in the morgue looking down at my brother's body feels... surreal.

I can't explain it, I know I am here physically but my mind can't fathom the fact that I am actually standing here staring at my older brother's lifeless body. The last time I saw him, he was hurling insults at me and swearing that he would never speak to me again for arresting him, that he would hate me till I die.

Guilt swirls inside me.

I feel Benny place a hand on my shoulder, offering his silent support. I hear him, Ro and X all speaking but I can't make out a single word as I stare down at my brother. Memories of us growing up and being closer than ever flash through my mind. Marcus was my hero, I wanted to grow up and be just like him. I made sure that no one would be able to trace his relationship to me. There were no loopholes, my entire existence as his brother was erased. I know for a fact Marcus would never have disclosed this information to anyone. Someone ratted my brother out.

I swear on everything in this fucking world that I won't stop until I find out who the fuck did this to you, brother.

I vow this silently. Leaning down, I press my forehead to his cold one and close my eyes. "I'm so sorry, brother," I whisper, before turning and stalking out of that morgue, with my friends hot on my heels.

"Where the hell are you going?" X asks as he catches up to me. I ignore him as I burst through the exit doors and head for my car. I don't say anything as I slide behind the wheel of my Camaro and start the engine. The three of them climb in. I grip the steering wheel in a vice like grip and slowly turn my head toward Ro who sits shotgun.

"Get. Out," I snarl.

"We ride together, always," he says in a firm tone.

I shake my head. "I'm going off book. My oath went out the fucking window the moment our mole snitched on my brother."

"What are you saying, Kace?" Benny asks from the seat. I slowly turn to face my partner.

"It means I'm not bringing anyone back to stand before a judge. I'm taking the mole and all these other fuckers down until I find out who the fuck murdered my brother!" I roar. My breaths rush out of me as anger courses through my veins. I latch onto it and hold it close, knowing if I don't, I'll break down and fall into the pit of despair where I will blame myself for his death.

Benny's eyes harden. "I got your back." I look at Xavier next, he nods firmly.

"I'm with you," he says. I look to Romeo last, who is already turned and facing forward.

"We gonna keep sitting here playing with our dicks or go take out some Albanian scum?"

I have no words. I put my car in drive and peel out of the lot. I don't even make it a block before my phone rings through the Bluetooth. When I see the caller ID, I debate letting it ring out but decide that if these three are going to put their lives on the line for me and break every oath and law, then they should know who my informant is.

I answer the call. "What?" I clip out, not in the mood for her shit.

"You have a tail, they know who you are and are going after your family." I can hear the slight hint of panic in her voice.

"You're bluffing," I sneer.

"Jesus Christ, they call you the Draugur. I know your brother is dead and I also know that Omar is tailing you and has men going after your parents and other brother right now."

"Why are you helping me, Chanel?" I feel my friends eyeing me warily, especially Xavier and Romeo since they met Chanel on Friday.

"Because I'm not a complete bitch, contrary to what you might think." Fuck, if what she says is true, I have no way to get my parents to safety, they are in California and there is no fucking way I will get to them in time. Dread churns inside me.

"I can't save them," I mutter as I accelerate and swerve in and out of traffic heading for the airport.

"Where are they?" A part of me doesn't want to disclose their whereabouts in case she uses them against me, but another part also knows she is my best chance at saving my family.

"California," I force out through clenched teeth.

"I do this, you set me free and never contact me again. Every file you have on me and my family is to be destroyed."

"You have my word."

"Meet me at the pier. I'll have Chaos extract your family and send them to one of our safehouses."

"Sin... please–"

She cuts me off before I can finish. "My issue is with you, not your family. You have my word that your family will be safe and under the protection of the *Memento Mori*." She ends the call and I'm left here reeling. I never thought I would ever ask anything of the mafia and yet here I am accepting the help of my ex-girlfriend—who isn't just an heiress to the biggest crime family but she is also the underboss to the new mafia that runs Miami. I pull a U turn and head back toward the pier to meet Chanel.

"I'm going to take a wild guess here and assume that was the same Chanel from Friday night?" Xav states from the backseat. For a split second I forgot about them being in the car.

"If you three are sure you want in on what I have planned, you have to understand that I am going off book. The badge means nothing until after I finish this shit, you good with that?"

"We're here, aren't we? I think you need to explain things to us, Kacey. I know you are hiding shit," Benny says. I nod my head and decide to tell them everything, it's the least I can do for my boys. They will never know how much their loyalty and willingness to help me on this crazy ass fucking revenge mission means to me.

"Two years ago I was sent undercover at UNLV to flip Rico Vargas." Their shocked intake of breath is warranted. I never discuss my jobs with anyone, not even my partner. All Benny is told is that I am on a job. The only person I speak to on a job is Quintin. "Long story short, the moment he went missing, I was pulled from the case and brought back here to go undercover for the Albanians."

"Wait, you're leaving shit out, what happened at UNLV?" Ro pushes.

I sigh and scrub a hand down my face. "I broke protocol and fell in love with a girl."

"Holy shit, the girl is Chanel, isn't it?" Xav presses.

"Who is Chanel?" Benny tacks on.

And this is where they are going to flip their shit. "Yes. Her name is Chanel Murelo. She is the daughter of Carlina Murdoch and Vincent Murelo aka, the infamous Blood-hound." The three of them start shouting and hurling questions at me. "Calm the fuck down!" I roar.

"You were fucking her?"

"Dude, she is the fucking mob?"

"Did you know who she was?" they all ask in unison.

I answer each of their questions. "No, I had no idea who she was until after we slept together and became a *thing*."

"Kacey, you are a fucking agent and she knows who you are. How the fuck did that happen?" Xavier is right to sound concerned.

"She overheard me on the phone to my handler. She wanted to kill me but..." I let my sentence trail off.

"But she was in love with you and couldn't bring herself to kill you, even though that is what her family would have expected her to do." I nod. Ro whistles before carrying on. "Her helping you puts a target on her back from her family."

"I know," I grit out. I don't know how she is going to save my family without outing herself to her family, but call me crazy and all that, but I trust her to get them to safety.

"You still have feelings for her, don't you?" Benny phrases it as a question, but it's not.

"I fell in love with her and somehow I just never fell out of love with her," I answer honestly. There is no point in denying it. She hates me and with good reason, but I could never hate her. I hate myself for hurting her and causing her pain. We pull up to the pier, I park the car and sit here for a moment just staring at her standing at the end of the dock. The lone lamp-post shines down on her, casting her in an angelic image. Sighing I climb out of the car as the guys follow after me. At the sound of our approach, she spins around.

"The fuck?" she snarls as she draws her gun and aims it us. My boys pull their guns and aim at her, without thinking I lurch in front of her and shield her with my body as I turn to face my friends, ready to shout at them to drop their guns but freeze when I see Vincent Murelo standing behind Ro and Benny with a gun in each hand pressed to the back of their heads.

"Think really hard about your next move," Vincent grits out. My boys look to me for guidance, I give them a stiff nod. The three of them slowly sheath their weapons and raise their hands as they step to the side. I move to stand with them and Vincent stands beside his daughter, who is currently glaring at me. This is my first encounter with Vincent and I'll admit it takes every ounce of my self-control not to stare at him. This man has taken more lives than I care to think of, and the fact he stands before us is kind of an... honor. The agent in me wants to demand he raise his hands and read him his rights, but the brother of Marcus Vaughn wants to beg him for his help.

"Who the fuck are they?" Chanel snarls.

"We've met before, sweetheart," Romeo says. I fight not to roll my eyes when Chanel scoffs.

"Who the fuck are they?" she asks again.

"Ro and Xav are cops. Benny is my partner," I answer.

"Why are they here?" Vincent asks.

"Because I trust them. They are here to help me find my brother's killer. No offense, but I don't need to explain shit to you," I snap. Chanel's brows raise to her hairline at my outburst.

"Yet you feel the need to explain yourself to my daughter. Why is that?" I gulp loudly as I shoot a look at Chanel, gauging how to answer that one. Her father may know she is working for the FBI but I have no idea if he knows how deep my relationship with his daughter is. The sound of my phone ringing breaks the tension-filled silence. I pull it from my pocket and glare at the name flashing before me. I answer without overthinking it.

"Owen," I snap in lieu of a greeting.

"What the fuck happened at the prison?" he shouts.

My restraint snaps. "You mean how the fuck was my brother murdered? When I told you he was compromised and you promised to have him moved to solitary?"

"I did place the fucking call! As soon as I got off the phone with you, I rang Quintin and told him. He assured me that Marcus would be moved and then transported to the prison in Alabama." My eyes seek out Chanel on their own accord. The moment our eyes lock, I feel like a haze of fog has been lifted and I can finally think clearly since Benny delivered the news about Marcus.

I keep my eyes on her as I answer my boss. "I'm taking leave to deal with shit–"

"Don't do anything stupid, Vaughn. It isn't worth it—" I end the call, not wanting to hear the rest of his bullshit story.

"If you're taking leave, who is going to destroy the files and evidence you have against my family?" She spears me with a look of warning, as she can read my mind and knows without a doubt something has changed inside me.

"I swear to you, I will burn every file and any information about you and your family—"

Vincent cuts in before I can finish. "You make this promise, but you had no trouble forcing my daughter to turn against her family using images of my fucking wife!" he roars. Vincent is a big fucker and I'll admit he carries an edge of darkness with him that has me feeling slightly on edge.

"I never sent her those pictures. I swear to you, I would never use such disgusting means to flip her." He eyes me questioningly, so I push on. "Those images of your wife were obtained by our boss. Chance Bennett had a mole inside the Bureau and I think whoever the mole is, was the one to send those images to my boss. I pulled every string I had to make sure I was the one handling Chanel."

"Handling my daughter, huh?" I balk at my error and shake my head while ignoring my friends who snicker behind me. I shoot the three dickheads a glare that has them snapping their mouths closed and face Vincent.

"It's not what you think—"

"So you have never done anything toward my daughter?" Chanel closes her eyes and shakes her head clearly just as uncomfortable about this conversation as I am.

"I... We... I mean–"

Chanel cuts in and saves me from floundering and making a dick of myself. "Enough." Her father scowls down at her but she ignores him as she looks to me. "I want all the evidence you have against my family. I kept my word and placed a call to have your family relocated which has raised a shit load of questions from my own family." Regret churns inside me as a look of unease crosses her face.

"Sin–" I start but Vincent cuts me off.

"*Sin?*" He stares down at his daughter. She looks up at her father and frowns. "How the fuck does he know what Royal and the twins call you?" he growls.

She darts her tongue out to moisten her lips, and fuck me if my cock doesn't stir in my jeans as memories of what she can do with that tongue flash through my mind.

"Technically, *he* is the one who started calling me Sin first." Vincent's eyes narrow as he looks at me.

"Just how fucking friendly were you two?" he grits out through clenched teeth.

"Dad–"

"Quiet, Chanel," he roars.

"Don't talk to her like that!" I shout. The frown on Vincent's face vanishes as he takes a step forward. Chanel darts in front of her father with her back toward me and a hand pressed against his chest.

Chapter Eight

CHANEL

I stare up at my father pleading with him to remain calm. I know this whole situation is fucked up and a lot for him to handle... Shit, it's a lot for me to handle!

"Move," Dad grits out. I shake my head. I feel Kacey at my back and close my eyes praying that he will be smart enough to sense the danger he is in, but clearly he isn't that smart.

"Step aside, Sin," he whispers. I peer over my shoulder at him and shoot him a look.

"Shut up, unless you want to die tonight."

"Answer my fucking question," Dad snarls, drawing both our attention back to him. I flinch at the angry tone of his voice, but he needs to realize I am not an eight-year-old child anymore—I'm a woman.

"What do you want me to say?" I snap.

"Did you fuck him before or after you knew he was a fucking fed?" he shouts right in my face. My breath hitches as my own father stares down at me in disgust. I loathe to admit I can feel tears pricking the backs of my eyes, but I fight them back... I will never allow anyone to see me cry! Kacey grips my waist and anchors me to his front. I'm too focused on my father to even comprehend what he is doing.

"Your daughter was never just some fling to me," Kacey grits out. There is only an inch of height difference between him and my dad—being sandwiched between the two of them is not my idea of a good time.

"She may not have known who you were, but I can guarantee you knew exactly who she was. Do you even care that she has risked her own life to help you?" Dad doesn't give Kacey a chance to answer. "You get her those files before we leave tomorrow night. Because of you she now needs to go back and face the wrath of her Don." Dad steps closer and leans forward so he is a hair's breadth away from Kacey's face. "If my nephew doesn't forgive her for this indiscretion and chooses to take action against her, I will make sure your entire family is reunited in hell while you watch." He doesn't wait for a response, just turns on his heels and stalks off back toward the car. It takes me a minute to gather myself before I pull away from Kacey, and turn to face him and his friends.

"Chanel–" I raise my hand stopping Kacey.

"Don't. I don't want to hear anymore bullshit from you. Get me the files, Kacey, then please... let me go. This is a job for you," He frowns, "but for me, this is my fucking life!" I run a hand through my hair and shake my head. "I betrayed the one person I swore I never would for you."

"I never asked you to save my family!" he defends.

Staring up into the blue eyes of the man I thought I would bring home to my family has an ache forming in my chest.

"You didn't have to ask. Unlike you, I would never use your family against you to manipulate you into doing my bidding. Get me the files, Kacey, and then we are done for good." I turn to leave but his words stop me.

"I'm sorry, Chanel." I slowly turn back to face him.

"Your words mean nothing to me, don't you get it?" I shout, waving my arms around. "I should have fucking killed you two years ago!" He reels back a step at the venom in my voice. "I let my feelings for you cloud my judgment and because of that stupid fucking error my parents are going to have to bury their only child." His eyes darken to the point they almost look black. He darts and grips the back of my neck, pulling me in close so he can rest his head against mine.

"Tell me how to fix this," he murmurs quietly.

"Chanel!" My father's voice booms in the quiet of the early morning. I free myself of Kacey's hold and smile sadly up at him. I wish I could regret ever meeting the asshole but truth is, I can't because loving him made me who I am today.

"Goodbye, Kacey Vaughn," I say as I turn and head toward my father.

"See you soon, Chanel Murelo," he calls after me but I don't look back. At least I did one last good deed before I die. I knew calling Chaos for help would alert Royal. I also know that facing my cousin is going to be harder than I ever thought.

Dad hasn't spoken a single word to me since we left the pier last night. I know he isn't angry at me, he's just pissed he can't control the outcome of this situation. As a father, I know he can't allow me to walk to my death but as The Bloodhound he also knows I can't run from this, which is why we are leaving tonight to head back to Royal's so I can confess everything. Chaos agreed not to say a word to him when I explained the situation last night, provided I told Royal within a week.

I enter the same pub I met Kacey at on Friday. It's not as packed here during the week, but I do have to push my way through a crowd of rowdy college students to get to the booth I know he will be sitting at. Sure enough, there he sits in the same booth as Friday night. Unlike the last time we were, here he doesn't wear a smug look as he sees me approach. This time he has a sad look in his eyes as he watches me approach. I slide in opposite him and rest my arms atop the wooden table. Kacey takes a shuddering breath.

"I had to call my parents today and tell them about Marcus." I keep the surprise from my face, I didn't expect that to come out of his mouth. I remain silent, sensing he isn't finished. "To say they were pissed that a group of people came into their hotel, dragged them out and moved them to a lavish cabin in the middle of nowhere is an understatement." He chuckles but there is no humor to it. "My dad refuses to speak to me and my mom thinks it's best that I keep my distance from Marcus's funeral. They also think it's best for Ash and his career as a pro baller that I stay away completely from the family." The pain and self-loathing in his tone has me feeling compelled to comfort him but I manage to keep myself seated, which is no easy feat. He turns away and looks toward the group of college guys who are cheering at something on the TV. "Do you ever wish you could go back to the first day we met and do things differently?" I suck in a sharp intake of air.

"Kacey–"

"I love hearing you say my name," he murmurs as he slowly turns back to face me. The look of pain that was present in his blue eyes a moment ago, is quickly replaced by a lustful one.

"I'm not here for a trip down memory lane, I need the files." He eyes me with a hungry look and sucks his bottom lip into his mouth. I'm captivated by the sight and unable to tear my gaze away.

"Follow me," he whispers huskily and stands. Irritated and wanting to get this little meeting over with, I follow him out the back of the pub to a dark parking lot. I spot his car parked in the back. There are only three other cars out here. My senses heighten as I look around and make sure we aren't being followed. When I turn back around to face Kacey, he has his gun drawn and pointed directly at me. I reach for my own but freeze when I feel the barrel of a gun pressed against the back of my head.

A quick look over my shoulder confirms my suspicion, his friend Romeo shoots me an apologetic look and shrugs his shoulder. "Loki seems like a fitting name now, doesn't it?" I grit out.

"I can't let you go back there. Help me bring down the Albanians and I swear to you I will hand over all the intel we gather on them to your cousin in exchange for your life." Shaking my head I stare at him like he is simple.

"That's not how shit works. Royal already has a meet with the Albanians in three week's time–"

"I'll explain everything but I need you to get in the car." His gaze bores into mine pleading with me to listen and not argue.

"When my dad doesn't hear from me, he will come looking, Kacey."

"I know," he answers without hesitation.

"Then you also know who my father really is. He will find me Kacey and when he does, I can't save you and your friends from his wrath. He won't bring the national guard, he'll bring the Murdoch mafia and make no mistake, Royal will bring *Memento Mori*."

"They won't need to do all of that." I frown in confusion. "Why?"

"Because we meet with your cousin in the morning." My blood turns to ice.

"You stupid fucking fool, you just signed all your death warrants," I mutter as I head for his car without argument.

Romeo and the other two dropped Kacey and me off at some abandoned warehouse near the docks. According to Kacey, this is where Xavier lives. I haven't spoken a word to him since we arrived. He gave me some towels and a shirt, then pointed me in the direction of the bathroom. I know it will only be a matter of time before my dad finds me, so I decide to waste time by showering. I am pleasantly surprised by the sheer opulence of the bedroom and bathroom. The outside of the building looks like it is condemned but inside, it looks like a brand new remodeled apartment.

I strip off and step under the spray of the shower. A small moan escapes me at the feeling. I push all thoughts of what tomorrow will bring from my mind and the clusterfuck I have made of my life. I feel a draft on my back and tense. I don't need to turn around to know it's Kacey that just stepped into the shower with me.

His arms band around me as he buries his face in the crook of my neck, inhaling my scent like a starving wolf. He reaches up and cups my breast with one hand as he lowers the other to reach my pussy but I grip his wrist halting his movements.

"Kacey—"

"If tonight is the last night I get to be with you, then let me be with you, Chanel, without any secrets between us... Please." I shake my head.

"I can't," I whisper, the broken tone of my voice has me mentally scolding myself. He spins me around and forces me backward until my back is flush against the tiled wall, bending at the knee so we are level.

"I need you, baby," he whispers as he slowly leans in, giving me every chance to push him away or stop this, but I'm powerless to do anything. I have never been able to deny this man anything and a part of me hates that, but another part also relishes the control he demands and forces me to obey without thought. His lips mesh against mine, forcing his tongue past my lips and demanding entry without permission. His taste assaults my senses and I moan. His hands grip my waist in a punishing hold. I wrap my arms around his neck as he grips the backs of my thighs and lifts me.

He breaks the kiss and stares up at me with longing in his blue eyes. "I can never be yours, Kacey. Come tomorrow, we will part ways and never see each other again. You know that, right?" His eyes flick between mine trying to detect a hint of deceit—he won't find it.

"I let you walk away from me before but I don't think I can do it a second time." The raw honesty of his words has my breath hitching.

"You won't have a choice. We can never be more than this moment, right here. Right now." His eyes darken as I push the wayward strands of his hair back off his forehead.

"Then give me everything you got, baby." I seal my lips to his and groan when he starts grinding his erection against me. I moan loud when the head of his cock slips between my folds and brushes against my clit. Kacey wraps his lips around my hardened nipple. A strangled cry tears from me as I push my chest further into his sinful mouth and grind down against his cock.

"Kacey..." I breathe out.

He releases my nipple with a wet pop and peers up at me through his thick lashes. "You need me to make you come, baby?"

"Yes." I sound like a wanton hussy but fuck, I don't care. It's been too long since I have felt his mouth on mine, or the feeling of his thick cock stretching me open as he slams inside my wet cunt. He places me back on my feet and I watch transfixed as he slowly lowers to his knees before me, hooking one of my legs over his shoulders.

"Such a pretty fucking pussy." The husky tone of his voice sends a shiver down my spine. He presses a single finger inside me. I cry out as I raise to the ball of my foot, but he grips my waist with his free hand and holds me in place. "You like how I finger this pussy, Sin?"

"Y-yes," I moan as he inserts a second finger.

"Tell me it's my pussy and I'll make you come all over my face, baby, just the way you like." I bite down on my tongue refusing to say it, I can't. "Answer me, Chanel," he demands as he bends his fingers at the perfect angle to hit my G-spot.

"It's my pussy!" I cry out as he hits that sweet spot again.

"Your pussy, huh?" I balk down at him when he yanks his fingers out of me. I open my mouth but he speaks before I can utter a word. "We'll see about that." My retort is cut off when he buries his face in my dripping cunt, I scream the moment he pushes his tongue inside my tight wet hole.

Fuck I didn't realize how much I had missed this until now.

Chapter Nine

KACEY

Fuck, I love the taste of her pussy!

I lick up and down her slit, loving the sounds that come out of her mouth. I hadn't planned to come in here and eat her pussy, I just meant to check on her but the moment I saw her naked and the water dripping down her body, I couldn't resist. I needed to touch her, feel her, hold her... Fuck, I just needed to be near her.

"Just like that, Kacey, make me come," she cries out as she reaches down, grips my hair and starts to ride my face, chasing the release only I can give her. "Fuck!" she screams as she squirts all over my face. I continue to lap at her clit and swallow her cum, moaning at the taste of it. Fuck, I've never tasted a pussy this good before.

Aftershocks wrack her body as I slowly climb to my feet, grip the back of her neck and yank her forward. Her mouth opens as she gasps. I spit her cum into her mouth and growl my approval when her eyes blaze with desire as she swallows her own release and moans.

"Admit it, you fucking love that I make you all dirty." She wraps her arms around my neck and jumps, forcing me to grip her ass. Locking her legs around my waist, she smirks down at me.

"Never said I didn't." My cock twitches painfully against her ass. "Fuck me and make me forget that you ever lied." She tries to sound nonchalant but I hear the hurt in her tone. I reach between us and line my cock up with her entrance.

"You let anyone else touch what is mine, Sin?" She pulls her gaze from my cock and stares into my eyes.

"I'm not yours, Kacey." I keep my eyes locked on hers as I thrust deep inside her tight little pussy. She screams so fucking loud and flops forward, resting her forehead against my shoulder as her pussy clamps down on my cock. She's too fucking tight. She can deny it all she wants, but I know without a fucking doubt, she hasn't slept with anyone else aside from me.

"You have been mine since the moment your virgin blood coated my cock and stained my sheets," I growl into her ear. A shiver runs down her spine and a whimper escapes her lips as I draw almost all the way out of her wet heat, then slam back inside her.

"Kacey!" she screams. Hearing my real name from her sinful lips has a haze falling over me. The urge to dominate her and make her mine for all to see consumes me. I know this is meant to be a goodbye fuck, and maybe for her it is, but for me, this is my way of showing her I can't let her go again.

I capture her lips and pour everything into the kiss, showing her without words that I am here and I want to try again, but this time there would be no more secrets. We will just be Kacey and Sin. She meets each of my thrusts and pushes down onto my cock, chasing her own orgasm. I created a monster the night I stole her virginity. Believe me, taking Chanel Murelo's virginity isn't something I take lightly, and it will be something I treasure for the rest of my life. She digs her heels into my ass to pull me in closer as she thrusts her hips back and forward on my cock, drawing a deep groan from me as I break the kiss.

"Kace, I need more," she pants.

"I know what you need, baby. Unhook your legs." She does as I say and whimpers when I draw my cock out of her. Spinning her around, I press her front flat against the tiled wall. Gripping her hips, I pull her ass back to me. "Spread your legs." She does as I command and fuck me if it isn't the most stunning sight I have ever seen—her ass is red from my grip, her pussy is weeping for me. I grip my cock in my hand and pump it twice before lining it up with her entrance again. I give her no warning as I slam back inside her tight cunt.

"Fuck!" she screams.

"Back that ass up and fuck me, baby." Flattening her palms against the wall, she does as I ask and presses back against me, chasing her own release. As her cries begin to grow, I feel my balls tightening.

"Kacey... please," she begs. I fist my hand in her hair and pull her back against me. With my free hand, I pinch her clit between my fingers and fuck her at a ruthless pace. "Oh fuck yes, Kacey... I'm coming," she cries out her release the same time I come deep inside her tight little cunt with her name on my lips. Wrapping my arms around her waist, I pull her closer and nuzzle the side of her neck. Fuck, I missed this.

I missed her.

We stay like this for a moment and just... be in this moment. Chanel isn't like most women. She is reserved, her emotions aren't worn on her sleeve and she never allows you to know how she feels. But with me, she let me see everything until I ruined it with the truth. She pulls forward and flinches the moment my cock slips free of her, then turns to face me. Her eyes are filled with a war of emotions.

"I'm sorry about your brother." At the reminder of Marcus's loss, the blissful feeling I was vibing with a second ago vanishes and is replaced by self-loathing.

"Yeah," is all I manage to say as I turn away from her and step under the spray of the shower. When I feel her arms wrap around me from the back, I drop my chin to my chest and allow myself to feel everything—all the pain, hurt, anger and regret. Tears burn the back of my eyes. I place my palms flat against the wall and allow the first tear to fall. Fuck the pain in my chest burns at the loss of my brother. I know he fucked up and made some shitty life calls but he didn't deserve to die. "They killed him because of me," I say brokenly. She slips around the front of me and cups my face between her hands. I know she can see the tears falling from my eyes but she doesn't comment.

"Your brother knew what he was getting into when he entered this life. Just like I knew the risk I was taking the night I found out who you were. We all make choices, Kacey."

"He chose wrong," I grit out.

"Some would argue I did as well, but here you stand before me." Dropping my hands to her waist, I push her back until she is flush against the wall.

"Do you regret it?" She nibbles her bottom lip and tries to escape me, but I grip her chin between my thumb and forefinger, forcing her defiant gaze back to me. "Do you regret it?" I ask again.

Her eyes flick between mine, trying to get a read on me, but I'm too fucked up right now for her to even get a read on what I'm feeling.

"Do I regret meeting you? No." I sigh in relief. "Do I regret falling in love with a lie? Yes." I drop my hold on her and step back.

"I never meant to hurt you, Sin."

Her eyes narrow. "If that were true, you would never have

pursued me, you would have left me the fuck alone, Kacey." She throws her hands in the air as I shut the water off. "I only found out days ago your name wasn't even Connor. You fucked my life up."

"I'm trying to fix my mistake!" I argue.

"How? You think coming back into my life after two years to force me to rat on my family is the way to earn my forgiveness?" She doesn't give me a chance to answer. "You signed my death warrant! You forced me to choose between those I love and someone I *thought* I loved." She brushes past me as she steps out of the shower and begins to dry off, while I stand here and just watch.

"What do you mean *thought*?" I growl as I follow after her and crowd her space.

"What?" she snaps angrily.

"You said you *thought* you loved me."

"Exactly. I thought I did but clearly I was wrong." Reaching out I grip the back of her neck and drag her into me as I bend and get right in her face. "I could break your fucking nose right now," she snarls.

"Bullshit." She opens her mouth to argue but I push on. "You can lie to yourself all you want, baby, but you and I both know you are full of shit. You loved–love me because if you didn't, you would have opened those legs for someone else. I'm betting my life on the fact my cock is the only one that has ever been inside you, and I am the only man who has ever seen you come."

Her nostrils flare as her anger begins to take hold. She fucking jabs me in the ribs, then lands an open palm hit to my fucking nose, again. "Fuck."

"Fuck you. You don't know shit about me or how I feel. Just like how you are so fucking dumb to think that you could kidnap me. My cousin was kidnapped, you dumbass, and since then Royal has had trackers implanted in all of us. He and my father are already on their way to get me, so I suggest you get dressed unless you want my dad cutting your sorry ass excuse of a cock off." I balk at her as she storms out.

"You fucking love my cock, you dirty little liar!" I shout.

"And I'm sure your brother loved breathing, but here we are." Ouch, that fucking hurt more than I want to admit.

Chanel and I are both sitting in the living room. It's in the center of the downstairs part of the remodeled house. From here we can see the entire downstairs, which is exactly where I want her, no, I need her for this plan to work. I fucked up with Marcus and my family and that shit fucking sucks, but I won't do the same with her. I need to fix this and this is the only way I know how.

Sure enough, as if on cue, the front and backdoor are both kicked in at the same time and then men in black ops attire crowd the room. Chanel is on her feet while I remain seated and wait for him. She flicks her gaze to me and frowns. The crease in her forehead tells me she knows I'm up to something, but doesn't call me on it when her father pushes through the circle of henchmen to come to his daughter's side.

"You good?" She nods her head in answer to her father's question.

"You didn't need to do all of this, I was fine," she says as she waves her hand around at the men surrounding us.

"He didn't, but I did." She spins around and watches as two men step aside to allow their Don through. Royal Murdoch stands tall and proud as he looks at his cousin. A second later, one of the twins follows after him—that one I know is Havoc because Chaos is the one who moved my family to a safe house.

"Royal," she breathes out.

"What the fuck is going on, Sin?" It pisses me off to hear him calling her *Sin*. That's my name for the devious devil. She flicks her gaze to me for a second before looking back to her cousin and sighing.

I watch as her *fuck the world* mask slips into place and she stands taller and holds her head high. "I fucked up and I'm owning it." Royal's brows furrow.

"You never fuck up," Havoc says.

She shrugs. "I did this time." Both her cousins turn to face me. I slowly push to my feet and relish in the sound of everyone in the room cocking their gun.

"Ah, the fed she let live." Chanel's eyes widen as she looks up at her cousin in horror.

"Y-you knew?" Royal pulls his cold stare from me to stare down at his cousin.

"No, Uncle Vin filled me in on what the fuck was going on. Never in my life did I ever think you would ever fuck our family over like this. Shit, not even Amelia would have fucked us like this!"

She draws her gun from the waistband of her jeans, keeps her eyes on her cousin as she points her gun at me. "Want me to put a bullet between his eyes? Want me to prove my loyalty to this family by killing him?" She doesn't give him a chance to answer. "I never ratted. He was the one who fed me intel. I never disclosed anything about the family." Her face contorts and she slowly turns to face me with her gun still raised.

"Something on your mind, baby?" I taunt. Vincent growls, while Royal and Havoc move to flank Sin on either side.

"You never pressed me for more than the whereabouts of Chance's body, why?" The speculation in her tone is clear.

"He was all I needed," I answer honestly.

"You helped us take the docks from the Albanians, why?"

"Because I want them gone. You and your family don't sell little girls or boys." The four of them snarl in disgust. "I never wanted to bring you in, Chanel. I called him–" I motion to Royal as I keep my gaze on her, "because I know the Albanians are planning a trap for the meet in three weeks."

"How the fuck would a pig know that?" Havoc snaps.

"Because my brother may have hated me but he left a note. The Albanians are coming after me and they know that Chanel has been working with me." Her eyes widen but I push on. "They think the *Memento Mori* is working with the feds to take them out, so they plan to ambush you."

"We set the location!" Royal grits out through clenched teeth.

"But you don't actually know who is going to be at the meet, do you?" I clap back, making his eyes narrow. He turns back to Chanel and stares down at her with a cold look. I know what comes next and I am prepared for it, ready for it even.

"Kill him." Two words from her Don and that's all it takes for my girl to shut down. She closes off every emotion she feels as she slowly turns back to me. Her face is a mask of indifference but her eyes display the torment she feels inside. She knows I know more than I just said about the meet being a trap, but she won't push me for more or it looks like she is stalling.

Our eyes collide. Her second of hesitation is all I need. I raise my hand and show them the detonator in my hand. "Pull the trigger, baby, and I'm taking you to hell with me." Her eyes blaze. Royal, Havoc and Vincent have their guns aimed at me ready to shoot but even they won't take the risk.

"Drop it now," Havoc shouts.

"You have no leverage," I snap.

"You sure about that?" Royal smugly replies. I meet his cold stare.

"The only leverage you hold over me is currently pointing a Glock at my head, unless you plan to kill your own flesh and blood then you really have nothing over me."

"Royal," Vincent warns, but to both our surprise, Chanel steps forward and places her own gun against her temple.

"Sin, No!"

"Chanel!"

"Stop!"

"Fuck." the four of us shout in unison. Dread churns inside me at the sight of her holding a gun to her own head.

"Baby, put the gun down," I plead. She keeps her gaze on me as she closes the space between us leaving a foot of space between our bodies.

"If I don't kill you, he will kill me." The conflicted tone in her voice spears me.

"Then kill me, baby, because I will kill him if he touches a single hair on your head." She tentatively reaches out to me. A whoosh of air escapes me thinking I have managed to talk her down, until she snatches the detonator from my hand, jumps back a step and drops her gun back to her side, while I stand here open mouthed.

"You didn't really think I would kill myself, did you, Loki?" I grind my teeth so fucking hard my jaw begins to ache. "I told you before, Kacey, I would never betray them. My choice will always be them, they are my blood—"

"Keep telling yourself that, Chanel," I snarl. "I fucking put my ass on the line for you. Owen wanted you arrested and thrown in a cell to rot but I fucking fought for you and kept you out of prison." I'm vibrating with rage as I stare down at the woman that fucked me emotionally. She is a virus that has consumed me and there isn't a cure for it.

"You forced my hand!" she screams, dropping her facade for the first time and allowing the hurt and anger to shine through in her words. "You blackmailed me, Kacey. Jesus

Christ, how can you not see that?" She doesn't give me a chance to answer. "I walked out on you two years ago because you are a fucking fed! You and I will never be anything. We are from two different worlds, Loki. If you can't see that, then you are not as smart as I thought." She turns away from me to face her cousin. "My fate is in your hands, Royal. I fucked up but I swear I never betrayed you or our family. Do what you must." She strolls out of the room without a backward glance. Honestly, the fact she didn't look once hurts more than her words. Something about this moment feels final, like this time I won't actually ever get to see her again.

Chapter Ten

CHANEL

The whole ride back to Royal's house was filled with tension. Havoc, Dad and Royal didn't utter a word, neither did I. I have nothing to say. In truth, my heart has been in my throat the whole time and the burning question in my mind is, did they kill Kacey? The moment we arrived back here, I had to tamper my anger when I saw my mom, Aunt Kiara and Uncle Bishop. I said nothing to them as I stormed up to my room. I'm currently sitting here exhausted beyond belief having had no sleep, as I stare out the window at the sunrise.

I've heard shouting coming from downstairs but I don't have the energy or the desire to go down there and find out what the verdict is. I knew from the start that hiding who Kacey was, and the fact he pulled me in as an informant, would sign my death warrant but I just couldn't fucking bring myself to rat him out. Every fiber of my being told me I was making a huge mistake, but like a moth to a flame, I fell into the trap of wanting to keep him alive.

I scoff at myself. I have no idea if he is still breathing. The moment I walked out of that warehouse-style home and jumped in Royal's car, I turned the radio up hoping to drown out any sounds coming from inside of that home. The sound of my bedroom door opening has me stiffening. I don't bother to turn around or acknowledge whoever it is. I am surprised when Erika moves to stand in front of me and leans against the wall to gaze out the window at the sunrise. We remain silent just watching the sun for a long time until she breaks the silence.

"I was right when I said someone had broken your heart, wasn't I?" I look at her out of the corner of my eye, expecting to see a satisfied look on her annoying face. I'm taken back when all I see is a look of understanding.

"We're not friends, Erika." A shuddering breath leaves her as she nods.

"I know, I just thought that maybe you could use someone who can relate to what you are going through," she says with a shrug.

"How can you relate?"

She pins me with a deadpan look. "I'm currently dating the sworn enemy of my family and the son of the man I was led to believe killed my family." I cock my head to the side and purse my lips, bitch does have a point.

"Point taken."

She turns to face me and all traces of humor are wiped from her face. I sit up straighter in my seat as we stare at each other. Before there was a wall I placed between us but right now, I am too fucking tired and wrung out over everything that has happened to keep up with any pretense.

"Royal is pissed." I drop my gaze to my lap, I had no doubt he would be angry at me.

"He has every right to be," I mutter.

"No, he fucking doesn't, Chanel." I snap my gaze back to her in surprise.

"I betrayed him—"

"No, you didn't. You fell in love with someone who lied to you. If I was in your position, I would have done everything you did because to kill Royal, would be like killing myself. I know you and him have a complicated relationship. If there is anyone in the world who is able to make him see the error of his ways, it's you." I shake my head but she pushes on. "Make him see, Chanel. Show him that you never betrayed him. Show him that you did this because you fell in love. Throw my relationship with him in his face if you have to."

"I marked him," I blurt out. Her eyes soften.

"I know." I jerk back in my seat.

"How do you know I marked Kacey?"

"Once marked, the kill is final or punishment will be inflicted. A loved one can never be marked. A royal flush is to be unanimous. The caller is the one to kill. If one shall fall, their card will lay in rest." I stare up at her in shock as she recites the laws of the *Memento Mori.*

"The caller is the one to kill," I mutter. She smiles and nods. "Kacey..." I let my sentence trail off.

"Is alive, Chanel. You marking him is what saved Royal from doing something that would make you hate him. Duty forces him to act as the leader, but the love he has for you is what gave him pause long enough to find out you marked your man."

"Do you plan to honor the call or accept punishment?" I jump to my feet at the sound of Royal's voice and spin around, finding him and Havoc both standing there in the doorway with grim looks on their faces. Surprise ripples through me when Erika moves in closer and inches in front of me.

"What was your punishment for letting me live when she marked me?" I stare at the back of Erika's head like she has lost her fucking mind. I have shown this woman nothing but disrespect and hatred and here she stands defending me and my treachery against my family.

Royal scowls at his girl. "That was different!" he snaps.

"How? Was I not feeding my uncle intel on you and your family?" She doesn't give him a chance to answer. "From what your mother tells me, Chanel *never* divulged any information about your family. She remained loyal to *you*." Not wanting to cause a rift between the two of them, I place my hand on Erika's shoulder, then move to stand in front of her with both my arms clasped in front of me, ready to accept whatever punishment—even if that means my life.

"If he kills you, I'll kill him." My brows jump to my hairline as London forces her way between Royal and Havoc to enter my room.

"Bellezza, what are you doing up?" Havoc asks but she ignores him as she glares up at Royal, who returns her angry look with one of his own.

"You are not allowed to hurt Sin!" This child is perfect. Erika bringing her home was the best thing. Royal and London still haven't managed to get along, I can't see why not because London is fucking amazing.

"Aren't demons supposed to stay hidden till nightfall?" Erika gasps and rushes forward to London's side at Royal's jibe.

"Royal–"

London cuts Erika off. "I got this, Momma." Royals brows jump to his hairline and his jaw slackens hearing her call Erika *Momma*. "You hurt Sin, I hurt you." Her threat is heavy and filled with venom. I have to bite my bottom lip to keep from laughing at the little spitfire.

"Go back to hell, demon," Royal snarls. Havoc, Erika and I all glare at the bastard.

London just places her hands on her hips and smiles brightly as she shouts. "Grandpa!" Royal's eyes widen and once again his mouth unhinges. Not thirty seconds later Uncle Bishop is shouldering his way between his son and nephew.

"What happened, sweetheart?" Uncle B asks London in a tone so soft I almost balk, I've never heard him sound like that before.

"Sweetheart?" Royal spits, earning a glare from his father.

"He..." London spits while pointing at Royal, "wants to hurt my Aunty Chanel." I choke back my snort. This kid is fucking perfection and knows how to play all these men. A second ago I was Sin and now I'm Aunty Chanel. Uncle Bishop opens his arms, London rushes to him as he scoops her up and turns to face his son who is rigid and glaring at both his father and... *daughter?* I honestly have no idea what London is to them.

"Make her cry or upset her again and I'll give you the ass whooping of a lifetime." With that said, Uncle Bishop leaves the room with London who looks back over his shoulder and winks at Royal. He slams the door closed and locks it before pinning Erika with a scathing look.

"Why couldn't you bring home a fucking puppy?" Erika laughs and shakes her head as she closes the space between them, then wraps her arms around her man. He's powerless to stop himself from holding her close. A pang of longing hits me in the chest—I had that once.

"She loves him, Royal," I hear her mumble against his chest. He places a kiss to the top of her head before finally lifting his gaze to me. Standing tall, I hold his stare. Never in my life have I ever felt this awkward in his presence. He has always been my comfort, my person I run to when shit gets hard, but right now, he is the one person in this world I want to be the furthest from. He steps out of Erika's hold and moves toward me at a slow pace. I hold his stare the entire time. I crane my neck back to hold his gaze as he comes to stand in front of me with a hurt look in his eyes that has my heart aching.

"Why didn't you tell me?" he asks softly.

I shake my head and shrug. "How could I tell *you*, the person I spent my whole life looking up to, that I got played by the first guy I fell for? I couldn't let you see me broken or weak. I dealt with it as best I could, until he forced his way back into my life. I fought him..." A lump begins to form in my throat. I am not a crier but right now I can't manage to keep my emotions in check. Royal says nothing as he allows me the time I need to gather myself before continuing. "I told him I could never betray you. But then photos of my mom were sent to me and I floundered for a second and agreed to meet him."

"What photos?" I pull my phone out of my pocket and show him the images. He clenches my phone in his grasp, so tight I think he may actually snap it. "How the fuck did he get these?"

"He said Chance sent a thumb drive. He thinks he somehow got it from your Grandpa's estate," I answer honestly.

"Who else has seen these?" he asks.

"Me, Dad, Kacey and his boss." Royal nods but I can see the cogs in his mind turning, he knows something but he isn't telling me. "I swear, I never told him anything–"

"How the fuck am I supposed to believe that?" he roars.

My emotions shutdown and I go into fight mode. "Because you fucking know me!"

"No, I don't. The person I knew would never have gone behind my fucking back and fucked a fed."

"I didn't know who the fuck he was at the start—"

"You should have come to me—"

"Fuck you!" I scream, cutting him off. "You never listened to me when I told you she was a liar." I feel like shit talking about Erika like this when she just tried to help, but hey, they don't call me a bitch for no reason. "I fucked up, I know that but I'm telling you, I can fix this."

"Prove it," he snarls.

"How?" I snap back.

"Omar will be at a gala tomorrow night in Orlando. Prove to me you can be trusted by getting in there and getting me the intel I need to take out these Albanians fucks and maybe, just *maybe*, I won't be forced to take the life of my best friend and drive a wedge between our family because she thought it was a good idea to turn to her fed boyfriend instead of her Don." I bristle and step into him as I allow my anger to take control.

"Make no mistake, cousin," I spit. "You may wear the title of Don, but you are not above me. You are my equal, as are the twins. I have proven my loyalty to you time and again and yet, because I don't have a cock swinging between my legs, you constantly undermine me."

He bends at the knees until we are eye level. "I have never undermined you, Chanel. I know without a shadow of a doubt that you are my better and always have been. All a cock would do is enhance your ruthlessness. Don't ever question my perception of you again." I stand here with my mouth open as I watch him storm out of my room. Erika shoots me an apologetic look as she races after her man, leaving me alone with Havoc. I take a deep breath before turning to face my cousin and prepare myself for his wrath.

"You may as well have a go at me as well." He stuffs his hands in his pockets and shakes his head.

"Nah, he said enough."

I scoff. "Ya think?"

"Want my opinion?"

I throw my hands in the air. "Why the fuck not?"

His eyes shine with understanding. "Take it from someone who fell in love with a girl that he had no business loving. I know how hard it is to fight loyalty to your family when your heart wants what it wants... it's fucking agonizing and hurts more than a hundred bullet wounds. I understand why you did what you did." I stare at him in shock. I never knew Havoc loved anyone. Everyone knows Chaos is in love with a girl he can't have, but I never thought Havoc had someone as well. My heart aches for my cousin at this moment.

"I had no idea."

He shrugs. "It's not something worth dwelling on. I deal with the pain because it's a constant reminder of what loving her would cost me. I would never allow her to come between me and my brother, no matter how badly I want her."

My jaw unhinges. "You're in love with the same girl as your brother." He doesn't confirm or deny, but the look in his eyes tells me I'm right. He turns to leave but stops in the threshold and peers back at me over his shoulder.

"He's alive, Sin." Pain explodes inside me. "He couldn't kill him. He tried to but the moment that fucker pulled your card from his back pocket and dropped it at Royal's feet, he knew then that you marked him for a reason."

I shake my head. "The rules didn't apply. I meant to take the shot..." I whispered.

"You can't kill your own heart, Sin. Trust me, I've tried." I say nothing as he turns and leaves me alone with my thoughts. When I marked Kacey, I had intended to kill him when the time was right. In a strange turn of events, I feel like Havoc is the only one who understands me and how I feel. I never thought I would ever see the day that the big fucker fell in love and wanted something for himself. He has always put his twin's happiness above his own and never taken anything for himself.

I spent the whole day and night holed up in my room. The next morning, I woke up to my mother and aunt forcing me out of bed and into the shower, saying they are running out of time to make me a lady. I gripe and moan the whole fucking way about them doing my hair and waxing me. I drew the fucking line at my mother trying to wax my pussy. A smile full of pride graces her face. I told her I had laser hair removal done, so there was no need for that. I've been sitting in this seat for hours as they primp, prime and talk about how they have waited years for this, while I sit here trying not to stab my eyes out.

"Knock, knock," Erika calls out as she saunters into the room with London hot on her heels. The little girl stares up at me with a huge smile on her face.

"You look beautiful, Aunty Nell." My heart skips a beat, hearing her call me *aunty* has a sense of protectiveness wash over me. She may have just came into our lives but fuck, I already have a soft spot for the kid.

"She's right, you do look beautiful." I flick my gaze to Erika who gives me a half smile. I stare up at her for a moment, letting all the loathing and bitterness I feel toward her go as I smile and nod. Her eyes well with unshed tears. She grabs my hand in hers and gives it a gentle squeeze. Clearing her throat and shaking her head, she laughs to lighten the mood and steps out of view for a second before returning, holding a dress that has my eyes widening.

"Fuck," I whisper. London holds a black pair of strappy looking heels out to me. I eye them both with horror.

"I know you would rather die than be caught in a dress and heels." I snort my agreement, earning a groan from my mom and aunt. "Your mom and aunt wanted you to wear something pink or green." I balk in horror, which has all three women laughing at my expense. "So, I thought I would save you and pick something I thought you would like better."

An hour later, I am dressed and ready to head to the gala. I feel like a baby deer learning how to walk in these fucking stupid shoes. The moment I enter the living room where my dad, uncle and cousins are waiting everyone's mouth drops open and they stare at me like I'm a fucking circus freak!— Royal, Havoc and Erika will escort me tonight—our parents are to remain here. Unlike us, their faces are known and any chance we have of getting close to Omar would vanish at the sight of them. All four men stare at me with wide eyes. Royal looks disgusted and Havoc looks like he might pass out. Uncle Bishop smacks them both on the back of the heads as he comes to me and places a kiss on my cheek.

"You look stunning." I smile my thanks. "You get your good looks from your mother's side." My dad growls and shoves him out of the way. My uncle laughs as he wraps his arms around my aunt and places a kiss on her cheek. Dad stands before me with a mystified look on his face. Suddenly feeling nervous and fucking exposed in this scrap of material, I shuffle from foot to foot.

"Vincent, use your words, baby," Mom teases as she comes to stand beside us with a proud smile on her face.

"I-I...You..." I sigh and drop my gaze to my shoes.

"I look like a freak, I know," I mutter bitterly. Dad scoffs, grips my chin and lifts my face so he can look me in the eye.

"Chanel Vincetta Murelo, you, my darling daughter, are the epitome of beauty." My mouth parts on a gasp as pride and love shine in my dad's eyes. "You radiate beauty on any given day, but right here, right now, you are breathtaking, my beautiful daughter. Just... just give me a moment to take you in, if this is the last time I get to see my daughter in a dress, let me imprint this moment to my memory." I stand here awkwardly as my mom comes to snuggle into my dad's side, as he smiles and nods.

"Thanks, Dad," I mutter shyly.

"I thought your mother was the most beautiful woman I had ever laid eyes but seeing you standing here, I may have been wrong." Mom gasps and feigns hurt, but giggles when Dad smacks her ass, earning a growl from my uncle and a disgusted look from me.

"On that note, I have some fucker to kill so I can get the fuck out of this thing."

Dad groans and throws his head back. "She was doing so well, looked like such a lady and then she ruined it by opening her mouth."

Chapter Eleven

KACEY

Romeo's voice crackles through the ear piece. "In position."
I look to the left and spy him over the rim of my
champagne.

"Nice ass, Vaughn." I shake my head at the sound of
Xavier's laughter coming through the ear piece we all wear to
communicate. Benny is stationed outside to give us the
heads up.

"Fuck you," I whisper into my wrist where the micro-
phone is. Their laughter rings through my ear. There are so
many people here dressed to the nines. I fucking hate wearing
this tux but it's not like I could get in here wearing jeans, a
shirt and my Converse. So many known faces filter around the
ballroom, noses in the air acting like their shit don't stink. My
phone vibrates in my pocket. I pull it out and send the call to
voicemail when I see it's Owen calling. The guys and I have a
hunch, and until I am proven wrong, I'm not wearing my
badge. I took an oath and vowed to uphold it till death, but
what happens when the ones you are supposed to trust betray

you, and the ones you are sworn to take down become the ones you trust?

"The Godfather has arrived." I roll my eyes, Benny is being fucking dramatic as always. I keep my eyes peeled for their entrance, trying to prepare myself for her arrival. No doubt in my mind she will be wearing a suit, leather pants or something like that. The moment Royal enters the banquet hall it's like a hush falls over the room. Erika Vargas is tucked into his side protectively. Royal Murdoch is a beast of a man, towering over his girlfriend, making her seem almost fragile. I can tell from the way he angles his body in front of hers slightly, that he would take a knife to the heart for the girl. His eyes scan the room and the moment they land on me, a snarl pulls his upper lip back. Rika follows his gaze and her brows raise at the sight of me. "Do. Not. Come. In. Your. Pants." I frown at Benny's dumbass comment.

Erika smiles slyly as she pats her man on the chest, then pulls him to the side. I begin to bristle under the scrutiny of Erika and Royal's gazes as they watch me. Havoc appears in the entrance and I'm surprised to see that he is even in a tux like Royal, the guy doesn't strike me as the type to play dress up. He's the fucking size of a silverback gorilla—broad shoulders and a permanent scowl that is always in place. He spots me and subtly lifts his hand to scratch his nose. I scoff when he uses his middle finger to do it. The fucker stares me down for a minute before stepping up next to Royal.

Does he ever smile?

"Xav, you or Ro need to snap a pic of this fucker's reaction for me." Benny's voice comes through our coms and still I have no idea what this dick is talking about.

"Oh fuck."

"He's coming in his pants," Ro and Xav both speak at the same time, but their voices are drowned out by the sight of *her*. Never in my life have I ever seen a sight more beautiful than the one standing in front of me. Her brown hair is flowing around her in curls that have me envisioning me wrapping my fist around them and slamming into her. Her big doe eyes are wide, the smoky-looking makeup enhancing them... But it's the dress. Fuck me seven ways to Sunday, that dress! It's a black silk dress, with a neckline that plunges to the middle of her chest showing off the swell of her ample chest. Long slits run up each side of her legs so when she moves, you see the full length of her glorious legs. My mouth dries the moment her eyes find mine. I watch as her chest releases an exhale, it's as if the sight of me has put her anxiety at ease.

Chanel Murelo isn't the type of girl to be nervous but right now, I can see it in her eyes how uncomfortable she is. I let my eyes travel over her again and groan at the sight of the black strappy heels she wears. Time seems to slow as we get lost in each other's gazes, but all too soon the spell is broken when a pansy fucker with a balding head steps in front of her, blocking my girl from my view. The moment I see his hand lift as if to touch what doesn't belong to him, I'm powerless to stop my feet from moving across the room. I'm nearly to her when Havoc steps into my path blocking her from me, again.

"Stay the fuck away from her. He won't spare you twice." His words are low enough for only me to hear. I look around just to make sure no one can hear us. The party is in full swing now, but there is an air of tension now that the Murdochs have arrived. They may not know who they are per se but they aren't stupid. Danger clings to them like a shadow, you don't have to know their names to know they are from the dark side.

"Fuck you. I won't stand here and watch some fucker touch *my* girl."

Havoc's brows raise. "Your girl, huh?" I meet his cold stare with one of my own.

"I didn't stutter," I snarl.

"You want to dress her corpse before you place her body in

a wooden box?" I growl low in my throat. "You fuck this up for her, he will kill her to teach *you* a lesson."

"If he touches her–"

Havoc steps into me so we are chest to chest, there is no mistaking that this isn't a friendly conversation to onlookers. "You will do nothing. You dragged her into your shit because you are a fucking pussy. All their lives, no one has ever been able to come between them, not even me or Chaos. Yet, somehow you managed to do what no one else has ever done."

"And what is that?" I force out through clenched teeth.

"Make her question her loyalty to her best friend and make him question her every move. Those two are like water, you can never separate them, but somehow you managed to do just that. You fuck this up for her and he will kill her. Duty compels him to honor the code we live by. She chose to turn her back on his trust to save *you*. Do the right fucking thing here, Kacey, and let her go so she can live. Because I can tell you now, you will never have her. My family will never allow a fucking fed to be with one of their own. You will never be what she needs."

"I'll never let her go," I say as I press my forehead against his. The big fucker just smiles.

"Well, that is a shame because she already let you go when she walked out on you the day we brought her back. She could have chosen you tonight, but she chose *him* over you again because he is her rock. You never stood a chance against their bond."

"Unless we want this whole thing blown before it begins, step the fuck back." The quietly snarled words from Royal have Havoc and I facing off for a second longer before we each take a step and force smiles to our faces so the partygoers see us as two men who were just fooling around. "You stay the fuck back and let her do her thing, you understand?" Pulling my gaze from the silverback, I meet Royal's glacial stare.

"You in the habit of pimping your cousin out?" I spit the words at him. He attempts to step into me but Erika dashes in front of him with her hand extended to me.

"You must be the infamous Kacey Vaughn." I shake my disdain for these bastards away as I shake Erika's hand.

"I am." She rolls her lips over her teeth and smiles fondly.

"You are trouble with a capital T and I am so here for it." I frown and shake my head but she pushes on. "She marked you, you are hers to end. Remember that, Kacey Vaughn." I feel like there is a double meaning to that when both males shake their heads and share a heated look, before turning their backs on me. Before I can question her, Chanel joins our little group. She stands in the middle of Havoc and me but leans closer to her cousin and doesn't glance my way as she speaks.

"Chaos just sent me the image of the target. He's at the back table with the mayor and Director of the FBI." My eyes widen as I turn to where she flicks her gaze and sure enough, my mentor and boss sit there.

Fuck!

I turn slightly so my back is to them and bring my wrist to my mouth discreetly, all four of them watch me with rapt interest. "I know who the mole is!" Chanel's brows furrow.

"Who is it?" Benny says.

I hold Chanel's gaze as I speak. "Quintin is the mole." I see the moment she remembers that name.

"He was the one I heard you speaking to that night at UNLV?"

"Yes, Quintin is–*was* my handler and I think he used me to get to you."

"You fucking prick," Royal seethes but I ignore him.

"Chanel, listen to me. I think Quintin is the one who sent you those pictures and set Owen up to take the fall for my brother's murder."

"That makes no sense. He's a fucking fed," Havoc hisses. I

turn to him and shake my head at his stupidity, this fucker doesn't get it.

"Quintin is the only one who knew where the fuck I was. He is the one who helped me conceal my brother's identity so no one would know. Yes, rumors circulated about the *Draugur* but that's all they were until someone ratted me out."

"Sucks when you're the one being ratted on, doesn't it?" Royal snarks. I grit my teeth and try to tamper my anger. I want to storm over to that table and beat the shit out of Quintin, then put a bullet in his head for what he did to my brother and planned to do to my family. He fucking betrayed me!

"Xav, I need you and Ro to get me all the intel you can on Q," I say to my guys. They both voice their agreement and say they will put in a call. I look at Chanel and shoot her a pleading look before I say, "I need to get into his office. If there is a master list with the files of your family and his intel on the Albanians, as well as those pictures of your mother, they will be in his office."

"I want every scrap of evidence you have against my family," she says in a tone that leaves no room for argument.

"Yeah, that is going to take some time since he works out of the head office and that shit is locked down tight."

"But I thought you were *Draugur*?" Royal taunts, earning a side sneer from me. Chanel shifts and pulls her gaze from me to look at her cousin. The resolute look in her eyes has me feeling uneasy.

"Now's my chance. I'll get it done," she says before brushing past me. I try to reach for her but fucking Havoc is there pulling me back and growling in my ear.

"You make a scene and you'll blow all of our covers. Live up to the name they call you and be a fucking ghost before you get her killed." I watch as the woman who has occupied my thoughts for years sways her hips, as she walks toward the cunt who killed my brother. She hypnotizes every man in this room as she makes her way toward Halil and Quintin. She radiates sex appeal without even trying. She is deadly in her normal daily clothes but dressed like she is, she is fucking lethal.

Havoc slowly releases me. I can feel him and Royal staring at me, waiting to see what I will do. Part of me wants to throw her over my shoulder and storm out of here so I can fuck some sense into her, but Chanel would shoot me in the dick if I did that. The other part of me knows she can handle herself, that this is the best chance I have of taking down the fucker who killed my brother and exposing the mole. Omar and Q's conversation ceases the moment they spot the beauty walking toward them.

"Get the fuck off the dance floor, people are staring!" Romeo's words snap me out of my stupor. I hustle from the floor and claim one of the tables at the back, not giving a fuck if I'm sitting in someone's seat. I have her in my sights and that's all that matters. Her cousins and Erika join me at the table. Ro and Xav let me know they are going to circle around since Q has no idea who they are. Both Q and Omar climb to their feet and place a kiss to either side of Chanel's cheeks, forcing me to grip the edge of the table or risk flying out of my chair to smack the cunts for touching her. Omar pulls a chair out, Q drops his hand to her lower back and guides her into the seat.

"You just gonna let those fuckers paw at your cousin?" I grit out through clenched teeth. Havoc shakes his head. Royal turns to face me and the emotionless mask he wears reminds me of his father.

"No one lets Sin do anything. If she didn't want them touching her, then they wouldn't be. Don't think for a second that just because you fucked her that you own her. She is our blood, our family. She belongs to the *Memento Mori* and will never belong to you."

"You don't know shit."

"The only reason I didn't end you is because you can erase what the feds have on my family and help take out the Albanians. Sin marking you had nothing to do with it. I am the Don of this family and mark my words, Kacey Vaughn, mark or not I will end you if you ever put her in danger or try to play her again. I knew something happened two years ago. She changed and started blocking me out. I will never allow a piece of shit like you to hurt her again. If she chooses to kill you, then we will deal with the fallout, because that is what she means to me."

"The fuck is that supposed to mean?" I growl.

"Does she mean enough to you to cross the line your moral compass says you shouldn't, for *her*?"

I open my mouth but snap it closed, because I don't know how to answer that. Would I throw away everything I have worked my whole life for?

"You're a fucking pathetic excuse of a human." My eyes widen as I turn to look at Erika, both Royal and Havoc are staring at her in shock.

"Excuse me?" I rasp out.

"You can't answer his question about risking it all for a woman you claim to love and yet, she risked it all for you without having to be asked. Chanel put her fucking life on the line for you. She risked everything to help you, but you can't even risk a fucking parking ticket for her." I frown at the bitch. She doesn't know and has no fucking right to judge. "You don't deserve her," She mutters as she turns away to look in the direction of Chanel. I can feel the judgment radiating off of the three of them and I fucking hate that shit. They have no idea what the fuck I went through, so I keep my eyes on my girl who is playing her part well and tell them what I did to keep her safe.

"When I first met Chanel, I had no idea who she was." I feel their gazes on me but ignore them. "I saw her across the quad at UNLV and thought she was the most beautiful woman I had ever seen in my life." Her cousins snort but I push on. "In my line of work, distractions can cost you your life, so I never pursued her. Days went by and I started to notice her more and more. She was never like the others who would dress for attention and show you everything their momma gave them. She was reserved and never mingled. I only ever saw her talking to both of you and Chaos. One day we bumped into each other in the library and then things just took on a life of their own."

"How the fuck did you find out who she really was?" Havoc asks.

"She became my obsession. Q started to notice that I wasn't sending updates regularly on Rico anymore and demanded to know why. My job has always been my first priority but with her, it wasn't important anymore. I wanted to become Connor Ryker for *her*. I only found out who she was the night I went to meet her and overheard her speaking to Royal on the phone about her parents. Once I heard their names I knew instantly who she was and told Q."

"Fucking bitch ass snitch," Royal growls out.

"Quintin wanted me to flip her but I refused. I couldn't do that to her so I told him I would continue to try to flip Rico and keep tabs on her knowing she would lead me to you three. Q agreed but when I stopped updating him all together, he knew I had fallen for my mark. He wanted to pull me straight away but then there was no one else who could do the job as good as me. The night she found out who I was, I left. I nearly lost my job because I refused to hand in my report on her."

"Why?" Erika asks. I pull my eyes from my girl who is laughing at something Q said and look at Erika.

"She thought I lied about everything and maybe I did, but I never lied about how I felt about her. I fell in love with my mark. I was chained to my desk for over a year until the Albanians became too much of a problem and they needed me to do my thing. I brought their organizations down—well, we thought we did but turns out we were wrong. That mistake cost me the life of my brother." Regret churns inside me as I say that aloud. I thought my job was everything until it cost me the woman I love and my brother. Now I'm not sure I wouldn't say fuck it to my moral compass and do whatever I needed to in order to save the one person who still takes my breath away the moment she walks into a room.

Chapter Twelve

CHANEL

"You are far too beautiful to be here on your own." I bat my lashes and smile coyly at Omar, acting like the perfect meek bitch. Fuckers like these two love it when a woman submits to them, it makes them feel powerful. Pathetic.

"My uncle left me no choice but to accompany him, only for him to get held up and leave me here on my own. Sorry, if I'm imposing..." I attempt to stand but Quintin places a hand on my bare shoulder and pushes me back into my seat.

"You are far from imposing, sweetheart. My friend and I were forced to listen to the mayors speak about how big their dicks are for over an hour, so believe me when I say, we are grateful to have you here with us." I force a blush to my cheeks and release the most disgusting girlish giggle that they eat up. As much as I would love to slit Quintin's throat for what he did to Kacey's brother, he isn't the one I'm after tonight. Omar is my target, but I am going to slip my card into Q's pocket tonight before he leaves because that bastard is marked already, even if he doesn't know it.

"What does your uncle do?" Omar asks. I roll my eyes and act the part of an airhead who only cares about money and not what someone does.

"He works in some big office doing paperwork for powerful people or something like that. I don't know. All I do know is that I get a hefty allowance each month. My parents dying was a blessing, they couldn't afford shit, but Uncle Henry can." I feel like an utter bitch for speaking like this but I have a part to play. I have to prove to Royal he can still count on me to get shit done. Omar snags some flutes of champagne from a waiter as he passes by and hands me one. I only take a sip because I have watched him the entire time since he snagged them. I wouldn't put it past these fuckers to slip something into my drink. I nurse my same glass as Q and Omar continue to drink excessively. Each time a waiter passes by I make sure to grab them each a glass. After the sixth glass, I decided to ask a waiter to bring us three glasses of whiskey neat.

I may not be able to handle the taste of champagne but I sure as fuck can knock a whiskey back and keep up with the big boys. Chaos is useless at killing and hunting but the man is a pro at hacking and drinking. I learned everything I needed to know about handling my booze from him. Which is why, two hours later I am still sober and my two friends here are slurring and swaying in their seats. The entire time I have sat here with these two, I've felt Kacey's eyes on me. Omar leans in closer to me and places a meaty hand on my thigh under the table and tries to whisper something in my ear but I can't hear a word he says over the sound of glass shattering behind me. I turn to look over my shoulder. Omar takes that as a hint to kiss me and I lift my hand ready to nail this fucker, but then remember where I am.

I ignore the sound of shit shattering and the sounds of gasps around the room as I allow this fucker to kiss me. I fight the urge not to gag. The moment his tongue prods my lips I pull back and smile at him, whilst blinking rapidly acting like his kiss stunned me stupid for a moment.

"Want to get out of here?" he whispers, his rancid breaths washing over me and I fight not to recoil from the stench.

"You two kids have fun, I got shit to do," Quintin says as he climbs to his feet. I follow his lead ignoring the frown from Omar. I don't think, I quickly pull him in for a hug as I discreetly pull a card that I have stashed in the waistband of my thong and slip it into his pocket. Quintin turns and leaves as Omar climbs up behind and places a hand on the swell of my ass and ushers me forward. It takes everything inside me not to rip his hand off me and break every one of his fingers. I flick my gaze to the side and spot Royal and Havoc holding Kacey against the wall as he rages against their hold.

"Fuck, I can't wait to get you out of this dress." A shiver of disgust rolls through me at Omar's words. The fucker mistakes that shiver for want and grins smugly. On our way out, I spot Romeo who gives a subtle nod, we stand outside as the valet leaves to retrieve Omar's car. I want to snort when a Rolls Royce pulls up, of course the fucker owns one of these.

Clearly, he is overcompensating for his little dick, I think as I slip inside and claim the passenger seat. I expected him to have a driver, but I was wrong. He climbs behind the wheel. I force myself to remain silent and not comment on the amount he has had to drink or the fact that he is drunk. On the way out, I spot Benny in a Range Rover—he pulls out just behind us. I'm not worried, Royal has trackers implanted on all of us so he would be able to find me anywhere. I know my dad and uncle would be tracking my every move as well. Omar makes small talk the whole way to his penthouse. He boasts about how amazing his view is and how he has connections to so many different celebs, and if I wanted to model, he would be happy to manage me. I smile, nod and play my part when in truth all I want to do is stab this fucker.

We pull up out front of a swanky looking place. A valet opens my door and helps me out as Omar rounds the car. He shoots the young valet a dirty look, before gripping my wrist. He drags me inside after him. I try not to bristle at the way he is manhandling me. I keep repeating to myself that the moment we get inside his penthouse, I can put the fucker down. The second the elevator doors close the bastard is on me, licking my neck and pawing at my tits. I grind my teeth so fucking hard my jaw begins to ache from the force of it. The moment his hand drops and he cups my pussy, I lose it.

My father always taught me to never allow a man to assume they have a right to touch me. He made sure from a young age that I was able to protect myself. Gripping his hand, I wrench it back. He shouts in pain as he pulls back. I jab him in the throat and relish in the strangled sound that comes from him. He drops to his knees and I release his hand, landing an elbow to the top of his head, causing him to sway. I don't relent, cocking my arm back and hit him right in the nose. The bastard falls to the side in a heap just as the doors open. Growling out my annoyance, I grab his arms and heave his fat ass out of the elevator with every ounce of strength I have. Before the doors can close, I grab his keycard from his pocket and toss it into the lift, knowing the others will be downstairs waiting.

Sure enough just as I get this fucker out of the entryway and into his zoo of a living room Royal and the others arrive. My eyes widen when Royal and Havoc are shoved aside and Kacey comes barreling toward me. He grips my face between his hands. I smack his hands away and jump back a step glaring at him. The bastard has the audacity to scowl down at me.

"The fuck was that shit, Chanel?" Kacey shouts. My brows raise as I stare up at him in stupor.

"Idiot," I hear Havoc mutter from behind us as he grabs an unconscious Omar and shoves him into a seat to tie down.

"Who the fuck do you think you are? You don't get to come in here and throw your weight around—"

"Oh, but any cunt is welcome to put their hands all over you like some cheap escort?" My anger snaps, without warning I hit him across the jaw forcing him to stagger back.

"You ever call me a fucking whore again and I'll break your jaw," I grit out. His eyes spit fire at me as he rubs his cheek.

"Oh, baby, I know you're not a whore. The only cock you've ever had is mine." My eyes widen as the sounds of gasps and choking sound out around the room from my cousins, Ro, Xav, Benny and Erika. "I said you were an escort, there is a big difference between the two professions, baby." This smug motherfucker is about to get his ass handed to him.

"No, in your line of work you just use people and then get them killed." It's a low blow, I know it is, but he needs to learn that I am not his. A haze overcomes his features for a second before he masks it.

"Don't worry, Sin, I never make the same mistake twice, unlike you." The double meaning isn't lost on me. Before the son of a bitch can get another lashing from me, Omar wakes.

"What the fuck?" the bastard snarls as he looks around the room, taking stock of all the strange faces in his home. When his gaze lands on me, his upper lip pulls back in a snarl. Kacey may be pissed at me but the protector in him takes over. He steps in front of me and shields me from Omar's view.

"You don't fucking look at her," Kacey snarls. I roll my eyes and step out from behind him. He snaps his hand out and grabs my wrist. I look to his hold on me then back to him with a brow raised. "I got this," he growls. I peel his fingers off me and shake my head.

"This is my show, it's time you learned who I really am, Agent Vaughn," I snap.

"You fucking rat. You will die," Omar shouts at Kacey. Everyone ignores him. Havoc and Royal step away from our victim at my approach. Unlike Kacey who remains on my fucking ass, they know I can handle myself.

"I ask the questions, you answer and we make this as painless as possible. You lie or fuck me around and I start taking pieces of you, got it?" The cunt spits right in my face. Before I can recover, Kacey is pummeling his face with his fists. Romeo, Xavier and Benny rush forward and pull their friend back.

"You motherfucker. Do that to her again, you cunt, and I'll kill you," Kacey rages.

"I think the agent might be rethinking his career choice," Havoc taunts but I ignore him. I ignore Omar for the time being and turn back to Royal who tosses me the duffle bag in his hand.

"Get the sheet out and secure it, he's gonna be a screamer," I say. Erika hands Havoc the bag she carries so the guys can get the plastic sheet out—easier to clean up that way and we don't leave any traces of DNA. I pull out the instruments I packed and place them on the ground.

"I put a shirt in there for you," Royal calls over his shoulder. Sure enough, I pull out one of his shirts and a pair of sweats. I turn my back to the others and push the straps of my dress down.

"Close your fucking eyes!" I hear Kacey shout. I fight the smirk from breaking free. I could have gone into a bathroom to change, but I just wanted to fuck with him some more after his stupid ass comment earlier. I stuff the dress and heels back into the duffle as I secure the sweats and tie them as tight as I can. I feel Kacey's gaze burning into the side of my head, but I ignore him as I grab the gag and machete from the floor. I eye

Omar as Royal and Havoc finish placing the plastic tarp beneath him. He tries to act calm but I can see the fear that lurks in the depths of his gaze.

"Search the place, see if you can find anything we need on Halil and his location," I say. Benny, Ro, Erika and Xav leave to do as I ask, leaving me, Kacey, Royal and Havoc alone with Omar in the living room. Omar keeps flicking his gaze between the three males. Shaking my head, I step forward and stop when I'm standing between my cousins. His gaze slowly comes to me and he growls before spitting at my feet. I open my mouth to speak but then Kacey comes from the side and punches Omar across the jaw. He grips his hair and yanks his head back so he can look him in the eyes.

"I warned you," Kacey snaps. I look at Havoc and nod. He steps forward and pulls Kacey back. If he can't contain himself, then I have no choice but to have Havoc remove him from the room completely.

"She doesn't need you to protect her," I hear Hav whisper to Kacey.

"I can gag you and start by taking your hands until you squeal, or you tell me what I want to know and I end it quickly," I say with a shrug of my shoulders.

"You fucking bitch, I'll never tell you–" A scream so fucking loud tears from him when I swing the machete into his knee cap and lodge it there. Royal tears the gag from my hand and rushes forward to secure it on Omar, as I turn and grab three of my daggers and the nail gun from the floor. Tears stream down Omar's face when I turn back to face him. He tries to speak around the leather gag but nothing can be understood.

"Now look what you made me do, Omar." I tsk as I step forward. The bastard drops his eyes to the daggers and the nail gun in my hands. I place the nail gun down on the sheet in front of him and then twirl one of my daggers in my hand, loving how his eyes track its movement. I wait for him to relax slightly in his chair before I dart forward and plunge it into the top of his thigh. He wails and thrashes in his chair, but it's no use. "No one will hear you scream, no one will come to your aid and no one here will help you."

"Hmmmm." I shush him and yank the dagger out. He cries out but it's muffled, thanks to the gag. I drop the other two daggers to the floor as I yank the machete free from his knee. His eyes roll backward, so I dart forward and drop onto his lap, ignoring the growl that comes from Kacey. I trace the tip of the bloody dagger down his cheek and smile when his eyes begin to focus on me again. I can feel his blood from his thigh soaking through Royal's sweats.

"How attached to your ears are you?" His eyes widen and he begins to try and buck me off, but I hold firm. "Omar," I say his name in a high pitched voice, like a mother would use to scold their child. "I thought you couldn't wait to get me back here and get me out of that dress to play?"

"Motherfucker," I hear from Kacey. I wiggle my brows at Omar and lean in to brush my lips against the shell of his ear.

"I think my friend over there is a bit jelly," I fake whisper.

"You weren't calling me your friend in my shower." I ignore the bastard's retort and the groans of my cousins as I grip Omar's ear and slice it off. I drop the useless piece of flesh to the ground and smile at him when I pull back. I drop my dagger to the ground and place both my hands on the tops of his shoulders.

"So, now that you know I am the one you have to worry about and not my guys, are you ready to talk or am I going to have to scalp you?" His eyes blaze with hatred, as I give him a second to think on my request. When he subtly nods, I climb off his lap as Royal removes the gag. The gray sweats I wear are covered in his blood. "Omar, where is Halil?" I ask.

"I don't know." I sigh and shake my head as I bend to

retrieve my two daggers. Royal slaps his hand over Omar's mouth as I lodge a dagger in the top of each of his thighs. "Fucking bitch," Omar seethes when Royal drops his hand from his mouth. I grab the other dagger from the floor and twirl it in my hand, loving how Omar eyes it with trepidation.

"You see, Omar, I am so used to everyone doubting me because I am the only female in the room and naturally, they assume I'm the weakest out of me, Royal, Havoc and Chaos." Havoc snorts and shakes his head, smiling. I shoot my cousin a wink before focusing back on my target. "That is the worst mistake to make, because I am the most savage and ruthless out of the four of us when it comes to extracting information. I am going to give you another chance to answer my questions before I nail your cock to your thigh and then sever your balls from your body."

"Jesus, Sin."

"Ouch," comes from my cousins but I ignore them.

"What the fuck?" Ro mutters as he and the others enter the room and take in the sight of Omar. I shoot the four of them a wink before looking back to my non-compliant friend.

"Are you ready to talk?" I ask.

"I don't know where he is. I swear I have no idea." Without warning I throw the dagger. It lodges in his shoulder as a roar of pain escapes him.

"Fucking hell, Sin, warn me next time!" Royal snaps from his position behind Omar.

"I'm a dead shot. There is no way I would have missed," I say. He shoots me a dirty look before moving away.

"I don't know where he is!" Omar screams.

"Okay. Then answer me this, how the fuck did you know who Kacey was?" Omar cuts a glance at Kacey and sneers before focusing back on me. I see the war in his eyes, he's debating if it's worth telling me or not so I prompt him. "Either way, you are not making it out of this room so you may as well tell me what I want to know. The more you corporate the less pain for you, fuck around and your cock will be nailed to your leg."

"She's fucking crazy!" I hear Benny sneer.

"Halil got a tip from our inside man in the bureau, we didn't know we had a rat until after we got busted."

"Who told you about Marcus?" Kacey asks.

"Fuck you, bitch!" Omar spits.

"Answer his question," I snap.

The bastard grits his teeth, wanting to defy me so I shake my dagger in his face. "We got intel from our man inside—"

"Quintin?" Kacey cuts in and asks. Omar grits his teeth and nods.

"So, he was the one who told you who Kacey was and that his brother was imprisoned?" I push.

"Yes." I nod accepting his answer. "We never had a problem with you–"

"But I had one with you. Miami is ours and you fuckers thought because Chance was no longer here, that you could remain?" Royal doesn't give him a chance to answer.

"Newsflash, bitch, you and your scum will be pushed out. The *Memento Mori* don't and never will deal in the skin trade. I will have this operation shutdown before it even begins again you sick fuck." Like his father, Royal will never allow the skin trade to happen on our turf. The Albanians want to bring it back. Uncle Bishop stopped that shit years ago. Chance was promised a cut if he helped them.

"Halil will kill you!" Omar snarls at Royal.

"We meet with your boss in just under three weeks, but we have found out that you bastards want to set a trap." Omar's eyes blaze. "I want to know where Halil is now. If you don't tell me and we get to the meet and get ambushed, I'll make sure to tell your boss that you sang like a bird."

"Fuck you, you don't know shit, bitch," he shouts. I

collect the nail gun and don't hesitate to pull the trigger and nail both his feet to the floor.

"I know enough to know that when an Albanian soldier falls, their families are cared for but if they are snitches, their families are killed. So I ask again, where the fuck is Halil?" It takes me nailing his cock to his thigh and nailing each of his balls to the chair before he finally gives up the location of Halil. True to my word, I end him. Pulling the dagger from his shoulder, I slit his throat and watch as his soul slowly leaves his body. Taking a life always fills me with a sense of power and makes me horny. This feeling is fucking addictive and I honestly can't get enough of it.

Chapter Thirteen

KACEY

I watch as she drops the dagger to the ground and steps back, smiling down at her victim. She's covered in his blood and for the first time I see her, the real her. She pulls a card from her pants pocket and tosses it onto the counter behind her victim, letting everyone know that the *Memento Mori* was here. For all my years of being an agent, I should be repulsed and taking her ass to jail. I have worked my ass off my whole life to get to where I am, only for it all to be a lie. I would never have been able to figure out who the mole was this quickly if it wasn't for her and her family. I can feel my friends staring at me, but I can't take my eyes off the woman who just single handedly killed a man in front of my eyes.

"Go shower, bring everything out with you. I'll call Benny." Royal says.

"Uh, I'm right here," Benny says. Both Chanel and Royal pin him with a dry stare.

"Benny is also the name of one of our guys who... will clean this situation up," Erika supplies.

"Got any spare clothes?" Chanel asks. Havoc and Royal both look at the clothes she's wearing. She groans and goes for the duffle bag that contains her dress and heels. I turn to Ro and toss him my keys, which he catches.

"Get my go bag out of the trunk," I say. He nods and takes off toward the elevator. "I got some clothes in my car." She darts her gaze to me and frowns before nodding stiffly, then makes her way down the hallway where Erika told her the bathroom is. It takes about ten minutes for Ro to come back up with my bag in hand. Taking it from him, I turn to head down the hallway but Royal blocks my path.

"Where do you think you are going?" I eye the fucker with a look of pure disdain.

"You don't own her," I grit out.

"Never said I did."

"Bullshit."

"You think because you got to witness her do this, that you are safe?" He doesn't allow me to answer. "You thought wrong. You got your answer, now it's time for you to leave." I square up to the bastard until we are chest to chest. I see the spark of intent in his eyes.

"Not. Without. Her," I enunciate each word so he doesn't misunderstand my intent. I am here for her as well as my answers. Before another word can be said, his fist lands on my jaw, then we are going at it. Havoc and my boys rush forward to break up the fight. Benny and Havoc try to hold Royal back while Xav and Ro grab my arms and pull me back.

"You're done. Get the fuck out now before I change my mind and kill you where you stand," Royal snarls. The elevator pings. The fight forgotten, we all draw our guns and turn toward the entry to see six men enter the room with frowns on their faces. Royal drops his gun and moves forward to greet the man. I'm assuming this is the guy he called to get rid of the body.

"Oh shit," Xav breathes out. I follow his line of sight and see Chanel standing at the end of the hall in a towel, the six men all looking toward her. Darting forward, I snarl at them and grip her arm, yanking her back to the bathroom ignoring her threats. I slam the door closed behind us and trap her between my body and the counter.

"Don't fucking touch—"

"You don't fucking show them what is *mine*," I shout right in her face, making her eyes narrow.

"I am not yours, Kacey. We will never be more than what we are now." Her words have a pit of unease forming in my gut.

"Why not?" The words are out of my mouth before I can stop them.

"Because, unlike me, you save people and follow the law. I kill those who wish to harm the lesser beings and don't obey the law. We are from two different worlds, Kacey. Why can't you see that?"

"Because, all I see is you, baby," I whisper as I lean my forehead against hers. "I can't walk away from you, Chanel. Not again." I hear the anguish in my own voice.

Her eyes shutter closed as a whoosh of air escapes her. "You don't have a choice. If you stay here and try to push this, it will be the end of me. You are the law and I am the person you have been taught to hunt. Could you look me in the eyes right now and tell me you would let me go if you were to raid one of our warehouses?" I stare into her brown eyes and mull over her words, I couldn't even let my own brother go so how can I answer that? A tired sigh escapes her as she pushes me back a step, then snags the bag from my hold, places it on the counter and drops her towel as she turns her back to me.

My eyes drop to the swell of her ass and I bite back a groan as she rifles through my bag. Before I can stop myself, I step forward and plaster my front to her back. She stiffens but doesn't push me away. Bending down I place open mouths kisses from her shoulder to her neck. She tilts her head, giving me better access. I nip at her earlobe and love the shudder that runs through her body. Gripping her waist in my hands, I turn her to face me. Her eyes are glazed over and I see the need inside them. Lifting, I place her on the counter and force her legs wider to accommodate my size. She opens her mouth but I'm too scared to hear what she has to say, so I silence her with my lips.

I groan into her mouth and tighten my hold on her waist as her tongue dances with mine. I grind my growing erection into her and relish in the moan that comes from her. Breaking the kiss, I push her back enough so I can capture her nipple in my mouth. A soft mewl comes from her as I lap at her nipple and twirl the other between my fingers. She thrusts her hips, trying to grind against me but I stay just out of reach, wanting to work her up so she is a panting mess. Out there she may be the boss but in here, I call the fucking shots.

My cock is painfully hard and begging to be released from the confines of these fucking slacks. Her fingers tangle in my hair as she yanks on the strands to pull me closer. I bite down softly and love the sound of the gasp that comes from her.

"Kacey, I need you inside me." Releasing her nipple with a wet pop, I step back, shuck off my jacket and make quick work of ridding myself of my shirt and pants. Her eyes drop to the bulge in my boxers.

"You want me to fuck you, baby?" I tease. Rather than answering, she slips off the counter and stands in front of me. She keeps her gaze on mine as she grips the waistband of my boxers and pushes them down. Slowly, she lowers to her knees before me and Jesus Christ, seeing her kneeling before me is an erotic sight. Most women would tease and draw it out, but not my girl. She grips the base of my cock in her hand and pumps it twice, drawing a hiss from me. I flop forward and place a hand on the wall behind her to steady myself. A bead of pre-cum glistens on the tip of my dick. She darts her tongue out and licks me, moaning at the taste.

"Fuck, yes," she mutters before wrapping her lips around my cock and sucking me as far as she can before she begins to gag. I tangle my hand in her wet hair and hold her in place as she locks her hands behind her back, flicking her eyes up to me.

"You want me to fuck your mouth, Sin?"

"Hmmm," is the only reply I get, so I do as she wants and fuck her face, groaning in pleasure. The sound of her gagging and choking on my cock, and watching as her spit drips down her chin is fucking sexy. When I feel my balls begin to tighten, I pull free of the wet warmth of her mouth and use my grip on her hair to pull her to feet. She's dragging in large amounts of air as she stands before me. Releasing her hair, I rub my hand through the spit on her chin and rub it all over her face before claiming her lips in a kiss that stamps my ownership of her. I break the kiss before she can deepen it and spin her around, push between her shoulder blades so she is folded over the counter, then kick her legs apart.

I massage the globes of her ass in my hands, loving the soft mewls that come from her. Memories of her kissing Omar flash through my mind. Gritting my teeth, I spank her ass twice on each side and don't rub out the sting.

"Did you like kissing him?" I growl. She turns her head to peer over her shoulder at me and glowers.

"I had to–"

Thwack.

She yelps and jolts forward but I keep her in place. "That wasn't what I asked," I growl.

"I didn't have a choice–"

Thwack.

She growls and tries to turn, so I smack her ass again. "Answer the fucking question, Chanel, or I jerk off and come all over this red ass while you stay on edge." Her jaw slackens as she stares up at me.

"No, I hated it," she grits out through clenched teeth. I slip my hands between her legs and cup her pussy. I can feel her arousal coating my palm and hum my approval.

"If you ever..." I push a single finger inside her tight cunt, "let another man..." I push in and out of her, working her up as I speak, "touch you again, I'll kill him and take out my anger on your pussy." I pull free of her heat. She whimpers as I glare down at her. "Do you understand, Chanel?"

"Y-yes." I land another swift thwack to her ass before I drop to my knees behind her and bury my face in her pussy. She jolts forward and cries out. I plan to make her scream my name so all those fuckers out there know exactly who the fuck their warrior princess belongs to. She pushes back against my face as I eat her pussy like a starved man. She reaches back and grips my hair to hold me in place as she grinds up and down on my tongue chasing her release. "Kacey!" she screams as she squirts all over my face. I hum my approval as I capture some of it in my mouth and stand behind her. I spit her release over her naked back and rub it in as I nudge her legs further apart and line my cock up with her entrance.

"This is for me, not you. You need to be taught a lesson on who the fuck you belong to," I snarl as I slam inside her.

"Fuck!" she screams so loud I know without a doubt everyone would have heard. I grip her hips in a punishing hold as I fuck the shit out of her, not caring if she comes or not. After her little stunt tonight, she doesn't deserve to come on my cock. My balls begin to tighten and I know I'm seconds away from coming deep inside her tight little cunt. Releasing my hold on her hips, I gather her hair in my hand and yank it, she moans her approval.

"Fuck yes, take my cock like a good girl, baby."

"Don't stop, please," she begs.

"Who the fuck does this pussy belong to?" I growl as I slam into her at a ruthless pace, sweat beading my brow as I chase my climax. When she doesn't answer, I use my free hand to redden her ass. "Answer me!"

"You. It's your pussy. Now make me come." The moment her pussy walls start to clench my cock, I pull free of her and grip my cock pumping twice before I throw my head back and roar out my release. Jets of cum spurt over her back and ass. She gasps in outrage that I didn't allow her to come. She tries to move, but I grip the back of her neck and hold down as I smear my cum all over her, mixing it with her own juices, then I gather some on my finger before pushing it inside her cunt.

"Shit," she moans as she rises to her tiptoes.

"You belong to me, Chanel. I am the only man who will ever see you come." I continue to fuck her with my fingers. "Now come all over my fucking hand so those motherfuckers know who owns every single one of your orgasms." As if my words are her undoing, she comes all over my fingers and squirts all over the bathroom floor. Pulling my fingers free of her pussy I meet her eyes in the mirror as I bring them to my mouth and suck them clean. A shiver rolls through her at the sight, while I moan at the taste of her sweet juices coating my tongue.

Stepping back, I allow her to stand. She turns on wobbly legs to face me, her face flushed and her eyes hazy. She darts her tongue out to moisten her lips and immediately the image of her on her knees minutes ago with my cock in her mouth flashes in my mind. My cock twitches with the need to be inside her again. I know we don't have time for another round so I take another step back.

"I need to shower," she mumbles as she tries to step around me. I block her path and scowl down at her.

"Not a fucking chance, you walk out of here with my cum

all over you so those cunts know exactly what the fuck we were doing in here." Her eyes widened.

"Kacey–"

"Try me, Chanel. I dare you." She balks at me and shakes her head.

"They already know!" she whisper shouts. Crossing my arms over my chest, I quirk a brow at her.

"Don't give a fuck. Now you either get dressed in *my* clothes or I'll dress you myself. Choose." She tries to look pissed off but her brown eyes swim with lust at my demands. I know she is a bad bitch and can hold her own, but she loves it when I go all caveman and force her to do shit. It calls to the beast inside her that hungers for me to control it.

Chapter Fourteen

CHANEL

Walking out of that bathroom, I couldn't meet anyone's gaze. Erika's quiet laughter had me cringing. They all knew exactly what we were doing. If they didn't, they sure as hell heard me screaming Kacey's name. That fucker has no issues walking out with his head held high and his chest puffed out. It's not like he's the one who has cum all over his body! The elevator ride was so awkward. Kacey refused to wait for the next one and he and the others climbed in with the four of us. Royal shifted to get further away from them but the moment he bumped into me he jerked away and shuddered in disgust, causing Erika to laugh at his expense.

I didn't even look at Kacey as I climbed in the back of Royal's car next to Erika. No one has uttered a single word. The guys keep checking the mirrors but have yet to comment on the fact Kacey and his friends are following us home. There is no fucking way they will be allowed inside the property or near it. Which has me worrying about what Royal has planned. He won't allow anyone to know where we lay our heads, so I know he has something planned.

"So, how was your night, Chanel?" I snap my head toward Erika and glare. Her smile is stretched wide across her face.

"Baby, don't," Royal warns but she ignores him and clearly can't sense the danger she is in if she continues to push me.

"Well, unlike those two salty cousins of yours, I am proud." Both guys groan while I frown in confusion.

"What?" She waves her hand and gives me a toothy grin.

"Girl, I knew the moment he saw you in that dress that he would lose his fucking mind and want to tear it off you. Tell me I'm wrong?"

"Jesus, Rika, stop, please. She is like a sister to me and I can't hear any more of this. Hearing what I already have has ensured I can never look her in the eye again." I can't help it, laughter bursts out of me at Havoc's comment. Erika joins me while the guys continue muttering curses beneath their breath. Erika reaches over and places her hand on my shoulder. My laughter dies off as I look at her.

"I'm happy for you." I have no idea why, but her words have a warmth washing over me. "He seems like a good guy. Well, duh, he must be if he managed to snag your attention." Royal and Havoc have stopped speaking and listening intently for my reply. Erika shoots me a look that tells me to speak my truth. I take a risk and trust her.

"Kacey is... not like anyone I've ever met," I answer honestly.

A snort comes from Royal. "Of course not. How many feds do you know?" The angry bite to his words has me recoiling within myself.

"Probably the same number of heiresses you know that wanted to kill you." Royal sputters at his fiancées snarky reply, while Havoc just laughs at his expense.

"I liked it better when they hated each other," Royal mumbles sourly. We round the final corner before pulling onto our street. I sit upright in my seat and pull my Glock from my waistband at the sight of six blacked out SUVs blocking the road and men surrounding them. One of the vehicles moves to allow us through and then quickly shifts back into place to block Kacey and the others from following us. I want to ask how he had time to organize this blockade but decide it's better to keep my mouth shut and not piss him off more than I already have.

Royal brings the car to a stop out front of the house and I cringe when I see my father and uncle standing there. My dad looks murderous, while my uncle looks uneasy which is unusual. I leap out of the car before it completely stops and rush toward my dad. He jumps back a step when I'm within arm's reach.

I freeze on the spot and ask, "What's wrong?" Panic begins to bloom inside me until my uncle starts to cough to mask his laughter. I feel the others come up behind me. Both of my cousin's snicker behind me but silence the moment my dad shoots them a scathing look. "What the fuck is going on?" I snap.

Royal places a hand on my shoulder drawing my attention to him. "I knew your...*friend* would follow us home so I rang your dad because he was with Marco and asked him to organize the blockade back there."

"And?" I snap, getting pissed off.

Royal smiles wickedly. "You were occupied while I was on the phone and my poor uncle had to hear his darling daughter *screaming* in the background." I choke on air, my mouth hangs open and my eyes are so wide they begin to water. I slowly turn to face my dad, who is standing there clenching and unclenching his fists at his sides.

"Dad–"

"Not a fucking word, Chanel!" he roars. Uncle Bishop loses the battle and laughs loudly. "Fuck you, Bishop!" Uncle B raises his hands in the air and turns to my dad, unable to stop smiling while I stand here wanting to die of shame.

"I told you, one day karma would bite you in the ass for constantly talking about fucking my sister and now she has finally dished out her revenge. Fuck me it's the sweetest thing." I ignore my dad and uncle's bickering as I turn back to Royal, who is shaking with silent laughter. His laughter dies in his throat the moment he sees the tears in my eyes. His face pales.

"Sin–"

Shaking my head, I cut him off. "We have done some fucked up shit to each other in the past... And I know I fucked up with hiding the truth about Kacey from you. But this..." I shake my head, swallow the lump of shame in my throat and push on. "You took a private, intimate moment of *mine* and made a mockery of me. I would never have done that to you!" I scream, turn on my heel and march back toward the gates, needing to get the fuck away from here—from *him*. I ignore him shouting my name because as a male it may be funny for them to do shit like this to each other, but that's my dad! My father should never have heard that shit and without a doubt, I know Royal did it on purpose. He could have called Marco directly but he didn't, he chose to call my father knowing he would hear me.

The gates open and I march down the street toward the blockade. At this moment I don't care about what I did to betray my cousin by hiding Kacey from him. Royal fucked me over worse than he will know. I am so ashamed and there is no fucking way I can ever look my father in the eye again after this. The closer I get, I can hear shouts and Kacey spewing threats at the guys to let him through. At the sound of my approach, they all stop and turn to me. Marco rushes forward to try to stop me, but I just pull my gun and point it at him.

"I've been instructed not to let anyone pass," Marco says as he raises his hands.

"Try and stop me and I'll end you where you fucking stand." Marco darts his gaze over my shoulder. I slowly turn around to see my father, uncle and cousins standing there. Royal at least has the decency to look sheepish and drop his gaze to the ground. My dad isn't looking at me, he has a look of hatred directed over my shoulder and there is no doubt in my mind he's looking at Kacey. Waves of tension roll off my dad. I cut a glance to my uncle and I'm not surprised to see the humor from earlier is replaced by an emotionless mask. He's in Don mode.

Lowering my gun back to my side, I stand tall and hold my head high as I look to my dad. I cringe when his gaze drops to what I'm wearing. Not only did he hear what I was doing, he now has to see me wearing Kacey's clothes!

"Let him through." Those words send a chill down my spine, I have never in my life been scared of my dad until this moment. He has no issue with me killing and breaking the law, but the knowledge of me sleeping with someone, he has a huge fucking issue with it! I don't dare take my eyes off my dad, even when I hear the guys behind stepping aside and the sound of footsteps coming up behind me. I pray that Kacey has a sense of self preservation and doesn't come to me. That thought evaporates as fast as my hope of him living to see tomorrow when he comes to stand beside me.

Kill me now!

Kacey places a hand to the small of my back. I want to step away from him and act like I have no idea who he is, but it's too little too late for that. Dad knew there was something between us when he first saw Kacey, but he had no idea I was fucking him until tonight! Dad's features turn deadly as he looks Kacey up and down with utter distaste. I spy him out of the corner of my eye. The fact he is standing tall and looking directly at my father tells me he is fucking suicidal!

When my dad steps forward, everything inside me stills. I swear my heart flips inside my chest. My plan was to run out and escape with Kacey and his friends for the night, just to let my father calm down, not for him to follow me out here. Uncle Bishop and Havoc flank my dad while Royal remains where he is. He tries to catch my stare but I refuse to look directly at him.

This is all his fucking fault!

"Sir–" Kacey tries to speak but my dad silences him with a deep growl. I may be furious at Kacey and hate what he did to me, but I also can't allow my father to kill him. I open my mouth ready to try to defuse the tension and attempt to make peace, but I don't get the chance.

"Vincent Murelo, get your ass back here now!" My eyes widen at the sound of my mother's angry voice. I peer around my dad to see my aunt, Erika and my mom storming toward us.

"Same goes for you Bishop and you." Aunt Kiara points at her son who is looking everywhere but at her. "I am so disappointed in you. How could you do that to your cousin?" Royal doesn't answer his mother as he turns to Erika. She crosses her arms over her chest and stares her man down.

"You told my mom on me?" he accuses.

"Don't take that tone with her!" Aunt Kiara snaps.

"Vincent, you will not harm that boy!" my mom states. My dad still won't take his eyes off Kacey or even acknowledge my mom standing behind him. Mom huffs out her annoyance and comes to stand in front of my dad, keeping her back to him. I don't know why but nerves thrum through me as she looks Kacey over, her brow scrunching and her lips pushing to the side, as if she is concentrating really hard. To my utter disbelief, Kacey begins to fidget under the scrutiny of my mother's gaze, but when faced with my father and uncle, he stands proudly and ready to throw down if need be.

The one to break the tension is Erika. She brushes past her man and bats his hands away when he tries to stop her from coming toward us. I keep darting my gaze between my parents and Erika, the latter shoots me a look that begs me to trust her and right now, I don't have another choice but to trust the woman I have been a downright bitch to. Rika stops in the middle of me and my parents, and shoots my mom and dad with a bright smile.

"Vincent, Carlina I would like to be the first to introduce you to Kacey Vaughn..." My dad seems to relax slightly and I do as well until Erika continues speaking, "Chanel's *boyfriend*." Everything happens in a blur. One second my mom and Erika are in front of us, then in the next blink of an eye my dad is in front of Kacey with the muzzle of his gun pressed against his forehead. All Royal's men surround us and have their guns trained on Kacey's friends.

It's at this moment I understand why my father is called The Bloodhound. He strikes without noise and has the poise of a lion. The look in his eyes has my breath hitching. I see no trace of the man that raised me, he is in full on killer mode and fuck me, I have never wanted to be more like my dad than I do in this moment. He is a force. I thought the name Murdoch inspired fear but I was wrong, my dad doesn't need a name he is just... *lethal.*

"Vincent—" my mom tries to defuse the situation, but my dad isn't having it. My uncle and cousins have my aunt and Erika behind them, protecting them.

"You think after what you did to *my* little girl that you can waltz in here and remain breathing?" My mouth feels like it has cotton balls in it. I keep swallowing trying to think fast about how to get Kacey and his friends out of here alive and breathing, but keep coming up blank. When Kacey doesn't answer, Dad presses his gun harder against him prompting him to answer.

"No, sir, I don't." His answer has me balking up at him. "You have every right to think what you do about me. I fucked up badly where she is concerned." Kacey flicks his gaze to me and I deflate, the resigned look in his eyes has my chest feeling like it may crack open.

"You will stay the fuck away from my daughter–"

"Dad–" He cuts a look to me that has me clamping my mouth closed.

"You put her life on the line, you betrayed her and tried to use her. You will never be welcome around her or my family." A lump begins to form in my throat as a feeling of anguish washes over me. "I'll allow you to walk out of here with your life, because she cares for you. Do not mistake my kindness for weakness. If I ever see you again—"

"You'll kill me," Kacey supplies solemnly.

Dad darts his hand out, grips the front of Kacey's shirt and growls, "No, I'll start with your parents, then your last remaining sibling before I come for you." Kacey's chest rises and falls with harsh intakes of air. "Scum like you isn't worthy of her. You have three minutes to get the fuck out of here. Any last words?" Tears prick the backs of my eyes, something about this moment feels so final like I won't ever see Kacey again and that... hurts.

"Yes, but my words aren't for you, sir." Havoc and Royal both whistle between their teeth, thinking that this man definitely has a death wish. "If this is the last time I get to see your daughter, please allow me to say goodbye."

"Why the fuck should I give you anything?" Dad seethes right in his face.

"It's not for me, sir, it's for her." Dad flicks his gaze to me.

Whatever he sees in my eyes has him growling and releasing Kacey with a shove.

"You have two minutes," he snaps. Kacey wastes no time turning to me and gathering me in his arms. I don't hide from my feelings, I let them out and wrap my arms around him and hold him tightly, not wanting to let go. Kacey places a kiss to the top of my head as he holds me against his chest then pushes me back. The pained look in his blue eyes kills me. I don't realize I'm crying until he brushes my tears away with his thumbs.

"Chanel Murelo, I love you." His words have a strangled sound coming from me, fuck it hurts to hear those words coming from him when I know it will be the first and last time I ever get to hear them. "I am so sorry, baby, for everything I have done, said and put you through."

"Kacey–" He shushes me and smiles brokenly.

"Let me finish, I'm on the clock." He tries to ease the heartache with a joke but it doesn't work. "I'm sorry for a lot of things, baby, but I am not sorry for chasing you around like a love sick puppy until you finally gave in and let me talk to you. You will always be the best fucking part of me. Never change who you are, my *sinfully dreadful* beauty, because you're worth fighting for, baby. Thank you for allowing me to not only be in your presence but giving me a chance to know what it's like to be loved by a real life goddess." The sob that tears out of me is silenced by his kiss. He grips my face tightly between his hands as I cling to his shirt, trying to anchor him to me. He pours all his love for me into this kiss. I do the same, telling him without words I fucking love him and forgive him for lying to me.

The sound of a gun cocking has him breaking our kiss with a sigh. He rests his forehead against mine. I keep my eyes closed, not wanting to see him walk away. His lips press gently against my forehead before he withdraws his touch. I feel cold and empty without his presence. It takes me a minute to work up the courage to open my eyes. When I do, I break. Ro and Benny flank him on either side as he walks away with his hands in his pockets and his head hung low. Xav shoots me a sad smile before following after his friends.

"Kacey!" I shout as I take off. My dad tries to reach for me, but I dodge him. One of Marco's guys tries to block me, so I punch the fucker right in the nose. Kacey's eyes are wide as he spins around to see me coming. I launch myself at him and he catches me with ease. I seal my lips to his and pour everything I am into this kiss so he can take a part of me with him. I hear my dad shouting behind me and know for Kacey's safety I have to let him go. Pulling back he gently places me on my feet and forces a sad smile on his face. "I love you," I blurt, shock colors his features.

He grips the back of my neck and pulls me flush against himself. "Say it again," he demands.

"I love you." His lips are on mine again, but this time there is a fire brewing inside me, a need so strong that I gasp when he pulls back and stares down at me with a fierce look in his eyes.

"I'll fight my way back to you, Sin, Don't fucking give up on me."

"Never," I promise. He takes one last look at me before turning around and walking away with my heart in the palm of his fucking hand. I may have just given him the power to destroy me, but I can't find it within myself to care, because admitting my feelings out loud for the first time, has me feeling lighter than I ever have.

I'm in love with a man who betrayed my family.

Chapter Fifteen

KACEY

I'm standing on the hill at the back of the cemetery. My parents didn't want me here but I couldn't stay away. Marcus was my brother and as much I hate what he did with his life, I still loved him. It fucking sucks to not be up there next to his casket with my parents and Ash, but I know my presence down there would just cause pain for my mom and dad so I chose to stay back and watch from a distance.

I was shocked to get a call from Havoc three days after walking away from Chanel to tell me that Chaos was bringing my family home to bury my brother. I knew the twins and a few of the *Memento Mori* guards would be here in case the Albanians showed up. They aren't that ballsy, so I know there is no chance of them showing their faces. I've been dedicating my time to hunting Halil. Owen called me and told me I had to come in. I know it's because they found Omar's body, the *Memento Mori* wanted his body found so Halil knew he was being hunted.

I know my only shot at finding out where the fuck Halil is

hiding, is to go back to the office, but how the fuck can I do that when I know Quintin is the mole and setting Owen up to take the fall for his botched warrant. If I don't take Q down, then all the Albanian soldiers we arrested will go free. These soldiers weren't just runners, they were key players in Halil's operation, which is why the bastard is hiding. We took down his main team and now, he is floundering. The sound of footsteps draws my attention. I peek out of the corner of my eye to see Royal walking toward me. Unlike me, who is dressed in a suit and tie, he wears jeans, Converse and a plain gray shirt with a pair of Ray Ban sunglasses that match my own.

"I've never seen her cry before," he says as he comes to stand next to me. I keep my gaze forward and watch the service. I want to punch his fucking face in but I know all that will do is start more shit. Unlike him, I don't have an endless flow of money that can buy my way out of a fucked-up situation.

"Lucky you," I deadpan. He turns to face me but I refuse to look at him, I don't owe this cunt anything.

"You've seen her cry?" The dumbfounded tone of his voice has me wanting to laugh but I manage to stop myself.

"Yes," I grit out.

"When?"

"The night she found out I was an undercover agent." He blows out a breath and nods. I can tell he's shocked by my declaration, but I don't say anything. I mean, what the fuck does someone like me, an FBI agent, say to the Don of the biggest crime family in Miami. I should be arresting him or trying to work an angle to take him and his business down but... I can't. I'm finally seeing clearly for the first time in my life, not everything is black and white and a lot of lines are blurred.

"Does she mean enough to you to give up what you love most?" His solemn tone isn't lost on me. The fact he isn't referring to her in past tense has me believing they didn't kill her for loving me. "I can see the question on your face."

"What question?"

"I think we are past the point of hiding who we truly are, Kacey Calvin Vaughn, born September 12th, 1999. You are the youngest agent to ever be recruited by the feds, and within four years of working at the bureau, you have imprisoned more kingpins than men triple your age. You're a good agent, Kacey, that is clear." I finally turn to face him, he does the same.

"You read my file, want a fucking pat on the back?"

"Ask me the question you want to know the answer to and stop being a bitch," he snarls.

"Is she alive?" My heart skips a beat as I wait for his reply. The fucker takes his time on purpose so I can stew on it.

"Chanel broke our code. She knew she fucked up when she let you live. She also fucked up worse when she didn't come to me about you trying to use her to rat–"

"That doesn't answer my question," I snap angrily.

"She fucked up badly and betrayed me. You may love her but know this, I was the first man aside from her father to love that girl. She isn't just my cousin, she is my underboss, my best friend and I fucking love her like a sister. If it were anyone else, I would have had the cunt begging for death. But, she isn't anyone else. Chanel is alive." A whoosh of air escapes me as relief washes through me. "She will never leave me. This isn't just a way of life for her, this is who she is! It's in her blood. She is the heiress and without her the *Memento Mori* is nothing."

"Why are you telling me this?" I ask him warily. He studies me for a second. Something about the way he is standing and looking at me sets me on edge.

"Because I want my best friend back." I lift my glasses and push them to the top of my head.

"What the fuck is that supposed to mean?" He runs a hand through his hair in frustration.

"There are bodies piling up around the city. Marco, Benny and Terry are fucking amazing at their jobs, but not even they can keep up with cleaning the messes she is leaving behind in her wake."

Frowning, I shake my head in confusion. "What?" He removes his glasses and places them on his head like mine. I can see the tired look in his eyes now.

"Chanel left the night you did. It's been five days and she has taken the lives of over a dozen Albanian soldiers trying to find the whereabouts of Halil and the information you would need to take down your mole."

I reel backward. "How the hell could you let her leave?"

He scoffs. "Have you met her? There is no fucking way I was stopping that crazy bull when she was a waving a gun around."

"She pointed a gun at you?" I blurt.

He shakes his head. "Worse. She pointed one at her father and told him she was going to prove that you were worthy of her." My fucking heart does a flip inside my chest. "Stop smiling!" he snarls, but I can't, she really does love me!

"How do you know it's her killing..." I leave my sentence trail off when he pulls a bloody card from his pocket and hands it to me. I flip it over. The words *Memento Mori* are inscribed on the back. These cards are custom made. The queen has a skull face and instead of it being the normal color red and the image being mirrored, it is just one solid picture of a skull wrapped in red robes. She doesn't hold the queen's scepter like normal cards, she holds a dagger like the one Chanel used to kill Omar. Smoke rises up from the back of the queen and the card looks like it's almost charred, but that's just the way it is made to look. The back of the card has the words but it also has smoke in the background, but you can clearly see a pair of eyes and a mouth. It's a skull face made out of smoke.

"It's her. She's been leaving her cards at every scene and if she finds any information, she leaves it for us to find."

"Why are you here?" I finally ask.

"Because we can't find her."

"Bullshit." I snap rolling my eyes.

"Do you really fucking think I want to be here?" he snarls.

"You have a tracker implanted in her, that's how you found Xav's house. So don't lie to me." He rubs the back of his neck and turns back toward the funeral happening below us. I follow his lead and watch as they slowly lower my brother's coffin into the ground.

"She removed the tracker." I don't respond because the sight of my mother collapsing in my father's arms has me choking back tears. "I know my timing is shit given where we are." I shoot him a deadpan look.

"Ya think?" I mock, shaking my head before looking back at my parents. I watch Ash and my dad practically carry my mother to their waiting car. I hate that I'm not down there to help console her and try to ease her pain. Guilt churns inside me, they blame me for the death of their oldest son and that fucking hurts like a bitch. Chaos, Havoc and the other guards flank my family. Both twins look up to us and give Royal a two-finger salute before carrying on to their own cars.

"I need you to help me find her, Kacey. She is one of the toughest fucking people I know and can hold her own better than any man on my payroll, but she is getting reckless. She has no one watching her back. These fucking Albanians drug women and sell them on the corner. If one of them were to get the jump on her and then figure out who the fuck she is, what the hell do you think they would do to her?"

Anger masks the guilt I was feeling a second ago as thoughts of Chanel being harmed run through my mind.

"What the fuck makes you think I can find her?"

"She's leaving clues behind," he admits bitterly.

"What clues?"

"Clues!" he snaps, like that is supposed to make sense. He turns to leave while I just stand here staring down at the gravedigger covering my brother in dirt. "You coming?" he calls out. I keep my gaze ahead as I answer.

"Text me the address, I gotta do something first," I say as I begin to make my way down the hill.

"Kacey?" I turn back to stare up at Royal, from this angle he really does look like a badass king standing tall and proud.

"Yeah?"

"I never had a sibling..." He shakes his head and runs a hand through his head trying to come up with the right words, so I wait. "I'm sorry about your brother and I hope you get the revenge you seek."

"Thanks?" It comes out like a question but what else can I say. I never expected him to say sorry for my loss given the fact we can't stand each other.

"On your hunt for justice, keep an open mind because it might shock you when you realize we aren't the bad guys you think we are." I say nothing as I make my way to Marcus's grave. I wait until they finish covering him in dirt and place all the flowers on top of his grave. I crouch down beside the mound of dirt and place my hand atop of it. I feel the first tear fall and without permission more follow and within minutes I'm on my ass with my knees tucked into my chest and my arms resting on top of them as I cry for my brother.

"I should have let you go," I shout and I pound my fist against the ground. "This is my fault. I should have listened to you that night and let you go, you fucking begged me! I had my head too far up my own ass because I wanted to prove that I could be a better agent than Dad and show him that I was the better son." A sob rips out of me. "I was so envious of you,

Marcus. No matter how many times you fucked up, Mom and Dad still loved you, They thought the sun shined out of your ass. I did everything they wanted of me. I followed in Dad's footsteps and became the best at what I do just so he would notice me, but he never did."

I sit here until the sun sets, talking to my brother. He and I were so close growing up but then shit changed when he got his first hit of ice. I don't blame the drugs, I blame Marcus for not being strong enough to say no and walk away from the life he chose to live, just so he could earn enough for his next hit.

"I promise, I will find the sons of bitches who did this to you. No matter what I have to do or what lines I have to cross, I will avenge you, brother," I say as I slowly climb to my feet and head to my car so I can go and meet Royal.

This time when I pull down the street, there are no cars blocking the path. Memories of that night assault me. As painful as that was to leave her behind, I'll never regret it because she finally admitted that she loved me too. I come to a stop in front of the black wrought iron gates with the letters MM engraved in them. A guard taps my window so I roll it down.

"Name?" he asks.

"Kacey Vaughn. Royal is expecting me." He nods and steps aside before pressing his ear piece.

"Marco, I got a Kacey Vaughn here. He says the boss is expecting him." It takes a second before the guy is nodding and motioning for me to drive through as the gates open. I park my car and climb out. This place is fucking huge, but what stands out to me the most is the lack of guards patrolling the grounds.

"I didn't think you would show." I snap my gaze to the front door to see Havoc or is it Chaos standing by the front door. He looks me up and down before nodding his head for me to follow him. I follow him inside, trying to look around as much as I can and fuck me, this house reeks of money. I would never be able to afford something like this on my salary. For the first time I feel unworthy. I will never be able to give Chanel a house like this, she would be lucky if I could afford a house with a white picket fence. "I heard my brother had to reign you in at the gala?"

Ah, so he is Chaos not Havoc.

"No idea what you're talking about," I answer, causing him to chuckle. He opens a door at the end of the hall and walks in. I follow after him, only to come to a stop at the sight of Royal behind a large desk. Havoc leans against the far wall, but the sight that has me freezing in the entry way isn't the sight of Bishop Murdoch sitting on one of the couches, it's the sight of Vincent Murelo gazing out the window that has me tensing up and feeling like I just walked into a trap. I slowly take a step back, ready to cut and run but stop when I feel someone creep up behind me. I spin around, only to come face to face with Carlina Murelo.

"You lay one finger on her and I will put you down," Vincent's threat washes over me and I don't move a muscle as Carlina studies me like I'm a horse for sale at the stockyards. She hums in the back of her throat before walking past me to stand next to her husband, who now stands in front of Royal's desk staring me down. If looks could kill, I would be dead.

I pull my gaze from Vincent to look at Royal. "What the fuck is this?" I demand.

"This is me wanting to murder you with my bare fucking hands for defiling my daughter, but restraining because my nephew assures me you are the only one who can help me find her," Vincent answers for Royal. I look back to the big fucker and scrutinize him.

"Rumors say you can track anyone, find anyone no matter where they hide, so why do you need me?" Vincent's upper lip pulls back in a snarl. Royal slowly climbs to his feet and rests his hands flat against his desk as he stares at me.

"Chanel was trained by the best. My uncle *can* find anyone but my cousin isn't just anyone. She learned everything she knows from her father, so believe me when I tell you that if she doesn't want to be found, you will never find her." Pride swells inside me knowing my girl can evade the best of them. "Don't look like a smug cunt," Royal clips out.

"No idea what you're talking about," I quip back. The twins mask their laughter by fake coughing.

"You clearly have a death wish," Bishop adds. I finally look at him. The man is covered head to toe in ink and wears a suit that fits him like a second skin. He sits there looking relaxed and uninterested but I can see the devil in his eyes. This man is the head of the fucking mob and from what I have learned about him, he is fucking cut throat and ruthless.

"I'd rather not die," I answer honestly.

"Then, if I were you, I would help my brother-in-law find my niece before he kills you, and stages your death to look like an accident so his daughter doesn't lose her shit." It's said in a light tone but I can hear the undercurrent of his threat. I nod and step further into the room, making sure to stay as far away from Vincent as I can when I approach Royal's desk to look over the papers Chanel has left behind. I feel the twins and Bishop close in and watch me as I shuffle through the papers and try to make sense of what I'm reading. There are plans written out here of how they plan to bring in another shipment of drugs and addresses to stash houses,

"Who the hell is he?" I turn to the doorway to see a young girl standing there with an angry scowl plastered on her angelic face. Her green eyes spit fire at me. Royal groans as he steps out from behind his desk.

"None of your business, demon, now be gone." My brows snap to my hairline as I glare at the back of the bastard's head.

"She's a child, don't speak to her like that," I snap. Royal spins around and shakes his head.

"You have no fucking idea what *that* is, it is not a child. She is the spawn of the fucking devil and out to get me."

"Royal!" He visibly cringes at the sound of Erika's voice and slowly turns to face her.

"Yes, dear?" I scoff and the twins groan while Bishop shakes with silent laughter, it's a sight to behold seeing this man laugh.

"Don't you *yes dear* me! How many times have I told you not to speak to her like that?" Erika looks like she is about to beat the shit out of Royal.

"She is out to get me!" Royal sounds like a petulant child, there is no way this green eyed, brown haired beauty of a child could hurt a soul.

"You're out to get yourself!" the little girl snaps as she moves to cling to Erika. Royal snorts and shakes his head.

"Sweetheart, what have I told you about teasing Royal?" Bishop says in a tone far too soft to come from a man like him. The little girl bats her lashes up at him and purses her lips before answering.

"Not to pick on him and make him look weak in front of other people," she answers. Royal throws his hands into the air and continues to argue with a child. I tune him out as I focus back on the papers, spreading them out across the desk.

"What are you trying to tell me, baby?" I whisper to myself. Saying that shit aloud was a bad idea because I now have a gun pressed against my temple. I flick my eyes to the side and see Vincent standing there sneering at me.

"My love, you agreed you wouldn't harm the boy if he

helped," Carlina says gently as she reaches out and grips her husband's arm, forcing him to lower his gun. I brush off the encounter trying to appear unaffected when in truth, I have never had a gun pointed at me this many times. Even as an agent, I very rarely had to draw my weapon. I comb through the papers making sure to keep my thoughts to myself this time. After a while things start to stick out to me. It's coded!

"I got it!" I shout. I point out to each of them what I figured out. "These aren't clues, they are text messages between Halil and Quintin." I arrange the papers in order so they can read the messages in order.

"I don't get it," Chaos says.

"Me either," Havoc agrees.

"Halil and Q are discussing you blowing up their shipment of coke, it's just coded," I say.

"How the fuck do you know the code?" Vincent snaps.

"Because Q is using codes that we use in the agency. Like, here he says reaper destroyed our powder on the water, powder means coke and water is boat. I'm assuming the reaper they are referring to is Royal." Royal admits that I'm right and he did in fact blow up one of their ships. "Down here, Halil says that he's *out of second chances and to keep it buried, let the wife go*. I believe that is code for they know Chance is dead and not to worry about going after Erika. I don't know why he would say that but I think Halil is happy to have Chance out of the way."

"Why?" Bishop asks me.

"With Chance out of the way, Halil doesn't have to pay him his cut. Chance was getting a kick back from a lot of illegal shit and with him gone that's more money in their pockets. I believe Quintin is getting a kick back as well to keep the feds off their trail" Bishop nods and looks slightly awed by the fact I figured this shit out.

"You still didn't find my daughter," Vincent snarls. I

straighten and meet his stare refusing to cower under the pressure of his gaze.

"I know exactly where your daughter is, sir. I also know what she needs me to do in order to help her locate Halil Kozma."

"Where is she?" he growls.

"She'll come to me." Vincent's eyes shoot fire at me.

"What are your intentions exactly where my daughter is concerned, Kacey?" I blink a couple times, shocked Carlina is actually addressing me. I see so much of Chanel in her mother.

"I have no intentions—"

"Bullshit," Vincent snaps.

Fuck it, I'm gonna lay it out for them. "Fine, my intentions for Chanel are to love her for as long as she will allow me to. I fucked up, I know that, but I am busting my ass and going against everything I believe in to help her."

"How the fuck do we know you're not here playing us right now?" I can feel everyone's gaze on me at Vincent's question.

"If I were undercover right now, I wouldn't be wasting my time here with you all. I would be with your daughter and exploiting her feelings for me to flip her and gather intel on all of you." Vincent attempts to grab me but his wife steps in front of him, forcing him to stay his hand.

"If your feelings for my daughter are true, you need to understand that a relationship with her will never work. She is who she is and that can never change. She will never be a normal girl." I can hear the remorse in Carlina's voice. She wishes her daughter could have had a normal life.

"Mrs. Murelo, your daughter will never be normal because she was born to stand out. If Chanel gives me a chance to prove myself, I'll..." I take a deep breath before uttering the words I never thought I would say. "I'll give up being an agent for her. I'll give everything up just to be able to be near her. If she chooses to walk away from me at the end of this, you have my word that I will do everything within my power to continue to destroy any evidence that is gathered against your family and do whatever I have to in order to make sure she remains safe."

"Prove it." Those two words from Vincent hold so much fucking weight. I know without a doubt I have to prove myself to him in order for me to have a fighting chance in hell with his daughter.

Chapter Sixteen

CHANEL

I use the cover of darkness to conceal me in the shadows as I scope out Kacey's apartment. He hasn't been back here in days, which leads me to believe that he is staying somewhere else. I left clues behind hoping Royal would be smart enough to know that Kacey would be the only one able to figure out my whereabouts. It was a long shot but I thought Kacey being the only one able to track me would give him some credit with my family.

I haven't spoken to any of them since the night I turned my back on them and ran. I know Royal is probably feeling like shit but he deserves it. Dad went too far. He may be able to control others' lives but not mine. I am not a child anymore and I can make my own choices. My burner phone begins to vibrate in my pocket. I fish it out and groan, I never should have called her when I ran.

"What, Erika?" I growl. She is the only person I have spoken to. I know it's crazy considering what I did to her but the girl really doesn't give up, and there is only so much one person can handle before they give in and cave.

"Kacey was here last night." Immediately my attention is captured and I perk up for the first time in days.

"Why?" I can hear the hope in my own voice.

"Royal found him and asked for his help to find you."

"Did you tell them where I am?"

"No, I wouldn't betray you like that, Chanel." Relief washes over me. I may have been too quick to judge her in the beginning.

"Thank you."

"You don't need to thank me, but I do have to tell you something." I tense.

"What is it?"

"Royal let slip that you were the one to cover the costs of his brother's burial."

"Fuck."

"He left straight after that and said he would deal with you when you came to him." A shiver runs down my spine but not in a bad way. "Your dad is pissed, Chanel."

"Yeah? Well, maybe he should learn that he can't fucking tell me what to do." Headlights shine in the distance and I end the call before peering through my scope. At the sight of Kacey's Camaro, excitement begins to brew inside me. He drives past his building slowly as if he knows I'm watching him, then speeds off. Smiling to myself, I pack up my rifle and all my things before rushing down the fire escape. I know exactly where he is going and it's about time I claimed my fucking man.

Pulling up out front of Xavier's warehouse home, I smile. I knew he would come here. I've taken out every Albanian that has tried to come after Kacey or his family and only one of them proved useful enough to get me those messages. We have tried to hack and find anything we can but thanks to the FBI covering his tracks, Halil is virtually being erased from existence so there is no trace of him.

Climbing out of the car, I head to the back door and find it slightly ajar. I let myself in and follow the sounds of laughter into the living room, where I find Romeo, Xavier and Benny sitting around drinking a beer. The three of them shoot me knowing smiles.

"He's upstairs in his room," Xav says.

"*His* room?" I query.

"That apartment was just a front, Chanel. *This* is Kacey's home." My eyes widened in surprise.

"What?" I breathe out.

"Go talk to your man," Ro says. Nodding, I head upstairs and go in the direction of the room I was in last time. I push the door open and come to a stop at the sight of Kacey sitting on the end of his bed, with his forearms draped over the tops of his thighs and his head hung low. He doesn't lift it at the sound of my approach or even when I close the door quietly behind myself. I lean against the wall and wait for him to say something. The silence stretches and I begin to worry that I have misread things, maybe he didn't mean what he said the other night and didn't want me to fight for us.

"You paid for my brother's funeral," he murmurs. It's not a question, just a statement.

"I did."

"Why?" He still won't look at me!

"Because I can and I wanted to help in my own way," I say, feeling slightly unsure if I did the right thing now. "If it helps, your parents think you paid for it. I made sure everything was in your name," I tack on as an afterthought, not wanting him to think I did it for credit or to try to bribe him for forgiveness after the way he was treated by my family.

He slowly lifts his head and when I see the distraught look in his blue eyes I want to drop to my knees and weep. He looks so broken. It's a strange feeling to feel my heart ache for another. Don't get me wrong, I'm not that jaded to not love my family but I've never felt this feeling before. It has me wanting to do anything I can to remove the sadness from his life and be his happiness.

"I buried my brother yesterday."

"I know," I whisper.

"I wanted to blame you and your family for his death." I inhale sharply and brace myself for him to lash out. "Truth is, Marcus died because of me—"

"Kacey, no–"

He leaps to his feet and shoots me a scathing look. "You don't know, you weren't there that night. I could have let him go but I didn't because I wanted to prove to my parents that I was the better son. I'm a fucking agent because it was demanded of me." He pounds his fist against his heart and I ache to hold him, tell him that none of this is his fault but I remain where I am. "I broke my own heart. My parents wouldn't even allow me to be there for his service. I had to stay on the hill and watch. I don't know what the fuck I'm doing anymore." He scrubs a hand down in his face.

"You're hunting the bastards that took your brother from you. You are great at your job, Kacey–" He scoffs and shakes his head, pointing a finger at me.

"I'm that good of an agent, you blew my cover out of the water."

"Kacey, stop," I plead as I step forward, but he shakes his head and takes a step back.

"Why are you here, Chanel?" He doesn't give me a chance

to answer, my breath lodges in my throat as my heart begins to lurch in my chest at the thought of him ending this thing between us. "You have a family that loves you, parents who would kill for you and here you are wasting your time on a crooked fed."

"You're not crooked," I say as I try to close the space between us, but he avoids me and steps to the side. "Kacey, don't do this," I plead when I see the look of determination in his eyes.

"I can never give you the life you deserve, Chanel. I can't afford the front door of the house you currently live in, let alone the whole fucking thing." Shaking my head I deny his claims but he pushes on. "This warehouse is all I have. I couldn't afford a house so I bought this and started to convert it. Want to know a secret?" I don't bother answering because I know he doesn't need me to. "Xavier, Ro and Benny helped me pay for this place because I couldn't afford it on my own. This is the glamorous life of an agent, baby. I risk my life daily, only to be used and lied to. Everything I have fought for is a fucking lie. I met you and fell head over heels in love. The moment I found out who you were, I didn't give a fuck because you weren't like the stories I heard about your uncles and dad."

"I'm not like them—"

"No you're not, baby," he whispers as he cups my face between his hands and smiles down at me. "You are so much worse," he murmurs. I recoil and stumble backward, away from him.

"W-what?" I choke out.

"You are the most lethal poison. You run through my veins and I hunger for you like an addict. I should have flipped you that night you found out who I was, but I couldn't. It was then that I knew I wasn't cut out to be an agent. I threw myself into my work to prove to myself that I could do my job and you weren't a distraction. I arrested my own brother just to prove that I could do it and keep my heart out of it. I love you, Sin... always will, but I am no good, baby. I'll fuck this up between us just like I fuck everything else up." Tears well in my eyes as I process what he's saying.

"You... don't want me?" His eyes close. I watch his chest rise and fall as I wait for him to answer me. The moment his eyes open and I see the hollow look in his eyes, I know he is about to break me, again. He digs something out of his pocket and comes to me, reaching out he grabs my hand and places a card and key in my palm. I stare up at him waiting for an explanation but he says nothing, instead he places a soft kiss to my lips before releasing my hand and stepping back.

"That's the key card to get you into the building and that key is to Quintin's office. You will find all the files and every bit of information on your family on his computer. Benny managed to find out that Q has been running off the book surveillance on your family so we know without a doubt the master files will be on his computer."

"Kacey–"

"Your best chance to get in and out without being detected is when Royal meets with Halil–"

"Please," I beg as the first tear falls.

"If I find out where he is hiding, I'll text you."

"You'll *text* me?" I scream as my tears fall down my cheeks unchecked. He stands there with a blank look on his face as I stand before him, breaking in half as he rips my fucking heart from my chest.

"I knew you would be spying on my apartment, which is why I lured you here so they could take you home." Utterly confused I stand here staring at him until a knock sounds on his door, Kacey moves to open it and when I see who is standing there, I shut down. The tears stop flowing, my heart turns to ice and I go into survival mode as I block out all the pain and stand tall. "Thanks for coming."

"You the reason for that?" Royal asks as he flicks his head toward me.

"I never meant to hurt her," Kacey whispers. I scoff and shoulder past him, but before I make it out the door, he grips my wrist and halts my movements. I refuse to look at him, instead I glare daggers at Royal.

My cousin got what he wanted. He got the old, angry, jaded and bloodthirsty Chanel back. He'll never have to worry about me going soft again because I will never let another man get close enough to me to hold any power against me.

"I love you and I'm so sorry I couldn't be the man you needed me to be. You deserve the world. I wish I wasn't such a fuck up. Your dad's right, Sin. I don't deserve you." Hearing that my dad was talking shit to Kacey just fuels my anger. I yank my arm from his grasp and bail the fuck out. I ignore Ro, Benny and Xav as I exit the way I came in. At the sight of my father leaning against my car, I grit my teeth and ignore the bastard. I head to Royal's car and ride shotgun. I feel my dad's gaze on me but I don't look at him. Fuck him and fuck Kacey Vaughn, they both deserve what's to come.

Royal exits the warehouse a few minutes later, exchanges words with my dad, then climbs in beside me. Dad drives away in my car. Royal doesn't follow him instead he chooses to take the long ride home. I look out the window and fight back my tears.

"I'm always here, Sin. Believe it or not, I wanted shit to work out for you–"

"Fuck off with your bullshit, Royal. You never wanted me to end up with anyone because then that meant you would be alone. Newsflash asshole, you have a fiancée!"

He swerves off the road and pulls into a random car park by the water's edge. "Get the fuck out. We're doing this shit now!" I leap out of the car and round the front of the car where he meets me. His eyes burn with anger so I allow my own anger to take control. I strike out and hit him right across the jaw. He stumbles sideways but I don't stop. I jump into the air and land a hit to the side of his face. I keep throwing punches and he blocks each of them, allowing me to keep coming at him.

"Fight back!" I scream.

"Not like this," he yells back. He and I have sparred together since we were kids. He knows I can take a hit but he has never fought me outside of the ring at Uncle Rook's gym. I need him to fight back, I need to feel the pain of his fists to distract me from the crippling pain inside my chest.

"Fucking fight me, you pussy ass bitch." He grunts as I land a roundhouse kick to his kidney. He jumps back and keeps his guard up as I attack him again and again until I can't hold my arms up. "Fight back," I sob out. He drops his arms to his sides and the pitying look in his eyes as he stares down at me has me dropping to my knees, heaving out gut-wrenching sobs. Within a second he is on the ground beside me, pulling me to him as he holds me close while I break down for the first time in my life. I have never cried in front of anyone, aside from Kacey.

"I got you, Sin," he says as he rocks me in his arms like a toddler.

"It hurts," I cry out. He growls and tightens his hold on me.

"I'm so sorry, Chanel, so fucking sorry." I can hear the anguish and pain in his voice. Royal has never had to console before so I know this is hard for him, but I just can't find it within myself to care or even to try and stop this meltdown, because it fucking hurts like a bitch. My chest feels like it's on fire and it's hard to breathe. No matter how much air I drag into my lungs, it doesn't feel like it's enough.

I don't know how long we sit here on the cold ground, I don't even notice it's raining until Royal carries me to the car and places me in my seat, before claiming his own and turning the heat up. We make the drive back home in silence. I feel his gaze on me every so often but I don't have the energy to move or fight him anymore. We pull up in front of the house. I don't protest when he comes around and lifts me into his arms bride style. The moment we step inside, I can hear everyone shouting at him and demanding to know what happened. I tune them out as I bury my face in his chest. Royal knows me better than anyone and right now he knows I need to be alone, so he ignores all their questions and carries me upstairs to my room. He places me on my bed where I curl up into a ball and cry. He scrubs a hand down his face in frustration, not knowing how to deal with me.

"I got it from here, sweetheart," I hear my mom say from behind me. Royal looks from her to me debating if he should leave me or not. "Royal, this is the part where you leave me to hold my daughter through her first heartbreak. If she needs you, I promise I will call for you." My mom's words seem to break through to him. He places a kiss on the top of my head before he leaves.

"I'll be right outside. I'll sleep on the floor if I have to, but I'm not leaving her until I know she is okay. She may be your daughter, Aunt Carlina, but she is my best friend. I promised her I would always be here for her and this is me keeping that promise." His words have a sense of calm washing over me, knowing even after everything I have done he still loves me.

"You are a fine young man. I'll call you when she is ready," Mom says before I hear the door click shut. A moment later I feel the bed dip, then my mom is snuggling up behind me, spooning me as she wraps her arms around me and places kisses to the back of my head. "Let it out, my girl. I'm right here, baby girl," she whispers and then, without permission, a sob tears out of me and my tears flow faster.

"Mom, it hurts," I cry.

"I know, baby." I can hear the watery tone of her voice and know she wants to cry for me, but she doesn't because she is a badass and remains strong for me so I can break.

Chapter Seventeen

CHANEL

I wake to the sound of voices arguing in what I'm sure they think are hushed tones. I can feel how puffy and swollen my eyes are from the tears I cried last night. At the sound of my dad's voice, I feign sleep, he's the last person I want to see right now. I am so embarrassed that I allowed everyone to see me in the state I was in last night. I'm not that girl who cries over a guy. I never allow emotions to get the better of me but last night... I couldn't contain the hurt. I never broke down two years ago when Kacey broke my heart but last night, I was powerless to stop the pain from consuming me for a second time.

"She needs time, Vincent," Mom growls.

"She's my daughter, Gucci," Dad says.

"You are part of the reason why she is in this state. I told you to stay out of it and leave the boy alone but you thought you knew better."

"Carlina—"

"No, you listen to me, Vincent Murelo. You may be the

Bloodhound out there but in here, I am the fucking Pitbull. Believe me, baby, I love you with my whole heart but if you so much as cause my baby to shed one more tear I will show you just what I am capable of. People may fear you but you and I both know, you are scared shitless of me and what I can do to you." Pride swells inside me. My mom is a boss bitch and I am so fucking honored that she is my mother.

"Jesus, Carlina. Calm the hell down. She will get over it." I cringe, of course he would think this is just a fling or a stupid little girl crush.

"No, she won't. When have you ever seen her profess her feelings?" She doesn't allow him to answer. "She ran to that boy and told him she loved him. She fucking allowed that boy past her walls and you had to go and throw your weight around because you still see her as the eight-year-old girl who thought her daddy hung the moon. She will always be your baby girl, Vincent, but if you keep her from what her heart desires, then you will lose her."

"He isn't good enough for her!" Dad roars. I can't listen to this anymore. I sit up causing them both to clamp their mouths closed. I climb to my feet and ignore my dad calling my name as I head for my bathroom and slam the door closed behind myself. I avoid looking at my reflection in the mirror as I strip off and step into the shower. I stand under the hot spray, allowing it to wash away the salt from my tears and hope it can also wash away the pain that still lingers inside my chest.

I feel tears prick the backs of my eyes but I refuse to allow them to fall. I won't cry over Kacey anymore. He made his choice and he chose wrong. I would have fought for us. I went against my family for him. I risked it all just for him to leave me again. I wish I could stand here and say I shot the man who murdered my heart, but the reality is that I could never harm Kacey no matter how much he has hurt me. When my fingers turn to prunes, I decide I can't hide in here forever and step out. Steam covers the mirror which I am grateful for. I wrap my hair in a towel and pull on my robe before leaving the safety of my bathroom.

My mom sits on the edge of my bed while my dad sits in my chair that overlooks the backyard. I say nothing as I cross the room to my closet. Closing the door behind myself, I dress quickly in a pair of jeans and a baggy shirt that has holes in it and hangs off one shoulder. Making my way back to my bedroom, my mom motions for me to take a seat in front of her as she waves my hairbrush. Sighing, I resign myself to the fact that I have no choice but to allow my mother this and let her brush my hair.

Saying nothing as my mom brushes out my tangles and hums to herself, I close my eyes and relax into her touch as she begins to braid my hair. Even after she finishes my braid, she doesn't move. She sits behind me as I sit on the ground. I know she wishes I was more like her and loved to do makeup and girly things but that just isn't who I am. I have always wanted to follow in my father's footsteps, but last night showed me I will never be able to do that because he doesn't view me as an equal.

"Your cousins slept outside your door and I'm sure they are still there now," Mom says softly. I look toward my door, I may not have Xray vision but I know without a doubt that they are still there. Shame washes over me as memories of last night run through my mind. I attacked Royal and I should never have done that. "Do you want to talk about it?" she asks gently.

"No," I croak out, my throat hoarse from all the tears.

"Chanel–"

I cut my dad off before he can say anything more. "Don't."

"Hear me out," he pleads but I can't.

"No, you got what you wanted. Kacey is gone and I'm back to being the virgin princess you think I am. Everyone wins, right?" I turn to face him and pray he can see resentment in my gaze as well as hear the bitterness in my tone. He flinches back and takes a shuddering breath. He looks to my mom for guidance but she just scoffs, letting him know he's on his own with this one.

"I didn't win shit. How could I when I see how shattered you are just from the look in your eyes?"

I push to my feet and shake my head at my father, never have I felt so estranged from him until this moment. "What did you expect?" I shout. "You wanted this, right?" I don't give him a chance to answer. "You told him to stay away from me and that he wasn't good enough for your princess. Well newsflash, Dad, you won because he believes you and kicked my ass to the curb." He visibly flinches but I'm not done. "Just so we are clear, he was fucking good enough. If anything, he was better than me. Kacey loved me for me, not my name or because of who I am related to. He saw the real me, flaws and all and guess what? He still fucking loved me for all my down-falls. He never judged me, not once. You see a badge when you look at him, when I finally got over my hurt and anger toward him all I saw was my future." His eyes widen. "I saw my person, I saw what I could become with him by my side."

"Chanel–"

"No, Dad, you won. You got what you wanted. I swear to God I will never allow another to get close to me again. I kept him a secret from everyone because I wanted to fool myself into thinking that I could be different. I was wrong to do that because I am proud of who the fuck I am, and guess what? He was fucking proud of who I am as well. You have my word, I will never betray the family again. I will remain loyal and serve Royal and do everything that is expected of me. I'm sorry for putting a stain against your name with the family for falling in love with the wrong person. I promise you, I will never shame you again." The tears in his eyes don't deter me. I turn my back on my father and leave my room. Sure enough I find Havoc, Chaos and Royal all sitting on the floor opposite my room looking up at me with pained expressions. "Who's getting in the ring with me first?"

For five days I have managed to avoid my dad and having a conversation alone with Royal. Unlike my aunt and uncle, my parents refused to go home until they knew I was okay. Despite me reassuring my mother that I am perfectly fine and feeling like my old self, she just smiled and said they were stay-ing. It's driving me insane with my dad hovering. Even when I'm in the makeshift ring–the backyard—sparring with the guys, he just stands there and watches. It pisses me off when he throws out suggestions and tries to critique my technique.

I've thrown myself into work. So far in a matter of days, we have managed to get rid of four wannabe gangs, two others were allowed to stay as long as they cut us in on the profits and agreed to work for us. It is going to take time for us to gain total control of Miami. The *Memento Mori* is already begin-ning to spread throughout the state. On top of that, I have also been searching for Halil. He was supposed to have made contact for our meeting but hasn't. Chaos has remained here with us to try help us find this fucker. He is the best hacker out of the four of us.

"I'm out, my eyes are going fucking crossed," Chaos whines. I peer at him from the corner of my eye.

"We haven't found him yet," I snap.

He stands from the sofa, then places his laptop on the side table. He looks across from us to see his twin brother sprawled out, sleeping with his mouth open. Chaos shoots me a wink before he heads up to bed. I'd rather stay here and keep searching than go to my room. Every time I'm alone, I can't stop thinking about Kacey. He hasn't texted or called, and there is no fucking way I would ever reach out to him. It's nearly three in the morning when Royal strolls into the living room, wearing only his sleep shorts. He frowns at me.

"Why are you still up?" I focus back on my laptop as I answer him.

"Unlike you guys, I want to find Halil and put an end to this shit rather than drag it out." He ignores me as he crosses the room and wakes Havoc. The bastard lies and says he was just resting his eyes before stumbling out of the room to head upstairs. Royal drops into the seat Havoc just vacated. I feel his eyes on me and try my best to ignore it, but after a while the pressure of his gaze becomes too much. "What?" I snap as I like my head and scowl at him.

He reclines further back into his chair, lazily draping his arm over the back of the couch. "Why are you avoiding me?"

I fight the urge not to flee the room. I fucking hate talking about feelings and he knows this. "I'm not," I lie.

"Chanel, every time I enter a room you leave it. The only time you speak to me is when someone is around, why?"

"You're reading way too much into this," I deflect.

"I am not, so cut the shit and tell me why the fuck you are avoiding me." The confusion is clear on his face. Fuck it, may as well be honest with him.

"Because I don't know what to say to you."

"What does that mean?"

I slam the lid of my laptop and chuck it on the seat beside me. "It means, I don't know what the fuck to say to you. I am fucking disgusted with myself for how I behaved and lashed out at you. I hate that I allowed someone to have such power over me to break me in half. I hate that you saw me at my lowest point and I fucking hate that I can't get over this ache in my chest that makes it hard for me to breathe because *he* isn't here." I'm panting and breathless from blurting that all out. Royal doesn't look at me with pity like I expected, he just stares at me with understanding.

"You saw me at my lowest, Sin." I scoff, he ignores me and continues. "When I thought Erika was a rat I allowed you and Aunt Koby to hurt the woman I love. Watching that shit broke me and tore me the fuck up inside. Unlike you, I was fucking weak and allowed my loyalty to this family cloud my judgment. Because of that loyalty, Erika paid the price. You were strong and let the man you love live. You are not weak, Chanel. You re the strongest fucking person I know, and the fact you allowed me to be there for you in your most vulnerable moment is an honor. I would never betray you by holding any of the shit you said and did over your head." I hang my head in shame feeling like utter shit.

"I never should have hit you, Royal."

He snorts, drawing my gaze back to him. The big baby rubs his jaw, earning an eye roll from me. "You pack a fucking mean right hook." We both laughed at that.

"I pack a better kick." He forces a shudder out.

"Don't I know it." I laugh, it feels good to laugh and banter with him, I've missed this. Once our laughter dies out, silence ensues. It's not awkward, but it is filled with a slight tension. "Do you really love him?" he asks quietly.

The breath rushes out of my lungs and I slouch back into the sofa. "I do," I say barely above a whisper.

"Love makes you do fucked up shit, Sin."

"Love makes you weak. I will never allow that shit to affect me again. Love nearly made me lose my family."

He shakes his head. "Love didn't make you weak, it sure as hell hasn't weakened me. With Erika by my side, I feel like I can conquer the world and the best part is, Sin, each night I get to come home to her and know there is someone just for me. You loving Kacey forced you to stand on your own without me. You sought vengeance for his brother and you did that shit on your own."

I mull over his words, trying to think back on a time previously that I had done shit without him and the twins, but come up blank. The four of us have always been a unit. College, we did that shit together. Starting our own family, we did that together. Everything I have done has been with them. Maybe he is right. I did go out and find a trail for Kacey to follow, I didn't need Royal or the twins. Did love really make me stronger?

"You know he has been texting me every day?" His revelation has my mouth parting. "He checks in to make sure you're okay. No matter how many times I tell him to fuck off and die, he keeps messaging."

"Just block his number," I sourly reply, hating that he can message Royal but not me!

"I would, but he is actually proving useful and helping us track down Halil. He even managed to slip you some keys apparently and according to Kacey, the best time to get into Quintin's office is when we manage to secure a meet with Halil."

"Why?"

"He says Quintin will want to be at the meet so he can finally see who we are."

"I already met him at the gala."

"Which is why you won't be there. You will be scrubbing his drive of all the information and planting a bug to clone his shit so we can remain a step ahead. Chaos has a thumb-drive for you. All you need to do is plug it in and then he'll do the rest."

"What's the catch?" I know there is one, there always fucking is.

"Your dad will be your overwatch and Kacey will be with you." I jump to my feet and shake my head.

"Fuck off! Don't try and meddle in my shit–" He climbs to his feet and pins me with a hard look.

"I'm not doing this to hurt you. Kacey has to be there. He is the only one who can take you in without being detected and your dad needs to be there in case shit goes wrong."

"If dad's with me, then who will be watching your back?" I deflect.

"Dad, our uncles, Aunt Koby and Aunt Anya will be with me. The twins will watch my six, but I need to know you can handle this, Sin. We will only get one shot. It's not like we can break into the headquarters of the FBI anytime we like," he drawls.

"Fuck!" The bastard smiles triumphantly, earning a glare from me when he claps his hands.

"So glad that is sorted. You might want to get some sleep and shower in the morning."

I scrunch my face. "Why?" He starts to leave the room and calls out as he rounds the corner.

"Kacey and his boys will be here in the morning to help plan this shit out so we are ready to go at a moment's notice."

Fuck!

"I hate you!" I shout.

"You're welcome, you salty bitch," he calls back.

"What's the time frame?" Chaos asks. I remain standing against the far wall staying as far away from Kacey as possible. I barely slept last night. This morning I am a bundle of nerves and I never get nervous! I make sure to be in the office before he arrives. The moment Kacey, Ro and Xav walk into the room, I feel my dad's gaze on me straight away. No matter how hard I try to keep my eyes off him, I can't. He looks fucking delicious in a pair of jean shorts, loose black shirt and low-cut Converse sneakers. His hair is a tousled mess. I'm too much of a coward to meet his gaze when I feel him looking my way, instead I stand with my back to them and gaze out the window.

Royal and the twins have been plotting out the best way to narrow down the search for the Albanian boss, while Kacey and his friends work out a pattern of where Quintin has been going, thinking he might be the one to lead them to Halil. Dad is just in here because he's nosey and wants to make sure Kacey and I aren't alone together at any time.

"Benny has been keeping tabs on Q and requested a transfer to the main office to keep eyes on him at all times. He says that Q has been acting off, he thinks something big is about to go down," Kacey answers. The sound of his voice has me closing my eyes and taking deep breaths just to try to remain standing and not collapse. His presence affects me and I hate that even after him throwing me away like trash, he can still hold such a power over me.

"We have been searching for him for a few weeks now. He isn't hiding at any of his stash houses. We raided one a couple days ago and it was empty," Royal tells them.

"He can't leave the state. We have every exit and entry blocked. That Albanian scum isn't getting the fuck out of here even with his ties to the feds," Havoc growls.

"Then where the hell is he?" Ro wonders aloud. A snort comes from me when a thought strikes.

"What's on your mind, Sin?" I hear Kacey snicker at Royal using his nickname for me and I fucking love that it grates on his nerves. He has no right to call me that anymore.

I slowly turn and face Royal, making sure to never look Kacey's way. I'll show him that he means nothing to me. "Maybe we should be asking the twins to place a call." Havoc and Chaos exchange a loaded look before focusing back on me.

"Why?"

"To who?" they both answer in unison.

I pin them both with a bored look. "Your little pet's family lives on the border of Miami. My bet is that Halil isn't holed up in one of his own houses, but with your little toy." Their faces drop as they pick up what I'm putting down.

"No," Havoc snaps angrily.

"What's going on?" Xav whispers to his friends, but they ignore him as I push on.

"Halil would know we are hunting him after taking out Omar. He would be stupid to risk staying in one of his own properties."

"She does have a point," Royal adds.

"Why the fuck would he be hiding out with the Dominico family?" Chaos snarls. I understand their reluctance about accepting what I am saying but they both know I'm right, even if they don't want to admit it.

"Because it's a place we would never think to look and let's be real, we know your pet's father hates the both of you, so why wouldn't he side with our enemy?" I hedge.

"Are we talking about the Dominico family as in Ricardo Dominico?" Kacey asks. I watch as my dad pushes off the wall and stands up straight, both the twins stare at him with accusation in their gazes.

"How do *you* know about the Dominico family?" Royal barks.

"They were the family that was trying to oppose your father when he took over Miami from your grandfather. We were scouting him for a while but could never manage to get a man on the inside," Kacey answers.

"If he is hiding out with them, how the fuck are we going to find that shit out?" Chaos voices.

"With the feds covering Halil's tracks and erasing him from existence, that would also mean that they are in with the

Dominico family. We need to get eyes and ears in there." Royal looks directly at the twins in expectation. Havoc shuts down, his face is completely devoid of emotion. Chaos looks like he wants to eat glass and keeps clenching and unclenching his fists. "Which of you are going to make the call?"

"Wait, you have an in with the Dominico family?" Kacey sounds stunned, clearly not even his lying ass was able to infiltrate their family.

"Just... give us a minute," Chaos grits out. Doing as he asks and not saying another word, I turn and leave the room, grateful to be able to get the fuck away from Kacey.

Chapter Eighteen

KACEY

Seeing her for the first time since she walked out of my bedroom has me aching to wrap my arms around her and hold her close as I profess my love for her. Being in the same room as her and not being able to touch or catch a whiff of her scent is the worst fucking torture, but I know I can't do that. I'm no good for her. She deserves to find someone who isn't a fuck up and can give her all the lavish things in life. Royal and I have come to some sort of understanding. I help him gather intel and he updates me on how she is doing. The messages I got from him the first day after he left my house had my chest ripping open and me finding solace in the bottom of a bottle of Jack Daniels.

Ro, Xav and I follow Royal and Vincent out of the office, leaving Havoc and Chaos behind to discuss whatever the fuck it is they need to. I'm still stunned that they have an in with the Dominico family. Much like the Murdochs, their family doesn't outsource help, you have to be related or known by them before you can get within a meter of them. We pass by the kitchen as Royal leads us out onto the back patio. The view from the back is just as fucking stunning as the front. This place must be worth millions.

"Have a seat," Royal says as he claims the seat at the head of the outdoor table. The three of us claim our chairs while Vincent remains standing, with his arms crossed over his chest and his glare pointed directly at me. It's fucking hard to ignore. Ever since I stepped foot inside the house, I felt his eyes on me. The man doesn't disguise his hatred for me either. If anything, he makes sure I know that I am not welcome here or near his daughter. "What's the progress on Quintin?"

"Benny is working on getting a copy of his planner so we will be able to track his movements. We wanted to plant a tracker, but all the cars are swept daily when they enter the garage of the building," I answer.

"How soon before we can get that?" I meet Royal's gaze as I answer.

"Quintin is being real fucking cagey and not attending meetings or leaving his office much."

"Why?" he asks.

"We think it's because he is running the master server from his office and scrubbing any evidence from the system," Romeo answers.

"We know that some of the cases involving the Albanians have been wiped. Which means, now that Q has pinned the blame on Owen for not getting a warrant—when in fact it was him that didn't procure it—the cases he wiped means the men we sent to prison will be set free," I elaborate.

"We need to get into that office," he snarls as he pounds his fist against the table.

"The keys I have, I gave to Sin." No sooner have the words left my mouth does Vincent snap. He smacks his hands flat against the table and bends over so he is right in my face.

"You don't get to say her name," he grits out through

clenched teeth. I war within myself to remain silent and just be a good boy and take it, but wishes are bullshit and never come true so I snap back.

"Why not? I pushed her away like you wanted and broke your daughter's heart, *sir*. I know I can never give her what you can or some rich fucker can, but believe me, sir, I gave her everything I fucking had and she never complained, only *you* did!" I spit at him. Before I even see it coming, his fist lands right below my eye socket and sends me sailing backward in my chair. My head smacks hard against the wood of the patio. Vincent tries to come at me again, but Royal and my boys hold him back as I struggle to my feet and have to use the railing for support. The bastard packs a mean fucking punch like his daughter.

"You stay the fuck away from my daughter–"

"Vincent!" He clamps his mouth shut as I slowly swivel around using the railing for support to see Carlina standing in the doorway, but she isn't alone. Erika, London and Chanel stand on either side of her. Chanel looks livid, her fists clenched at her side and her face is contorted with anger as she stares at her dad. Her mother looks like she is ready to skin her husband alive. "Did you hit him?" Vincent opens his mouth but no words come out. Not knowing when to keep my mouth shut, I blurt out,

"No, I fell over." Carlina pins me with a dry stare. Chanel scoffs while Erika and the little that clutches her hand giggle. I know, I sound like an idiot but I'm no pussy and can take a hit, just ask Chanel.

"What he said," Vincent tacks on.

"Jesus, you are fucking pathetic," Chanel bites out. Her father and I both look at her and I know from the intel Royal supplies me with, that she hasn't spoken to her father and blames him.

"Chanel–" Vincent tries but she cuts him off.

"No. I did what I said I would. I moved on and stepped up to be the best second, I could be for Royal. *You* are the one that can't let go." Fuck, that stings. "He is here under Royal's invitation, not mine. What the fuck more do you want from me?" She doesn't give him a chance to answer. "I have done everything I can for you to see me as an equal but still, you treat me like I am fragile. I'm not a little kid anymore, Dad." Her voice is thick with emotion. "I gave him up... for you," she mutters the last part and fuck me, it kills me inside.

Vincent's face pales. He pulls out of the guy's arms and rushes toward Chanel, but Royal is quick and cuts in front of his uncle, placing a hand on his chest. The two of them stand there for a second silently just staring at each other.

"She is trying. I am not asking you, Uncle V, I'm telling you to leave her be and let her go. You may not see it, but she is fucking hurting inside because you can't allow yourself to see that it doesn't matter what you think or feel about him, she loves him." Royal's words have my brows raising in surprise. I cut a glance to Chanel to see her with a look of shock on her own face.

Vincent nods stiffly. Royal steps aside and allows him past, then shoots me a loaded look that says more than words. He didn't do that for me, he did that for her. I suspected he was up to something when he invited us here today. He could have just called but he demanded that we come to him. Carlina shoots her husband a look of warning as he comes to a halt in front of his daughter. Chanel looks up at him with a sour look on her face. I hate that I can see pain in her eyes, I never want to be the cause of her hurting.

Vincent tentatively reaches out and cups her cheek. She doesn't melt into his touch even though I can tell she wants to. "The last thing I ever want to do is hurt you. I know you think I am being hard on you and trying to punish you for growing up and becoming a... woman." That word sounds tainted coming from him. I have to fight to keep the smile from my face. "There are only three people I have ever loved in this world: my sister, your mother and you. I'm a simple man, Chanel. I don't need lavish homes, fancy cars and expensive clothes. All I need is you and your mother, with both of you by my side, I would be richer than any man."

He drops his hand to his side and steps back giving her some space as he runs a hand through his hair trying to find the courage to express himself. "You could never put a stain next to my–our name, I knew the day we found out we were having a daughter that one day my princess would grow up and become a queen and find her own king. I guess I just... didn't expect for you to grow up so fast and not need me." The hurt in his tone has her darting forward to wrap her arms around her father and hold him close. Vincent pulls her closer and rests his chin atop her head. "I have never been prouder of anyone in my life. You growing up isn't a bad thing, baby girl."

"I'll always need you," she whispers. The way Vin's eyes shudder closed is indication enough that he needed to hear those words from her.

"I have never thought you were less than me or any one of these boys." He pushes her back and places his hands on the top of her shoulders, as bends at the knees so they are eye level. "You are better than me, truth be told, Chanel. You proved it when I couldn't even track you and Royal had to turn to... *him* for help." As if she can't help it, she flicks her eyes to me for a second before she quickly rips them away. "You can hunt, track and eliminate better than I ever could. You are not my equal, my dear daughter, you are my better." Her brows rise in surprise. "I may be the *Bloodhound* to the world but, baby girl, you will be known as the *Hellhound*." Gasps sound out, pride swells in my girl's eyes as she looks at her dad. Fuck, I admit I even stand here with a goofy grin on my face.

"You mean that, don't you?" she asks.

"With every beat of my heart. It just took me a minute to realize that you didn't need me to protect you anymore because you have proven you can protect yourself."

"Thank you." Those two words from her hold so much weight. Vincent smiles, drops his hands from her shoulders and straightens. The happy look he was just sporting on his face vanishes, bringing a frown to my face.

"Now, you may be the new and improved Hellhound who can outwit her old man, and might just be the only person on this earth that can evade me, but I am still your father and regardless if you throw a tantrum or not, I cannot deal with... *boys*." Laughter bursts out of the three girls, even London has a smile on her face. Vincent scowls at each of them, especially his wife. "Stop laughing, Gucci. I'm being serious!"

Carlina places a hand on her husband's chest and smiles up at him. "I know, babe. That's what makes this so comical, because you can allow your daughter to hunt and kill but the thought of a boy sniffing around her, you go all caveman and alpha male."

"I don't care what she says, he isn't good enough for her and the fucker calls me *sir*!" He shoots me a glare over his wife's head. I remain still and calm, not wanting to anger him further and risk getting another eye blackened. "You help end this but you stay the hell away from my daughter," he grits out.

"Will anyone ever be good enough for your baby girl?" Xav asks. My stupid friend must have a fucking death wish. Vincent smirks and nods at Xav before turning back to me with an evil glint in his eyes.

"A eunuch." I choke my own spit. Chanel coughs to mask her laughter.

"What's a eunuch?" London asks Erika, but Vincent beats her to answer the little girl.

"A real man, darling. When you grow up, Papa V will find you the best eunuch there is and I swear to God, grandpa will be so happy and welcome your man with open arms." Royal begins to snicker and shoots his uncle a frown. Vincent stares his nephew down for a minute. "Ah, so you lecture me on my daughter and giving her freedom to love whom she chooses, but when it concerns *your* child..." He lets his sentence trail off, knowing he just won that round against Royal.

"I don't want a man. Uncle Havoc says boys are disgusting and that girls are way better and nicer." Royal and Vincent both splutter at London's answer, while me and my boys can't contain our laughter.

"I'll be having words with Uncle Havoc," Erika grits out.

"You will do no such fucking thing," Royal abolishes. "Havoc is right, boys are disgusting. Right, Sin?" The fucker shoots me a wink before looking back at my girl and imploring her with a puppy dog look to agree with him. Chanel shakes her head at her cousin, then kneels down in front of the little girl.

"It doesn't matter what gender they are, if they love you and treat you like the queen you were born to be then they are good in my book–"

"Chanel!" Royal warns, but she ignores him and pushes on.

"Just remember what I taught you about stashing a dagger under your pillow and how to go straight for their jugular."

"Jesus Christ," Romeo says in horror. I look around this strange group of people and begin to wonder if my prejudice against crime families was warranted, or was I just looking at it from the wrong side?

The twin's step outside and the easy feeling in the atmosphere changes. Each of them wear solemn looks. It takes Chanel a split second to be on her feet and by Royal's side. I see it now. Her loyalty isn't out of obligation or because they are blood, he has earned it and she has earned his. I never understood her blind trust in him until this moment. He may have a fiancée by his side, but Sin is his shadow as he is hers. They are one and the same.

"Havoc made a call," Chaos says robotically. Havoc turns and looks away and it's then that I see a bruise beginning to form on his cheek. Did they have a spat?

"He's hiding out there, isn't he?" Royal phrases it as a question but he already knows the answer.

"Yes," Chaos grits out.

"What aren't you telling us?" Chanel pushes. She looks the twins over with accusation.

"It's nothing," Havoc snaps, earning a glare from his twin.

"Fuck you!" Chaos shouts. Havoc spins and gets right in his brother's face, seething with anger.

"I told you she wasn't worth it. We started a fucking war with the Columbians because of her, and here we are again about to start another war over a bitch who can't fucking tell us apart!" The anger is clear in Havoc's tone but I can also detect a hint of anguish.

"She didn't have a fucking choice—"

Havoc cuts Chaos off. "Was that before or after my girlfriend opened her legs for you, brother?" My mouth drops open at that declaration.

"Get fucked. Lailani doesn't deserve this shit." Chaos bites back.

"She deserves everything she gets. She had a chance to run after we got rid of that Vargas bastard, but she stayed because she is nothing but a weak little girl. She will never love you, Chaos, she told you so herself."

"I don't give a fuck about you both wanting to fuck the same pussy, sort your shit out later and tell us what the fuck you learned!" Chanel shouts as she pushes between them. I step forward, ready to protect her if they decide to throw a hit while she is in the middle, but her mother cuts a glance to me and subtly shakes her head.

"Answer her!" Royal snarls.

"Halil is with the Dominico's and there is no way that Ricardo is going to give up his new son-in-law." Chanel and Royal both share a quick look and school the shock from their faces.

"He married his daughter off to one of the Albanians?" Erika asks.

"Yes," Havoc answers. "Her two younger brothers were supposed to form an alliance a couple years back but they failed, so she had to step up and take their place." A disgusted look crosses Chanel's face.

"Holy fuck," I whisper out loud, drawing everyone's attention to me. Chanel refuses to meet my gaze and seems to find her boots more interesting.

"What?" Xav asks, but I keep my stare on the brown-haired girl that stole my heart.

"Ricardo Dominico wanted you to marry one of his son's. Clearly after meeting your father, that was declined which is why he started coming after your family." Vincent growls at me but I ignore it. I know I'm right. It never made sense for Ricardo to start a war with the Murdochs over territory, but now I understand. The war started because his offer of marriage was declined. I look at the twins. Clearly both of them have a thing for Ricardo's daughter, so why didn't they take the proposal or was there never one for her? I look to Royal and that's when I get it. There was a proposal for the daughter, but it wasn't for the twins, it was for Royal.

Chapter Nineteen

CHANEL

I want to punch Royal in the fucking throat and watch him choke on his own saliva as I stand over his dying body and smile down at him!

"Just take the spare room down the hall from Chanel." The motherfucker has a death wish. I stand here breathing through my nose, trying so hard not to murder my aunt and uncle's only child. The smug bastard can feel the holes I am glaring into the side of his head but doesn't have the balls to acknowledge me.

Oh, you dumb fuck, I am going to help London murder you in your fucking sleep!

"Nah, you don't have to do that, we can drive back–" Royal cuts Kacey off before he can finish.

"Nonsense. The three of you have had a long day and we haven't even finished planning. You don't mind them staying, right, Sin?" He finally turns to me and the cunning look in his pale blue eyes makes me want to commit mass murder. I give

Royal a toothy smile that has the triumphant look in his eyes slowly fading away as he takes in the savage look in my eyes.

"Of course not! We really do have a lot to plan tomorrow... *after* you and I get out of the ring." Chaos and Havoc snicker behind Royal. I turn on my heel and stomp up the stairs, not giving Kacey and the others a choice but to follow me. I can feel Kacey's eyes burning holes into my ass the whole way. I stop in front of my door and point to the one next to mine, then across the hall. "Those are your rooms, enjoy," I force out before disappearing into my own room and slamming the door closed behind me. "Fucking Royal!" I growl into the empty room as I make my way into my bathroom.

He waited until my mom dragged my dad to bed and Erika left to tuck London in before announcing that Kacey and his friends were going to be spending the night! I pull my gun from my waistband and place it on the bathroom counter before stripping off and tossing my clothes in the hamper in the corner. I make quick work of washing my hair and scrubbing myself before stepping out of the shower. I reach for my robe, but freeze when the sound of my window creaking open hits my ears. Immediately my hunter instincts kick in, I reach for my gun and quietly step out of the bathroom not giving a fuck that I'm naked. The fucker is about to be dead in a second anyway, so it doesn't matter.

Taking a steadying breath, I slip out of the bathroom with my gun raised and finger on the trigger ready to shoot. "Fuck," he gasps out at the sight of me. Anger washes over me at the sight of him standing in front of me.

"How the fuck did you get in here?" I snarl as I slowly lower my gun back to my side.

"Your door was locked so... I used the pipe to shimmy across and hoped your window was unlocked and what do ya know, it was open as if you were expecting me or something." The humor in his tone grates on my fucking nerves.

"Get the fuck out, Kacey. You're not welcome here or wanted." A look of hurt flashes across his face. Ignoring it, I turn and march back into the bathroom. Putting my gun back on the counter, I snatch my hair towel off the rail and bend at the waist to flick my hair forward so I can wrap it in my towel. I begin to twist the towel, then freeze when I feel him behind me.

I stay bent over, unable to move. I know without a doubt he has a perfect view of my pussy right now. His jeans brush against the backs of my bare thighs and ass, then he grips my waist. Still, I remain where I am, unable to get my body to move even when my mind is screaming at me to shoot him. He slowly runs his hands up my sides leaving a trail of goosebumps in his wake. Just as he reaches my arms, his hands vanish from my body, then he's taking a step back. I finally get myself under control and stand, not caring as the hair towel falls to the floor and I turn to face him. He holds my robe out to me.

I look from it to him, then decide to take it, not wanting him to be able to see me like this. He lost that fucking right. I secure the robe, grab my gun, then shoulder check him on my way past to my wardrobe. I slip into a pair of cheeky panties and tug my sleep shirt over my head, then pull the elastic from my wrist and tie my hair in a messy bun atop my head, not giving a fuck that it will be a knotted mess in the morning. I take a shuddering breath as I ready myself to head back into my bedroom and pray to God that he took the hint and left, because I don't have it in me to fight with him.

Wishful thinking.

There he sits on the end of my bed with his face covered by his hands. At the sound of my approach, his head snaps up. His brows draw in at the sight of me.

"Nice shirt." I look down and mentally facepalm myself. I didn't even think when I put this on. It's the shirt I used to sleep in when I would stay over at his apartment. I don't even know how I ended up with it to be honest, but I sleep in the faded band shirt every night. I don't answer him as I move to the window and lean against the wall gazing out at the night sky. The stars are bright and out in force tonight. "Sin–"

"Don't speak, Kacey." I keep my gaze on the late-night sky as I work up the nerve to finally tell him how I feel. I've never been good at talking about feelings. "Two years ago, I allowed myself to fall in love and trusted someone other than my family. I have never trusted anyone who isn't related to me, but I trusted *you*." I hear his sharp exhale. "I thought at eighteen years old I was being crazy and there was no way I could be this in love with someone after nine months. I gave you my whole heart. I let you see the real me. I gave you a part of me no one else will ever get to have. I gave you all of my firsts. Now, two years later and after everything you said to me, I know you won't be my last."

"Like fuck I won't."

A humorless chuckle leaves me. "Don't bullshit me. I give you this though, you were right about not being enough for me." A pained sound comes from behind me but I push on. "If you were the man I thought you were, you wouldn't have pushed me away when I so fucking clearly chose you over the people I pledged my life to." I tear my gaze from the sky and slowly turn to face him. He stands mere feet away from me with a pained look on his face. "I fell in love with a lie. I forgave you for that lie and loved you for who you truly are, but you couldn't give me that same respect."

"What do you want me to say?" he shouts as he throws his hands in the air. "I will never be able to give you the life that you live right now. I'm a fuck up, Chanel. My own family wants nothing to do with me because they are smart enough to realize being close to me means they get hurt."

"I'm not them!" I scream.

"I know that!"

"Then why the fuck are you here?"

"Because I can't stay the fuck away from you. I love you–"

"Don't fucking patronize me, Kacey. You don't know what the fuck that word means."

"Yeah, I do. It means *you*. You are the closest thing I have ever had to happiness. You drive me fucking insane because you walk around acting like you are some badass and hey, babe, I know you are. But let's be real, behind closed doors you need *me*. I need you just as much but I will fuck it up. I am a fuck up."

"That wasn't your decision to make! It's my choice to love you and be with you. You don't get to decide that for me!" Fuck, torturing someone is so much easier than having this fucking conversation.

"Loving me will cost you. Just ask my brother... Oh wait, you can't because he's dead!" My eyes widen as understanding dawns on me. He pushed me away because he thinks him loving me will get me killed. His family abandoned him and he's scared I'll do the same.

"You stupid asshole. I'm not your family. Unlike them, I don't give up. You are worthy of being loved, Kacey–"

"I can't–"

"Shut the fuck up!" He clamps his mouth closed. "You have a decision to make right now because I will not keep doing this. You either choose me or you get the fuck out and never come back because if you do leave, I swear on my honor, the next time I see you we will be on opposite sides. I'll kill you where you stand." He tugs on his hair and begins to pace my room while I stand here with my heart on my throat. I keep my face blank, not wanting him to see that I'm beginning to panic that he won't choose me.

"You don't understand what you are asking of me."

"I understand exactly what I am asking."

"I'm an agent." The air rushes from my lungs. I nibble on my bottom lip as I finally understand what is really troubling him.

"That's what this is about, me being a Murelo and you being an FBI agent? You can't be with me because your job won't allow it." He frowns in confusion. "Get the fuck out and go back to your job, Kacey. Have a great life." I turn my back to him and stare out the window fighting back fucking tears. I hate that my eyes constantly leak these days.

A strangled gasp leaves me when the back of my neck is gripped and I'm forced back against the wall as he crowds my space. His breaths are coming in short rapid pants, blue eyes burning with anger.

"You shut the fuck up and let me finish for once." I cock my head to the side and stare up at him with a blank look on my face. "Fuck everything else, if being an agent means I don't get you then fuck it, I quit." My mouth parts in surprise. "I may not be able to give all of this shit–"

"I don't need this. All I have ever wanted was *you*," I admit. His face softens as he gently reaches out and cups my cheek. Leaning down, he rests his forehead against mine.

"I'm a fuck up, baby. I failed at being a son and an agent. I'll probably fail at being a boyfriend but if you give me a chance, I swear I will never stop trying to be better for you. I love you, Chanel, and I am so sorry I thought you would be better off without me. I allowed my insecurities to get the better of me because I thought years down the road when you finally wanted a house, I would never be able to give you that."

"You stupid prick, I don't need a building to have a home."

"What?"

Reaching out I place my hand over his heart. "My home is right in front of me. You are all I need, Kacey." A smile splits across his face.

"You really mean that?"

I match his smile with one of my own. "Yeah." He doesn't use words, instead he captures my lips in a kiss that has my toes curling, grips the backs of my thighs and lifts me without breaking the kiss. He walks us back toward my bed and slowly lowers me down. He stands between my legs, gazing down at me with a goofy grin.

"We really doing this?" he asks.

"If we do this, Kacey, you have to be all in because I won't keep allowing you to hurt me. If I am what you want, if this is what you want, then you need to fight for it because if you ever hurt me again, I will fucking kill you."

"You say the sweetest things, baby."

"I'm serious!"

"I know, baby. Just please don't give up on me, Chanel. I will fuck up but I swear I will try every day to be better and do better, just please... don't leave me like they did." My face slackens. I reach out and grip his shirt, yanking him down to me. He braces his elbows on either side of me to keep from crushing me with his weight.

"I will never turn my back on you like your parents and Ash did. Unlike those weak bastards, I fight for what is mine and you, Kacey Vaughn, are mine." A possessive glint roars to life in his gaze at my words. I feel exposed and vulnerable right now baring my feelings for him. I've never been this open before and it scares me, but I don't want the fear of striking out to keep me from going after what I want, and Kacey is what I want most. I just fucking hope I am what he wants. I can't do this dance with him again, my heart and mind can't survive that.

"You give me the type of feelings people write books about. People spend their whole lives searching for someone whose demons match their own and yours match mine perfectly. True love doesn't have a happy ending, baby, because true love never dies." A lump begins to form in my throat. "Letting you walk away from me two years ago was the biggest fuck up I have ever made. Allowing you to walk away again the other night was the stupidest thing I have ever done. You are a once in a lifetime chance, baby, and I won't allow you to slip through my fingers again."

I don't use words, instead I wrap my arms around his neck and pull him in so I can seal my lips to his. I pour every ounce of pain I have felt for the past two years not having him with me into this. After a minute, I switch it up and allow him to feel my love through the kiss. The kiss turns from sweet and loving to hungry and demanding, our hands roving all over each other. He grinds his erection against my pussy. I break the kiss and whimper not caring I sound like a desperate feline.

Pushing off me, he stands and stares down at me with a ravenous look in his eyes. He reaches behind himself and grips the collar of his shirt, then yanks it off in that sexy way guys do. My greedy eyes feast on the sight of his body—dear lord have mercy on my pussy. That greedy bitch flutters at the sight of her man shirtless with his V on display. The jeans he wears hang low on hips but I see the sight of ink peeking out just above his briefs. Without thought I sit up and unbutton his jeans pushing them and his boxers down. The sight of his hard cock doesn't even distract me from the sight of *my* name and *my calling card* just above his pubic bone. I flick my gaze up to his in shock.

Reaching out, he cups my cheek in his hand and smiles shyly down at me. "That's my name *and* card," I mutter like an idiot.

"Nothing gets by you, baby," he teases.

"Kacey, that's my fucking name and card tattooed on your body and not just on any part but right by your dick!" I sound like a crazed woman but I'm so fucking shocked I don't care.

"I had planned to get your name across my heart but that

seemed too cliché and nothing about us is normal, baby. So, I got your name and card right where I knew you would appreciate it."

"Why?" I breathe out.

"Because every part of me belongs to you, Chanel, and I wanted to be *officially* marked by you." I pull my gaze from his to stare at my name. *CHANEL* is tattooed in bold italics and beside it is the queen of hearts. I run the tips of my fingers over it. Kacey shudders and groans at the feeling of my hands so close to his erection, so I decide to reward my man. I grip his cock in my hand and squeeze it tight. A hiss escapes his lips.

"The tattoo would have been perfect if it said '*property of*' above my name." He purses his lips but I don't wait for a reply. I wrap my lips around him, he groans in pleasure as I take him as far as I can into the back of my throat. Kacey loves it when I choke on him, the sound of me gagging gets him off. Fisting his hand in my hair, he yanks me forward so I gag, spit dripping down my chin and tears clouding my vision.

"Show me how much you love your property, baby," he growls. I obey him and bob my head up and down on his cock, loving the sounds that come from him. I cup his balls and squeeze them lightly. "Suck them!" Releasing his cock with a wet pop, I continue to stroke him as I suck on his balls. "You're fucking perfect." He yanks on my hair pulling me back. I pout. "Arms up." He grips my shirt and yanks it off me, leaving just my cheeky panties.

I shimmy back on the bed and rest back on my elbows, loving the way his hungry gaze eats up the sight of me. He reaches forward and grips my panties, yanking them down my legs. He balls up the material in his hand and brings them to his nose, inhaling my scent. His eyes roll back into his head.

"Show me my pussy, baby." Bending my legs at the knees I rest my feet flat on the bed and spread my legs wide. I know he will be able to see how wet I am for him, I can feel my arousal dripping. "Fuck, baby, I need to taste you."

"Yes," I beg. He drops to his knees at the edge of the bed and buries his face between my thighs, licking me from top to bottom growling his approval. "Fuck, Loki, just like that," I cry out when he sucks my clit into his mouth. I drop back onto the bed moaning. He reaches up and twirls my nipples between his fingers as he continues to devour my greedy cunt. I know I won't last long, I'm too turned on to try and drag this out. So, the moment I feel my orgasm cresting, I grab onto that bitch and scream out his name the moment it shreds me apart, squirting all over his face.

He doesn't bring me down slowly, instead he stands and grips my legs, dragging me to the edge of the bed so my ass balances there, and positions my legs so they are over his shoulders. He pushes forward so I'm bent like a staple and slams into me. I cry out and relish in the burn from his sudden intrusion inside me.

"Fuck, baby, you're strangling my cock." I can see the strain on his brow, we're both too worked up to drag this out.

"Fuck me hard and fast, Kace," I plead as my pussy shudders around his cock. He draws almost all the way out of me before slamming back inside, both moaning in unison. Twice more he does this before he turns savage and fucks me at a ruthless pace that has the air rushing from my lungs.

"I need you to come, baby. I'm not gonna last," he grits out through clenched teeth.

"I'm coming!" I scream just as the words leave his mouth. Two more thrusts, then he is roaring my name as he comes deep inside my pussy, filling me up. We're both breathless and panting. He pulls out of me without warning, my legs dropping to the bed in a useless heap. He pushes two fingers inside me. I arch off the bed and moan as aftershocks continue to rip through me. He yanks his fingers free and brings them to my lips, smearing his cum over my bottom one.

"Suck." I open and do as he says, moaning at the taste of both our releases mixed together. Fuck, that taste is so addictive. I whimper when he pulls his fingers out of my mouth but am quickly silenced when he kisses me. His tongue swirls across mine, tasting the both of us, and groans into my mouth. Hungry for him again, I lock my legs around his waist and pull him into me. I need to feel him inside me again. I want him to fuck me so hard that I forget where he starts and I end.

Chapter Twenty

KACEY

I wake to the feeling of the sun on my skin. A smile stretches across my face before I even open my eyes because I can feel Sin tucked into me with my arms around her. I slowly open my eyes and stare at her, she looks so angelic. I cringe when I see the hickeys and bite marks over her neck and collarbone. There is no fucking way her father is not going to see them.

I'm a dead man!

Not wanting to wake her, I quietly try to slip out of the bed but freeze when she speaks but doesn't even open her eyes. "You make more noise than a toddler and can't sneak out of my bed for shit." *Fuck it, may as well die with empty balls,* I think as I jump on top of her and nestle my way between her legs. She lazily blinks her eyes open and smiles up at me.

"How many people have you had to sneak out of your bed?" I try to sound light and humorous but the truth is, I'm dying to know if she has had someone else in her bed.

"Just one." I growl.

"What's his address? I'm gonna kill the fucker," I snarl.

"Now, Loki, what fun would it be if you killed yourself?" She laughs when my face slackens, so I tickle her until she is a withering mess beneath me and begging for mercy. Her laughter dies and I stop moving the second someone bangs on her door. Our eyes meet for a second and I can tell we are both thinking the same thing, what if it's her dad?

"Chanel!" At the sound of his angry shout, I leap off her only to roll straight off the bed and land on the floor with a thud. She quickly slips off the bed and does nothing to mask her laughter as she snags her robe off the back of the bathroom door.

"Don't you dare," I warn her but she winks and heads for the door. I scramble to find my jeans and manage to pull them up and zip them up just as she opens the door, but the button is still undone. Rather than be discreet and open the door just enough for him to see her, she swings the fucking thing wide open. I pale the moment he tears his gaze from her to look at me. I watch his eyes darken at the sight of me half undressed in his daughter's room. I really don't want to fight with Vincent. He fucking hit me yesterday and I was surprised I didn't end up with a full-on black eye. Don't get me wrong, my cheek and my eye are slightly bruised but not badly.

"Oh this is just–"

"We'll meet you downstairs shortly, Dad," she singsongs as she spins on her heel, heading for the bathroom, leaving the bedroom door wide open and me and Vincent alone as she closes her bathroom door. I debate jumping out the window and making a run for it, but then I remembered the promise I made to her last night, if this is going to work between us, I need to prove to her father that I can be man enough to fight for his daughter and weather whatever he throws at me.

I open my mouth to say something but still when his gaze drops, and I know the exact moment he spots his daughter's name and calling card because his face contorts. A range of emotions splay across his face, outrage being the most prominent.

"I love her," I blurt out.

He slowly lifts his gaze to mine, his mouth presses into a firm line and his eyes crinkle at the corners. I don't fear Vincent per se, what I do fear however is his hatred for me becoming a factor in my relationship with his daughter. I know Sin is a badass and can hold her own but I also know she loves and idolizes her father. She told me so herself.

"You may be the *Draugur,* but I am the Bloodhound. You only continue to breathe because of her. Until you prove yourself worthy of her, you will never have a free pass with me."

"I can do that," I answer honestly. He rakes his gaze over me in disgust and that shit pisses me off. "I know I'm not who you hoped would end up with your daughter. I don't blame you for doubting me given our past. I also know I can never give her the life she deserves but I will bust my ass every single fucking day to put a smile on her face and make sure she knows she is loved unconditionally by me."

"When your boss asks you to flip on her, what then?"

I stand tall and hold his gaze so he can see the seriousness in my own. "When this is all over and Quintin is brought to justice, I will hand in my resignation. I learned the hard way that the good guys aren't always the ones carrying badges." His gaze bores into mine.

"My opinion of you has nothing to do with your bank account and everything to do with the fact you have hurt my daughter, not once but twice." I flinch, I fucking hate hearing how much pain I have caused her. "I may have money in my bank account, but I never spent much of it. I lived in the forest isolated and alone until I met my wife. I only knew true wealth when I allowed myself to love her and create a life. You hurt the life I created and for that, I will make you pay. I just haven't figured out how yet." He leaves me standing here mulling over his underlying threat as he turns and walks away.

"Well, at least he didn't throw hands this time." I snap my gaze to the side and glare at my sinfully dreadful woman.

"For the stunt you just pulled, you're going to be making it up to me by closing that door and getting on your fucking knees," I growl.

I sit out on the back patio of Royal's house, with my laptop on the table and a beer in my hand. I came out here after Ro and Xav left. I'm grateful for my boys coming here with me but they had to head home and get back to work. I was going to head out with them, until my girl shot me a look that begged me to stay without words, so here I am.

I scroll through the records of the Jones case, compiling all the evidence I can gather against Quintin. Killing the director of the FBI isn't that easy, so Royal and Sin agreed it would be easier if I arrested him and we allowed the court to decide his fate. With that decision made, I'm now tasked with compiling intel on him. Benny checked in earlier and told me he managed to plant a bug in Q's office. I've been listening all day but nothing he has said is anything I can use it court since the bug was planted without a warrant. All I need is for him to make or receive a call from Halil.

"I'm surprised she didn't kill you." I look up to see Chaos coming toward me with two beers in his hand. I thank him when he hands me one.

"Why are you surprised?" I ask after finishing off the luke-warm one I was nursing. I wait for him to answer as he takes a seat across from me.

"Chanel doesn't do second chances and from what I hear, you are on your third and final."

"I guess I'm just lucky," I answer, then take a sip of my cold beer.

"Nah, man, you're fucking insane," he says, then laughs. Cocking my head to the side as I'm confused I ask, "What?"

"Dude, anyone who knows my cousin knows not to get on her bad side, because she will nail your ass. You are fucking crazy because you legit fucked her over twice and still came back." I scrunch my face in distaste. "Teach me how the fuck you do it."

"Do what?"

He rolls his eyes. "Not be terrified of her! I was dropping my sacks when I had to tell her and Royal that I wanted to go back to UNLV and play ball. That chick is fucking crazy. I would rather take on ten dudes then go to battle against her." I can't contain my laughter.

"You make her sound like a psycho," I rasp out through fits of laughter.

He stares at me with a serious look. "You do realize who you are sleeping with, right?" he deadpans. Our attention is snagged when Royal and Havoc stroll out the back door and join us, the sun beginning to set behind us. They claim their seats and within minutes we all fall into easy conversation. I'm surprised to find it's not forced and I'm actually enjoying it. "Dude, I was just telling this dumbass." He says as flicks his head in my direction, "that he is fucking crazy for coming back after fucking her over, not once... but twice." Both Havoc and Royal nod their heads in agreement.

"She isn't *that* scary," I defend. The three of them all turn to stare at me. "What?"

"Idiot."

"Dead within a week."

"He really is a ghost," the three of them all mumble out.

"You three act like she is some heartless animal. Believe it or not, she is actually really fucking sweet." I frown when the three of them snort and start to laugh like I have just told them the funniest joke in the world.

"He said she's sweet," Chaos wheezes out.

"She is fucking sour not sweet," Havoc adds between bursts of laughter.

"The girl should have been born on All Hallows Eve," Royal says before throwing his head back, laughing harder. The twins join him, laughing their asses off.

"And you three should have been born on Aprils Fool's Day, but here we fucking are." At the sound of my girl's voice, their laughter dies off instantly and they all straighten in their seats, clear their throats and look everywhere but at me when she makes her way toward us. She smacks the backs of each of their heads on her way past. They all grunt but say nothing. To my surprise she doesn't sit in one of the vacant chairs, instead she opts to sit in my lap. I don't think as I wrap my arms around her waist and bury my face in the crook of her neck, placing a kiss there. She giggles and I smile against her.

"Eww."

"She just fucking giggled."

"Hell froze over." I pull my head up and frown at the three of them sitting there with wide eyes and open mouths.

"What the fuck are you staring at?" my girl snaps as she shimmy's further back on my lap. I grip her waist and hold her still, if she keeps wiggling like that, I'm going to be sporting a fucking boner in front of her cousins!

"Uh, you!" Chaos deadpans.

"Didn't Aunt Koby teach you it's rude to stare," she snaps back.

"Fuck off, I'm not even going to blink because I don't want to miss the sight of the ice queen's heart finally thawing." She growls at Chaos, Havoc and Royal can't contain their laughter. My girl huffs and crosses her arms over her chest.

"They're just hating because they are scared of you, baby, and want to know what my secret is to not getting killed by you." She turns and peers over her shoulder at me.

"I never said I wouldn't fuck with you." I recoil, the three fuckers at the other end of the table laugh like a pack of bitches at my expense. For the next forty or so minutes the four of them trade insults and Sin promises to mark each of them if they don't shut the fuck up.

"She marked you so we couldn't kill you," Chaos says.

"No, I marked him because I had planned to do it," she defends.

"Why didn't you do it then?" Royal taunts.

"Because I remembered how fucking amazing his cock is and decided I needed one last ride, and then of course, one taste wasn't enough." The three of them shove back from the table and begin to shout and cuss about how disgusting she is and ruined the mood. They promise to inflict pain on me if they ever hear us fucking. Now, I can't contain my laughter. The three of them treat her like a sister and like any siblings, the thought of her fucking makes them sick. I find it comical because I'm the one fucking her.

"What's so funny?" At the sound of Vincent's stern tone my laughter dies in my throat. The boys close their mouths and reclaim their seats. Vincent runs his gaze over each of us, and the moment he spots his daughter on my lap his eyes narrow. I expect him to have a go at me and demand Chanel sit on her own chair, but he doesn't. "Are you all laughing about his tattoo?" My eyes widen and Sin gasps. Her reaction prompts her cousins to demand Vincent spill the beans, of course Carlina, Erika and London have to come and join us and bask in my torment.

"Who got a tattoo?" Erika asks as she sits on her man's lap. London sits between Vin and Carlina.

"Kacey did. Why don't you show everyone," Vincent says in a sarcastic tone.

"Nah, no one needs to see that," I quickly say, cutting in.

"Oh hell no, we need to see it now," Chaos says as he rubs his hands together.

"Don't be a pussy," Royal taunts. Chanel climbs off my lap and peers down at me with a brow quirked. Of fucking course she is all for me showing everyone. Begrudgingly I climb to my feet, lift my shirt and pop the button on my jeans. The guys begin to shake silently with laughter. As I pull the band of my boxers down, they see the tattoo and they all go silent.

"Oh. My. God," Carlina gasps. I quickly fix my clothes and drop back into my seat, not a second later the three dicks break out into fits of laughter. I pull Chanel back onto my lap and bury my face in the crook of her neck, ready to plant a kiss on her neck, but stop at the sound of Royal's voice.

"She fucking marked him!" Erika starts to laugh with them. Carlina tries to fight it, but even she loses the battle and laughs along with the idiots.

"Why did you get Aunty Nell's name there?" Royal begins to choke on his own laughter. I smirk and open my mouth to answer London, but he cuts me a glare and grits out.

"You answer that and I swear to God, I'll say fuck it to the rules and take you out myself."

"Oh, please answer her," Vincent snarks, earning a glare from his wife.

"He got my name there because of his job. He can't allow people to see anything personal on him, so that was the safest spot to get it." The lie slips past Chanel's lips with ease.

"Oh, I would have totally got it on the bottom of my foot." I can't help but smile. London is clever beyond her years and honestly, Royal is going to have his hands full with this one. The rest of the night is spent drinking some beers and eating some amazing food that Carlina and London made for dinner. I'm surprised how freaking easy it has been to vibe with these guys. I was surprised to learn Chanel had ordered me some clothes to be delivered here. I was planning to get the guys to bring me some things tomorrow. Carlina even asked me questions about my family and my childhood. I was included in every conversation except when Vincent instigated it. The awkward tension came when it was time for everyone to call it a night. Vincent glared at me and I was tempted to go to my own room and wait an hour before sneaking into Sin's, but she wasn't having it. She placed a kiss on her father's cheek, gripped my hand, and led the way to her room.

Chapter Twenty-One

CHANEL

It's been a week since Kacey and I made up and I won't lie, it's been the best fucking week of my life. Every night, he fucks me into submission until I am boneless and ready to pass out. Every morning, he takes me again just to remind me who I belong to, his words not mine. I mean, the man literally has my name and card tattooed on him so there is no mistaking who *he* belongs to. Kacey and I have avoided talking about him going back to work. I know he needs to, but a part of me is hoping he will change his mind and career choice. My dad barely tolerates him and honestly, I don't understand why he and Mom are still here.

"Mom, you have to take him home because he is making shit so awkward," I whine to my mom as she continues to prepare lunch in the kitchen with London.

"I don't want Papa V to go," London says and pouts at my mom, who smiles and places a gentle kiss on the little traitor's head.

"You can always go with him," Royal says as he saunters into the room, shooting his mini me a dubious wink.

"I heard that!" Rika scolds as she follows after him. She is red faced and her hair a mess. There is doubt in my mind they just fucked. Erika ignores Royal as she heads over to my mom and London, washing her hands to help them.

"Your father wants to help with this problem before we leave you kids," Mom answers in her no-nonsense tone that she thinks makes her sound scary. That tone hasn't worked on me since I was three.

"Haven't been a kid in a minute, Aunt C," Havoc says as he, Chaos and Kacey enter the room. Kacey comes up behind me, wrapping his arms around my waist and placing a kiss to my neck, that sends a shiver down my spine.

"Stop that shit!" Chaos snaps, garnering my attention. Mom looks at me with a weird look and smile on her face, while the twins look disgusted.

"Stop what?" Kacey asks.

"Whatever it is you're doing to her. It's gross and she's been acting like a... like a... girl lately and I don't like it." Laughter bubbles out of me at the horrified look on Chaos' face.

"I am a girl, you dumb fuck," I clip back after I get my laughter under control.

"Yeah, but you never used to act like it," he deadpans.

"Oh my God, she might start wearing skirts," Havoc adds, earning a glare from me.

"Eww, what if she starts doing her makeup?" Chaos says to his brother.

"Could you imagine if she missed a shot because she broke a nail?" My mouth unhinges at Royal joining in on mocking me.

"Could you imagine if she actually killed the three of you right now and painted a masterpiece with your blood?" All of our gazes snap to London in shock. The little girl just smiles and shrugs her shoulders, like she didn't just stun a whole room full of killers.

"She needs therapy," Kacey mutters, earning a glare from Royal.

"Mind ya business and worry about your own shit and not what my kid does or says." Again, we all stand here with our mouths open, gazes trained on Royal in shock. He scrunches his face in confusion as he looks around the room. "What the fuck are you all looking at?"

Erika's face softens as she closes the space between her and Royal, wrapping her arms around him and burying her face in his chest. He shoots me a pleading look to help him out.

"That is the first time you have ever referred to London as *yours*," I say. His face contorts for a second and then he looks at the little girl in question, who is staring up at him with stars in her eyes.

"Only I get to fuck with you, no one else," he says.

"Ditto, Papi," London sasses back. We all stay congregated in the kitchen watching Mom, Erika and London cook. The twins call me out for not being able to cook. Kacey defends me and says he can cook so there is no need for me to worry about it. It feels fucking amazing to be able to be here with Kacey and my family in the same room. The moment is shattered when Kacey's phone begins to ring and I see the caller ID. My stomach drops, he takes a step back and shoots me a sympathetic look as he steps out back and answers the call.

"Who was that?" Royal asks, sensing the turmoil inside me.

"Owen," I answer in a clipped tone, as I turn and watch Kacey pace the length of the patio, running a hand through his hair. His face is pinched in frustration and I know without a doubt that he is being called back.

Where does that leave us?

The twins come to stand on my other side. The four of us

stand here, silently watching Kacey. "We call you out and give you shit, Chanel, but just know that if he ever hurts you again, I'll rip the motherfucker's spleen out and smile as I'm doing it." The venom in Chaos's voice tells me he means every word and will stay true to his vow if Kacey fucks up.

"What's the plan, Sin?" Hav asks.

"Hope he quits his job because if he doesn't..." I let my sentence trail off, not wanting to finish the last part.

"I'll do it." I look up at Royal and shake my head.

"I appreciate it but if anyone is going to kill him for choosing wrong, it's me." A pang hits me in the chest. I hate the fucking idea that I might have to take the life of the man I am in love with, but I also have to protect my family. Kacey is in too deep now to allow him to walk away and remain breathing. The moment he pockets his phone and steps back inside, he eyes the four of us skeptically before finally setting his gaze on me. The fact he is keeping space between us and not drawing me into his arms, tells me more than he knows. He's about to leave.

"I have a way into the Albanians and I'm taking it."

Okay, that was not what I was expecting him to say.

"But they already know who you are," Havoc says.

"Yes." I eye him skeptically, studying him trying to find out what he isn't saying.

"You're not going undercover, you're going in as the bait to lure them out," Royal announces. Kacey's gaze never leaves mine, the second his blue eyes shield all of his emotions from me, I tense.

"Yes. It's the only way to bring Halil out of hiding and finally be able to bring them down." His tone is clipped and void of emotion even, though I know this must be tearing him up inside.

"No. You're not doing it," I declare.

"Sin—"

"Shut the fuck up, Kacey. I said no." My voice is high pitched and I'm pissed off that my emotions are bleeding out of me but this is too much. If he does this we won't be able to be with him and have his back.

"Chanel, I love you but this isn't your call to make. I'm going." I stand here wide eyed and mouth agape as he turns and heads up the stairs, effectively ignoring me and my demand.

"Did he just say fuck you Chanel without actually saying *fuck you Chanel*?" Chaos mutters.

"Oh yeah, that was a big fuck you to Sin." I ignore the dumbass twins as I race up the stairs and storm into my bedroom, slamming the door behind me to find Kacey walking out of the closet with a duffle bag and some clothes.

"I said no!" I shout. He ignores me and dumps the contents on the bed before he begins to fold them. After a minute of being ignored, I close the space and grab the items he's folded, tossing them across the room. He glares down at me. I can feel the anger radiating off him.

"Stop throwing a fucking tantrum, Chanel! You need to realize that your word isn't God's law. I am a grown ass man and good at what I fucking do. This is my job–"

"What about me?" I scream. "You walk the fuck out that door, you choose your job over me. If you leave, Kacey don't you dare fucking come back!" I can feel the emotions I have been trying to keep locked down inside me rise to the surface, fear of him leaving me again is starting to choke me up.

"I'm doing this for you!" he roars. "No one has been able to get to Halil because he is hiding out with the Dominico's. This is our one chance to bring him out of hiding. We have to do this."

"You don't have to—"

"I have to do this for my brother! Can't you see, this isn't just about you and your family, but for me. I need vengeance for my brother. I love you so fucking much, Chanel Vincetta Murelo, but don't stand in my way. I am going to take this son of a bitch down so Marcus can rest easily and then you and I don't have to keep looking over our shoulders. This is my last job, Sin. I told Owen I would help him with the mole and taking down Halil, then I'm out." His gaze bores into mine. It takes me a solid minute before his words register in my mind.

"You're quitting your job?" I whisper.

He reaches out and cups my face between his hands, a timid smile stretching across his face. I reach out and grip his shirt in my hands, clutching it tight. "Yeah, baby. I told you I wouldn't let you walk away from me again and I meant it. My job is a problem for us, so I eliminated the problem because *you* are the most important thing in this world to me, baby." Fuck, the twins are right. I am acting like a girl! Tears leak from the corners of my eyes as I smile up at my man. He wipes the smile from my face with a kiss that steals the breath from my lungs. Before I can deepen the kiss and show him with my body just how happy his choice has made me, he pulls back when a knock sounds at our door. "Yeah?"

The door opens to reveal Chaos. I frown at the sight of him. "What do you want?" I snap.

"Royal wants a word with Kacey before he leaves. He thinks he has a plan to take out the mole and the Albanians in one hit." Kacey and I agree, our moment is ruined and I know there is no way I'm getting fucked before he leaves, so I decide to help him pack. The entire time my nerves are going haywire inside me. There is so much that could go wrong. I have asked him at least a dozen times what's the plan and how he is going to do this but he just keeps saying, I'll find out in due time and he doesn't want me to worry.

How the fuck am I not supposed to worry?

Kacey clasps my hand in his and leads me downstairs to Royal's office. I'm surprised to find everyone here. My dad stares at our joined hands before flicking his gaze away. I refuse to allow his salty ass mood to affect me for what little time I have left with Kacey.

"Okay, so let's get to it because I'm assuming we don't have a lot of time to get shit rolling and into place before this happens?" Royal asks Kacey.

"Yeah. Look, what I can say is we have about four days to get shit into motion. I don't have all the details but what I do know is Xav, Ro and Benny made a call to loop Owen in on the whole mole situation."

"What does that mean, Kacey?" Kacey turns to Chaos to answer him.

"It means Owen's ass has been on the chopping block thanks to Q. The guys made a good call because Owen has managed to assemble a task force to take down the Albanians and Q in one hit, which is why I have been brought back in."

"How do you tie into all of this?" Dad grits out.

"I am the only agent aside from Quintin that has met Halil. I know both targets and can give a positive ID so all units can move in." We spend the next thirty minutes hatching a plan. Kacey has agreed to keep us in the loop with everything, and Royal was okay with that so he has tasked Havoc with shadowing Kacey and making sure he is safe at all times, or he is to pull him out.

"Keep my brother safe," Chaos snarls as we all head out.

"The calling card tattooed on his neck is yours so, if anyone is going to get him killed it's your own card." At Kacey's reply, Chaos snaps his trap closed and scowls. I try to lead Kacey out but he halts me and turns back to my dad. "Vincent, can I have a word?" Silence ensues until my dad nods. Royal begins to usher everyone out. I stay where I am until Kacey looks down at me. "I need to talk to him alone, Sin."

I shake my head. "No."

He pulls his hand free of mine, places a kiss to the top of my head and darts his gaze above my head and nods. Royal and Havoc each grip my arms and drag me from the room, ignoring my threats of maiming them and cutting their cocks off.

Chapter Twenty-Two

KACEY

"She won't take this well, you know that?" I meet Vincent's gaze and nod.

"I know but if this is the only way to ensure she gets the fuck out of there safely, then I need you to do it." He eyes me up and down but this time there isn't hatred, just a form of respect in his gaze.

"You may just make it in this family after all." My mouth parts as he stalks past me and leaves me alone in my stunned state. Maybe he doesn't hate me that much after all. I snap out of it and make my way out of the office. I find Havoc at the front door rubbing his jaw and glaring down at my girl.

"You got anger issues!" he seethes down at her.

"Nah, I just got an issue when my cousins think they can control me," she shouts. Standing here staring at her and the way she holds herself against these large males, is awe inspiring. She may be smaller than them but she is fierce and deadly. These guys know without a doubt that she can hold her own and take any of them on without batting a lash. My girl is fucking incredible.

"Don't fuck my daughter over." I jerk to the side in fright and peer down at Carlina, who keeps her gaze focused on Chanel and Havoc as they continue to argue, while Royal slips away quietly and hides behind Erika. "If you hurt her again, Kacey, I will be very upset and believe me, my husband will do anything to keep me from being upset... even if it means killing an FBI agent to make me smile again."

Jesus, I see where Chanel gets her charm from!

"You have my word. I swear to you, I will never intentionally hurt your daughter, Mrs. Murelo. She is the reason I'm putting my life on the line—"

"Don't feed me your bullshit. I have five brothers and each of them were once whores until they met their match. Prove your love for her by coming back to her alive." She doesn't wait for a reply, walking away without a backward glance.

"Believe it or not, she is the hospitable one," Chaos jokes from my other side.

"This family is... out of this world," I say for lack of a better world. "Havoc, let's go," I say after shaking Chaos's hand and nodding goodbye to Royal and Erika. London rushes past me and launches herself at Havoc's legs, holding him tight.

"Don't leave me," she begs. Havoc untangles her and drops to his knees in front of the little girl. Sin walks over to me and huddles into my side as we watch the giant of a man be brought to his knees by a tiny little girl.

"Bellezza," he says softly as he rests his hands on her shoulders. "I will never leave you. I'll always come back, I swear." She may be only nine years of age but she is smart beyond her years. I look over at Royal and Erika. I'm surprised to see a pained look on the brutes face. I know he and London haven't always seen eye to eye, but I think the cold hearted fucker is more attached to the girl than he wants to let on.

"You better. If I have to come hunt you down and hurt people to get to you, I will." A proud smile crosses Royal's face. In some families, her words would inspire parents to seek professional help for their child, but not this one. London fits perfectly into this crazy as fuck place. One day I think she may just be twice as ruthless as her Aunt Nelly, just as cunning as her twin uncles and fearless like her father. This girl is going to rule the world, you can see it already. We all live in London's world.

Saying goodbye to Chanel fucking sucks ass. Havoc sleeps the whole way back to my place by the docks where we meet my boys. Ro shows Havoc to his room while Xav, Benny and I stay downstairs to go over the plan for tomorrow.

"So you're just going to meet Owen at the office?" Benny asks me. I take a sip of my beer before answering him.

"Nah, he's sending me an address where I'll meet him and the special ops team to go over the plan and run through possible extraction points if I need a hot evac."

"Dude, it is going to be a hot evac no matter what," Xav deadpans.

"Yeah, I know. But this is the only way I can get them to come out of hiding. Chaos has been tracking the Dominico's and the only one he can get a read on is one of Ricardo's sons." I turn my attention to Benny as I pull out the key card and key from my back pocket, then hand it to him. "I gave these to Chanel so she could break into Q's office and get all the intel on her family, but given the recent change of events, she is going to be my eyes in the sky and you are going to gather the intel and destroy the drive for us." Benny's brows jump to his hairline.

"Are you out of your fucking mind?" He doesn't give me a chance to answer. "I know your allegiances have changed since you and your gangster girlfriend got together, but mine haven't. This is a federal offense, Kacey. If I get caught, I could spend the rest of my life behind bars—"

"Owen approved it. He knows what I had planned and approved the request for you to burn the drive and lock Quintin out of the system." He visibly relaxes at my words. "I would never ask any of you to go against your oaths. After this mission, I'm out."

"What?"

"Since when?" they both say in unison. Ro enters the room with Havoc in tow and frowns at me.

"Why are you giving up the badge, brother?" Ro asks.

I shrug. "Because I found something worth fighting for and I'm not going to give her up, I love her and if changing my career means I get to keep her, then so be it," I answer honestly. Havoc has a smug smirk on his face and nods his respect, my boys may not understand why I am doing this and that's okay, I don't need their permission and I sure as fuck didn't ask for it. I spend the rest of the night catching up with the guys and going over our plan for tomorrow. Havoc has agreed to keep what he hears quiet, because he agrees that Chanel would lose her shit and go on a killing spree again. At around eleven, I leave the guys and call it a night. I need to shower and call my girl.

I climb into bed in a fresh pair of shorts and FaceTime my baby. The moment her gorgeous face fills the screen I feel a sense of relief wash over me. I know she is pissed I left her behind, but the underboss in her knows this is the best call to make for her family.

"Hey, beautiful." She smiles and holds up her index finger before turning away from the screen.

"Wheels up at daybreak. I want the area scoped out and all entry and exits marked. Ricardo went against us so we strike while he is distracted with Halil. Don't fuck this up, Marco. You get in and get out." I say nothing as she continues to lay out her plan. As she shifts the phone, I see Royal and Chaos standing off to the side, allowing her to run the show. The respect each of her cousins have for her isn't just from being blood, she has proven herself to each of them and shown them that she can lead and is a badass in her own right. "I want an updated report an hour after you land. Once the go ahead is given, we'll be on the next flight." She doesn't wait for a response, she stalks out of the room, then finally pays me some attention. "Hi."

"You answered a FaceTime call from me while you were barking orders at a room full of capo's?" She smirks and wags her brows.

"What can I say, I didn't want you to think I was avoiding you." I watch as she lays down on her bed and holds the phone above her. Memories of how I fucked her in that very bed run rampant through my mind.

"That the only reason?" I push.

"No," she whispers.

"You gonna make me work for the answer or share it freely?"

"That depends."

"On?"

"Do you miss me as much as I miss you?" The vulnerability in her tone has my chest aching and arms burning with the need to hold her. She finds it fucking hard to express herself and I will never take for granted the fact she is trying to do it for me.

"I miss you way more, baby."

"Bullshit. You'll get bored of me one day." I scowl at the little shit through the screen.

"Baby, I dropped a tear into the ocean and when they find it, that's when I'll stop loving you." Her eyes glaze over as my words sink in.

"I lied, Kacey," I tense.

"About what?"

"I was wrong. You will be my first and last love. There will never be another man out there for me, which is why I need you to stay the fuck alive until I can get to you. Can you do that for me?" I can't keep the smile off my face.

"Sin, you know I have managed to stay alive without you, right?" Her eyes harden and she grinds her teeth.

"Just promise me, Kacey. I need to hear you say it."

I do as she demands. "I promise, baby. I won't die unless you are the one killing me."

Walking into the office this morning feels strange. I feel like I'm an imposter here.

Benny not being here doesn't help me feel at ease, Owen kept him at head office so he is ready to move at a moment's notice when the meet happens.

"This whole operation is off the books until we can prove Quintin's involvement." I grit my teeth and clench the armrests of my chair.

"So, what you're fucking saying is, if shit goes wrong then I'm on my own?" Owen purses his lips and nods stiffly. I fly out of my chair and smack my hands flat against the boardroom table and hunch over to glare at Owen. "If shit goes sideways, who the fuck pulls me out?" I shout. Owen shoots a loaded look at Leonie; the latter at least has the decency to look sheepish as she looks to me.

"We can't run this on the books, Kacey. Quintin is the fucking director of the FBI. We can't run this on the books. It has to stay confidential until we have solid proof that he has been on the payroll. I swear to you, Kacey, we will do whatever we can to pull you out but you knew this would be a risk."

"Owen never said I would be on my own from the moment of transfer. If they intercept the prison transfer van, who the fuck gets me out?" I snap at Leonie, the tight set of her shoulders and the way Owen refuses to look at me tells me all I need to know. "I get captured, I'm on my own, is that it?" They both nod solemnly. I drop back into my chair and scrub a hand down my face. The plan is to stage a look alike prison transfer and broadcast it across all the stations that an agent has been caught pocketing product and cash from raids, to draw the attention of the Albanians. My mug shot will be plastered with the information.

"Yes, we will be with you every step of the way, Kacey. Trust us." I look at Owen and mull over his words. Six months ago, I would have taken his word and run with it but now, I have no faith in the system. Call me crazy but I'm placing my fate in the hands of my girlfriend and her crime family to save my ass from being executed.

"I wish I could, Owen, but given the fact you purposely left out the part of me being on my own to get me back here doesn't really put me at ease. I'll do this job and get you your mole and the head of the Albanian cartel, but after that I want my record wiped and my benefits paid in full."

Both of their eyes widen. "You're quitting?" Leonie splutters.

"I've been the Draugur for years now. I don't want to be a ghost anymore so, yes. This will be my final job for the

Bureau." I stand and walk out of the room, with my head held high and feeling lighter than I have in years. This was the last thing keeping me from being with my girl and now I have just eliminated that. For the first time in years, I'm excited for the future.

Chapter Twenty-Three

CHANEL

"What the fuck do you mean Kacey has been arrested?" I yell into the phone, Terry clears his throat before answering me.

"We managed to pick up a call, he's being transferred from the local precinct to Miami Dade in the next four hours." I end the call and shove my phone in my pocket. I rush down the hall into Royal's office to find him, Chaos, Dad and a few of Royal's guys standing around his desk, they all look at me but I only stare at Royal.

"We move now. They arrested Kacey, the Albanians will take him out in transit." I push out. I ignore the shouts of the others as I stare at Royal waiting for him to decide.

"Why'd you let Erika live?" his question throws me.

"The fuck are you talking about?" I snap.

"Why the fuck didn't you take the shot after she got back to her feet at the airfield. Don't fucking lie to me." I take a deep breath and grind my fucking teeth.

"Because I knew you fucking loved her and I couldn't hurt you like that!" I snarl.

"You have my word, if he flipped on us, I won't take him out for the same reason you couldn't hurt me. You marked him, Sin, he's yours to do with as you please. But, the Albanians are free for all. The only trace of presence to be left is the cards, are we clear?"

Within twenty minutes we have all the gear packed into the cars. I'm about to hop in with Royal and Chaos when dad grabs my arm and pulls me back. I spin around and scowl up at him.

"You can't stop me—"

Dad cuts me off. "You two go, we got the bird coming to get us there quicker and clear the area." My brows raise in surprise. Dad drags me away from the car as it peels out of the driveway and pulls me around the back of the house where four other men wait. I recognize them as the best snipers Royal has on our team. Gun cases line the ground. Dad rushes forward and pops one of the trunks open and begins to hand me all my tactical gear. I suit up without complaint and press the coms into my ear so we can remain in contact at all times.

"Who's in charge?" Spencer asks as he looks between me and my dad. I open my mouth to say my father is but he beats me to it.

"Chanel is. This is her mark so we go on her command." I stare at my father with an open mouth. He smiles proudly down at me. "You can do this. I trained you to be the Hellhound that you are. Lead me and these men on this mission and bring us home." I snap my mouth closed, stand tall and nod my head.

"I got this," I say as the helicopter draws in closer. We all grab the cases and crouch low as we rush forward to get in. The moment we are secured inside, the pilot lifts us in the air but I can't help but look back toward the house to see my mother standing on the back patio.

"She is the reason I never wanted this life for you." I

turn to face my father who keeps his gaze on his wife. "Leaving her behind to worry after me kills her. If I am killed out there, she will never know if I am dead or just captured. If I am killed, she will never have a body to dress, hug one last time or to bury. I never thought you were less than me, Chanel. I always knew you would grow up and surpass me. I just didn't want it to happen so soon. Never make a rash move, think everything out because I refuse to tell the love of my life, I was unable to bring her only child home safely."

For weeks Dad and I haven't seen eye to eye but right now, I sit here and stare at him in a whole new light. He was hard on me because he wanted to ensure I came home alive and safe. He pushed me harder than the boys because he never wanted to be the one to tell my mother I was killed in action. I don't think as I wrap my arms around him and pull him against me. He's stiff in my hold for a second before he sighs and returns my embrace.

"In position."

"Set."

"Ready."

"Clear on the east," comes from the four guys, each perched on roofs, hills and scattered around the area.

"Bloodhound in position on the south side." Hearing my dad's voice over the coms brings a smile to my face.

"Hellhound in position on the north side." Silence greets me after announcing my position. I keep my eye on my scope and take calming breaths. I push all my emotions down and lock them away to keep focused and my mind clear. If I keep thinking about what is at stake here, I'll fuck up.

"Chanel, change to channel two." I do as my dad says and flick my radio to channel two so we are able to speak privately.

"Yeah?"

"Breathe, clear your mind and remain calm. He is no one to you right now. He is the mark you are sent to save, he means nothing to you–"

"Dad—"

"No, the moment you start feeling for him you will miss the shot, as you trust in him and his skillset to save his own ass. You're the overwatch and that is it. Keep your mind clear and aim steady." I absorb his words and do as he says.

Time passes by slowly as we wait for a sign of the convoy of cars to come through. Royal and the others will be nearby, waiting for my call. Havoc is with Kacey and that is my only sense of relief knowing that Hav will have his back and make sure no harm comes to him.

"Two O'clock, I got a VW parking up on the corner." I adjust my scope and look to where Dex said. I keep my eye on the van, waiting for the driver to exit the vehicle. I wait with bated breath but I can feel it in the pit of my gut, this isn't some random van parking, this is part of Ricardo's men setting up to intercept Kacey.

"Four O'clock," comes through. I attempt to adjust myself but then another call comes through.

"Six O'clock, we have two blacked out SUVs."

"I got another on my six." Fuck, there are too many. I switch my radio to channel six.

"Royal, come in?" I say.

"I'm here, Sin."

"We got five in total, more are trickling in."

"Fuck, your man must have really pissed them off." I growl.

"Not the fucking time," I snap.

"I got you, Sin. I'm looping Havoc and Chaos in now." A second goes by before the twins join in.

"I got the men setting up a perimeter to block them in." Chaos's words put me at ease, the advantage is back to being ours.

"I'm on Kacey's ass. He's in the middle van heading your way in three minutes. The moment we hit the warehouse district they'll make their move," Havoc says.

"Terry and Benny are set to collect the prize the moment we engage."

"What prize?" Chaos asks Royal.

"You didn't tell them?" I whisper shout.

"Tell us what?" Havoc demands.

"We'll deal with this later—"

"No, Royal, tell us now," Chaos shouts.

Fuck it, I see the convoy in the distance and need both the twins heads in the game so I tell them. "Benny and Terry are snatching Lailani to use against her father while he is distracted. Beat the shit out of Royal later, but right now get your fucking heads in the game and take these cunts down."

I ignore the twins' shouts as I adjust my scope. I spot the van carrying Kacey in the middle. I flick back to the channel with my team and tell them to shoot to kill.

"Spikes are out," comes from Chaos. A minute later the first van hits the spikes and spins out, that's when everything goes down. The VW side door is open and men with rifles step out. I take out the first three, forcing the others to take cover behind the van but they can't hide. Dex is set up behind them and takes them out. Cars come squealing from the other direction, windows down with guns out shooting. I take out the tires on the first car, it flips while the other five dodge the wreck. The three vans are sitting in the middle of the battle. I spot Havoc's car blocking the road and him shooting at the car behind him that has been tailing him. I watch his six and take out two fuckers that dare to try to take out my cousin.

"Cutting it close, Sin," Havoc grits out after taking care of his tail and rushing for Kacey's van, but he gets pinned down behind the third van.

"Just keeping you on your toes," I snap back as I continue to take out the Albanian scum. More cars come barreling in, we're overwhelmed. I look around for Royal and the others but they're nowhere in sight. "Royal, where the fuck are you?" I shout but he doesn't reply. My attention is snagged when the van with Kacey in it has its door thrown open. Two guards jump out with their guns drawn. A third jumps out and reaches back in to grab Kacey. My breath hitches at the sight of him in an orange jumpsuit with handcuffs on his wrists and ankles. A haze overcomes me. I go numb as my focus hones in on the men trying to rush him. I take down each without hesitation, putting down any fucker that tries to get to my man.

More cars come barreling in. Panic tries to grip me but I fight it back. Royal should have been here by now! I swap out my mag and continue to take shot after shot, praying to God for the first fucking time that I am able to save my man, because I don't think I could survive losing him, not again.

"I'm hit!" comes from one of my guys.

"They have our positions. We need to move!" Calvin shouts.

"Hold your positions and guard the package!" I clap back, not giving a fuck if they found us, my main focus is to protect Kacey.

"Chanel, fall back now!" Dad roars. A lump forms in my throat as I watch the Albanians and Ricardo's men close in on Kacey. I swipe the tears from my eyes.

"I can't, Dad," I wheeze out, my vision is blurred from my tears.

"He's surrounded. Our positions are up. We need to

move. Trust me, Chanel. I will get to him." I take one last look at Kacey as he's being forced to move by the guard with his hand on the back of his neck. They are scrambling for shelter but one of the guards is taken down. Kacey and the other guard don't stop moving. I look for Havoc but I can't find him. "Trust me, Chanel."

"Fuck!" I grab my rifle and rush from the roof. Sure enough, as soon as I hit the ledge of the building, I'm forced backward when a shot rings out. I run to the other side swinging my rifle over my shoulder and using the fire escape to make my escape. Shots ring out around me. I grab my sidearm and fire back as I leap from one landing to the next ignoring the stairs, I have no time. I hit the ground and roll to the side so I can take out the two fuckers at the end of the alley. I race out the front and check from side to side before making a dash to the building where my dad was stationed, which is the same direction Kacey was moving. I just need to get to him. All thought flees my body when I watch Royal and the rest of the guys move in. It isn't the sight of them that has panic gripping me, it's the sight of London leaping out of the back of one of their cars.

Chapter Twenty-Four

KACEY

"We need backup now!" Kyle shouts into his radio. I shake my head at the idiot.

"Do you really think they don't have signal jammers? No one is coming, get these fucking cuffs off me now," I snarl. He looks around us trying to decide if he should or shouldn't listen to me so I push on. "There is no fucking special ops team coming. Quintin is out there with Halil. The mission is a bust. Get these off me now so I can help." My words seem to spur him into action. He pulls the key from his pocket and undoes my cuff. I wish I had a change of clothes, but I don't. I'm a fucking neon sign out here in this jumpsuit. I peer around the corner of the building to see Royal and the others creeping in, he was smart to hold his team off until they were sure no others were coming or they would have been ambushed on both sides.

"London!" At the sound of my girl's voice my eyes widen, she's a hundred yards from me with a panicked look on her face. I follow her line of sight and my jaw drops.

London stands at the side of one the blacked out SUVs. I spot Quintin as I race toward London. For a second I think I'll make it to the little girl, until Halil comes out of nowhere. Shots ring out around us but I don't hear anything as he stands mere feet away from me with his gun raised. I hear nothing but the blood pumping in my ears, this is it.

This is the moment I die.

I watch his finger shift to squeeze the trigger, then searing pain explodes through my shoulder. As I lurch forward from the force of the shot, my eyes widen when I see the bullet that just shot me go straight through my shoulder and lodge itself inside Halil's chest. He and I both dropped to the ground at the same time. I grunt in pain and reach up to apply pressure to the wound, as I try to turn to get on my feet and get some cover. The back of my jumpsuit is gripped and I'm yanked to my feet and dragged to the side of the field, taking cover behind a building. Vincent shoves me against the building as he peers around the corner letting off round after round until his mag is empty.

He spins around and looks me over. "You good?" he asks.

I nod. "Yeah, nice shot," I deadpan.

The fucker smirks. "You deserved it."

I grit my teeth. "You really didn't need to shoot me, you could have taken the kill shot," I snap.

He shrugs and smirks. "I could have, but *you* did give me permission to take you out before you left if it meant saving my daughter."

My eyes widen. "She wasn't about to be killed!" I shout.

"A thank you for saving your life would be nice," he snarks.

I splutter. "You shot me!"

"It was an accident," he defends.

"I know for a fact you never miss a shot, even your

daughter says you are the best." He rolls his lips over his teeth to keep from smiling.

"We all have our bad days, Kacey. Today must be mine." My nostrils flare in anger. This fucker took great joy in shooting me. He is a marksman and never misses a shot. Motherfucker did this to teach me a lesson for hurting his daughter. "Halil is down but your mole is still out there. We need to take them down and get that piece of shit."

"We need him alive. If Quintin is killed, then we can never prove he was the mole. The bastard wiped his drive, Benny couldn't get anything from his computer."

"What does that mean?" he asks.

"All my sanctioned missions are wiped. Without him alive to confirm that I was undercover, I will hit the FBI's most wanted list and all the operations we ran to lock up the fuckers slinging rock and guns will go free from prison."

"Fuck!" he clips out. Fuck is right. Owen and Leonie fucked me on this one. They assured me that with the drive I would be good, but now without that drive, I'm on my own unless I can bring Quintin in. How funny, the people I spent my life putting away and taking down are the ones here now saving my fucking life.

"London is out there," I blurt out. Vincent's eyes widen, he tosses me a gun before racing around the corner, leaving me alone. The fucker shot my shooting arm so I am useless out here. I poke my head around the corner only to come face to face with Ricardo Dominico. I raise my gun ready to shoot. Even if I miss the first shot, thanks to using my shit arm, I'm sure I'll hit him eventually. The first shot rings out but it's deflected by the Jeep. The bastard is going to escape. I shoot at the tires but it's no use, my aim is way fucking off!

Ricardo's men–what's left of them—begin to retreat. Fucking pussies. I look around for Quintin, he is the one that I need alive. I spy Royal with a panicked look on his face, running toward me from fifty yards away. I look closer and that's when I spot London against a wrecked van, with Quintin pointing his gun at her. I take off trying to get to her but I know I will never reach her in time. The pain in my shoulder is void as I push myself to move faster to get to her. I see Chaos and Sin out of the corner of my eye also rushing toward the little girl. Chanel lifts her gun ready to shoot Quintin, but then a hulking form dives in front of London just as a shot rings out. A split second later another shot comes from Chanel, then Quintin is falling to the ground in a heap.

"Havoc!" The pained cry comes from Chaos. I skid to a stop and try to roll Havoc off London but I can't move him. Royal is there in the next second, rolling his cousin off his little girl. He lifts her and checks her over, blood coats the front of her but none of it's hers. "No, no, no," Chaos cries as he drops to his knees beside us and lifts his brother's torso so Havoc's back is to his chest. Chanel drops down beside me. Tears stream down her cheeks as she looks at her cousin. Blood pours from his neck, his eyes are drooping shut.

"Havoc..." Sin cries out as she leans forward and places her hand on his wound, to try stopping the flow of blood. I cut a glance to Royal who is clutching London against his chest. She's crying for her hero—Havoc just saved that little girls life. Royal meets my gaze. I can see it in the depths of his eyes he knows as well as I do that Havoc isn't going to make it.

"Ch-aos." Havoc coughs and blood seeps out through his teeth. Chaos tightens his hold on his brother, running one hand through his brother's hair as he shushes him.

"Don't talk, save your strength, brother. We can laugh about how much of a pussy you look like right now, tomorrow." Chaos looks to the rest of us with a plea in his eyes to help him. "Get a fucking chopper!" he screams. "Someone do something." He looks down at his twin who has now turned pale and can barely keep his eyes open. Realization crashes into

Chaos, he's about to lose the other half of himself. Havoc musters enough strength to tilt his head back slightly and stare up at his twin.

"Lo-ve... you... broth-er," he chokes out. We all watch as the last breath leaves Havoc's body and he goes limp against Chaos. Sin sobs beside me. I wrap my good arm around her and draw her into my side as she screams into the crook of my neck. London wails in Royal's hold. She tries to break free to go to her hero, but Royal holds her back. Tears trek down his own cheeks as he stares at his cousins. Chaos looks down at his twin in shock.

"Tell me you love me tomorrow." His calm, even tone has me stiffening. I dart my gaze above the twins to see Vincent standing there with a broken look on his face as he stares down at his nephews. "You're going to be fine, you big ass baby." Vincent's gaze meets mine as Chaos continues to stroke his brother's head and place random kisses on the top of it.

"Havoc! I'm sorry, come back. Please, don't be dead," London screams. Chaos snaps his eyes to her and that's the moment it hits him. The war of emotions that was in his gaze a second ago is replaced by anger and hatred.

"He isn't dead, you little shit. He's fucking resting so don't fucking say that shit!" Chaos screams. London recoils into Royal, who holds her close. He doesn't snap back at Chaos, knowing that this isn't the time to tell him his brother is gone. Sin continues to sob into me, my heart breaks for my girl. Havoc was one of them and now they have lost their fourth horsemen.

"Someone call Knight!" Vincent screams after his fourth attempt at trying to get Chaos to let Havoc go. Everyone left him alone when he pulled a gun and shot Terry in the leg for trying to take Havoc from him.

We had no choice but to get every man to lift both Havoc and Chaos into the back of one of the SUVs since Chaos refused to let go of his brother. We couldn't stay there. With Quintin dead, the mission was a bust. We may have taken out the mole and the head of the Albanian cartel, but none of that matters because we have no proof that the mission was sanctioned. Chanel is huddled into my good side with her father sitting on her other side with his hand on her knee, offering his silent support. Royal sits in front of us with London in his lap, who cried herself to sleep. Two of his men sit up front driving us, but remain silent the entire way.

The atmosphere in the car is tense and filled with pain. We follow behind the car holding the twins. As we pull into the driveway, the twins car cuts across the lawn and heads around the back. Our car comes to a stop in front of the house where Erika and Carlina wait, both rushing forward the minute we stop. Royal gets out and goes to Erika who is crying. Vincent steps out next and goes to his wife who is shaking as silent sobs tear out of her. I help Chanel as best as I can out of the car, her eyes puffy and filled with anguish. She doesn't go to her mom like I thought, instead she grips my hand and leads me around the back of the house. The others follow after us. We stand back as we watch Royal's guys gently drag Chaos and Havoc from the back of the car. Chaos still hasn't let his brother go.

"How far away is Knight?" Vincent mutters.

"He should be here within the hour. Bishop and the others are coming with him. They got on the first flight," Carlina chokes out.

"Did you tell them?" Royal asks in a monotone.

"No. I just told my brother that his son needed him. They know something is up, which is why the whole family is coming." Carlina cuts a glance to me. I see the question in her gaze and shake my head. She wants to know if her daughter is okay and I don't want to lie. Carlina shifts to Vincent's other side where he wraps his arm around her shoulders and pulls her close as she clasps her daughter's hand in hers. Erika huddles into Royal's side, stroking the top of London's head as she sleeps in his arms.

The sight of Chaos sitting on the lawn with his brother clutched against his chest breaks something inside me. The guys bow their heads in respect as they step away and move the car around the front. We all stand here watching Chaos stroke his brother's head and whisper things into his ear. Every now and then Chaos laughs at something he says.

"He can't let go," I say quietly.

"All their life we always thought it was Havoc who couldn't function without Chaos. I see now we were wrong," Chanel rasps out, her voice hoarse from the tears she has cried. I look around as men who fought alongside us today come to form a large circle, making sure to give Chaos space. They all clasp their hands in front of them and bow their heads. Royal releases a loud exhale, then turns to Erika. He gently transfers London into her, places a kiss to his fiancée's head and looks at my girl.

"He needs us." Those three words have her standing tall and locking her emotions down, then stepping out of my embrace to walk side by side with her cousin. I keep my gaze on them even as Carlina speaks.

"I called Amelia. She knows about what happened and offered to come here and treat the wounded." I know who Amelia is because of Chanel. It must be handy having a doctor in a family like this. I don't respond. As Royal and Chanel near Chaos, he snaps his head up and points his gun at them. The feral look in his eyes has me on edge.

"Stay the fuck back!" he roars.

"We're here for you–" Royal tries, but is ignored when Chaos cocks his gun. The men around us shift and reach for their weapons. Sin raises her hand, halting their movements. Chaos darts his gaze around him as if he is only just noticing that he is surrounded. I feel for him. I know what it's like to lose a brother and it fucking shreds you up inside. I move forward without thought, I pass Sin and Royal ignoring their calls for me to stop. Even when Chaos points his gun at me I don't stop until I'm mere feet away.

"He will never truly be gone because *in Havoc lays Chaos.* You both are a part of each other. His memory will live on through you." His eyes crinkle at the corners.

"You don't know shit, he's fine. He's just resting and then he'll be good–"

I cut him off. "Look at him Chaos," I say in a hard tone.

"I am!" he shouts.

"No, you're avoiding seeing what is right in front you. Look at him!" I shout. Chaos's gun begins to shake as he slowly lowers his gaze to his brother's, meeting his twin's lifeless eyes and his breath hitches. Tense minutes pass by as we all stand by and wait for the weight of Havoc's loss to hit him.

"Havoc, Chaos?" At the sound of their names being called by their father, I spin around to see the rest of the Murdoch family rushing toward us. Knight and Koby lead with Rook, Gage, King, Bishop, Kiara, Anya, Allison and Clare following close behind. They all slow to a walk at the sight of us. I step aside so they can see.

"Oh God," comes from Koby as her knees buckle. Bishop rushes forward to grab his sister in law before she can hit the ground. Knight's wide eyes are trained on his sons. Disbelief is evident is his gaze as he slowly inches forward on shaky legs. "My baby!" Koby screams in agony. Bishop holds her close as screams tear from her, the sound will haunt me for the rest of my life. Chaos lifts his gun and points it at his father as he draws near, but Knight either doesn't see it or just ignores it as he drops to his knees in front of his twins.

"Don't you fucking cry, he's fine. He just needs to rest, he... he just... he's fucking..." Chaos chokes out, I see it in his eyes. He's starting to feel the loss now that he has allowed himself to finally see what is in front of him.

Chapter Twenty-Five

CHANEL

Royal clasps my hand in his as we stand here breaking internally for our Chaos, the loss we feel is nothing compared to the loss Chaos feels. Havoc and Chaos weren't just brothers, they were twins. Each of them loved the other more than they could ever love another. Uncle Knight reaches out and places his fingertips on the tops of his son's eyes and draws his lids down, closing them for the last time. His shoulders begin to shake with silent tears. Chaos stares at his father in horror. The moment he finally accepts the loss of his brother can be seen when the anger in his gaze vanishes and is replaced by pain. He looks like a broken little boy as he sits there with his twin clutched against his chest.

"Dad," Chaos cries out. Within a second, Uncle Knight has the distance between them erased and holds both his boys to him as they cry. Aunt Koby staggers over to them looking like a pale ghost. Her knees give out beside her husband. She says nothing as she reaches for her son and tries to pry him from Chaos, but he won't let go. "No, he stays with me–"

"He is my fucking baby. You give me my son now, Chaos. He is your brother but he is half my fucking heart and soul. I gave him life. Now, you give him to me so I can hold my baby boy." Her words have Chaos releasing his hold slowly. She pulls Havoc in close and buries her face in the crook of his neck, a gut wrenching scream tearing from her as she clutches her son's body to her.

I feel an arm wrap around my shoulders and look up with tear filled eyes to see Kacey standing there. I don't think as I bury my face in his chest and cry for my cousin. I hear my other aunts and uncles close in on us but I can't bring myself to come out of the safety of Kacey's chest. If I hide in here long enough maybe I can trick myself into thinking this is all a bad dream, and when I wake up tomorrow, Havoc will be in the kitchen cooking breakfast with London, mocking me about having sex hair.

I don't know how much time passes before Aunt Koby's screams finally quiet down. The pain in her screams kills me inside. I should have taken the shot sooner... if I did, Havoc would still be here!

"Aunt Koby?" At the sound of Amelia's voice, I pull away from Kacey and watch my cousin step forward with three men and a woman trailing after her with a stretcher. Aunt Koby eyes the strangers. Uncle Knight stands and blocks his wife and sons from view as he faces off with his eldest niece. "Uncle Knight–"

"Who the fuck are they, Amelia?" he cuts in and snaps, his tone holding a cold edge.

Amelia doesn't bat an eye at his tone. "They are friends of mine and the best at their jobs. They are here to take Havoc–"

"Touch my brother and I'll slit your fucking throats!" The three men visibly pale at Chaos's threat.

Not one to be deterred, Amelia pushes on. "They will

treat Havoc with the utmost care, they will make sure he is cared for—"

"I said no!" Chaos screams.

"Knight?" Aunt Koby whispers. He spins around and kneels down beside his wife who has Havoc's head resting in her lap as she runs her fingers through his hair.

"What is it, baby?" Uncle Knight asks gently.

"This isn't like when Rook went missing, is it?" I dart my gaze toward Uncle Rook and feel sympathy for him when his chin meets his chest.

Uncle Knight clears his throat. "No, baby. I would give anything for it to be like that just so I knew our son would come back, but I can't lie to you." Aunt Koby lifts her tear stained face to her husbands.

"My baby is really gone," she sobs out. Uncle Knight reaches out and grips the back of her head pulling her to him so he can rest his forehead against hers.

"I'm so sorry I wasn't there to save our boy." The devastation and regret in my uncle's voice has a lump forming in my throat. He pulls back and stares into his wife's eyes for a minute before he says, "Bishop, Royal, King, Gage, I need you to hold Chaos." Aunt Koby's mouth opens but he pushes on. "Rook, Vincent, I need you to hold Koby."

"Fuck you!" Chaos screams as my uncles and cousin grab him, dragging him back a few steps.

"You touch my baby and I'll fucking kill you!" Aunt Koby screams as Uncle Rook and Dad gently restrain her as Uncle Knight climbs to his feet and turns to Amelia, ignoring the screams and threats coming from his son and wife.

"I go with him. I will not leave his side for a second. I failed my son in life but I will be dammed if I fucking fail him in death." Amelia nods and motions for the four strangers to step forward. I stand here numb and angry as I watch Havoc be lifted on the bed and covered in a red velvet blanket. Amelia nods to her friends then they begin to wheel Havoc away with Uncle Knight following after him. The sight of his brother leaving is what finally breaks Chaos.

"Dad, please!" he begs. "Don't take him, I swear to God I'll never fail him again just please... don't take him!" Sobs rip out of him as my uncle ignores him and motions for the undertakers to continue wheeling him out. Aunt Koby is a mess in my dad and uncle's arms. To my utter shock, Kacey pulls away from me and heads straight for Chaos who is thrashing to get free. Kacey reaches out and places a hand on his chest and to my shock, Chaos stops fighting.

"I know you are dying inside right now, but your mother needs you. Pull it together until your father gets back to take over." Chaos snaps his head to the side to see his mother on her knees screaming for her son. "Go to her, she lost one son already tonight. Allow her to see Havoc through you. Give her the comfort of seeing your brother in your eyes." Immediately Chaos stands tall and his cries stop as his arms are released. He says nothing as he passes Kacey, scoops his mother into his arms and heads for the house.

Chaos took his mother to Havoc's room where they have holed up. I left Kacey to be treated by Amelia as I escaped to my room to clean up. I've been standing under the spray of the shower, praying that it can wash away the crippling pain inside me. When the pain becomes too much, my legs give out and I drop to the floor sobbing and crying out at the injustice of this whole fucking situation! I want to blame Kacey for being the reason for this fight today. Another part wants to blame Royal for taking too long to get to us and for not checking the cars. If he did, London wouldn't have been able to sneak into the back. I blame myself most of all for not taking the shot sooner.

"Ah, baby," I hear from behind me a second before a cold draft hits my naked back. A minute later Kacey is at my back shirtless and only in a pair of jeans. He wraps his good arm around my waist and draws me flush against his front. He says nothing as I cry in his hold. By the time I get my tears under control, my eyes are puffy and my throat is hoarse. I turn around and face Kacey. He reaches up and cups my cheek in his hand, I melt into his touch. "I am so fucking sorry, Chanel."

"Don't be sorry, just make me forget for a minute. I need to not feel this pain, Kacey—" He grips the back of my head and hauls me forward, claiming my mouth in a heated kiss filled with love, passion and pain for my loss. I ignore the last one and focus on the fire in my veins he is igniting with this kiss. I need this escape just for a moment. I shift and straddle his lap, reach between our bodies, not breaking the kiss, as I clumsily fumble with the button on his jeans. On the third attempt, I manage to get it undone. I yank his fly down and reach into his boxers, pulling his hard cock free. He groans into my mouth, no foreplay needed. I just need to feel him inside me, consuming me until I'm mindless and can't feel anything but him.

He breaks the kiss and stares directly into my eyes. Sky blue eyes meet coffee brown. "Fuck me, Chanel." Kacey doesn't need me to tell him that I need him to take the lead, right now he knows I need him to be in charge and tell me what to do so I don't think. "Put my cock inside that fucking pussy now, baby." I rise on my knees and line him up with my opening. We keep our eyes locked on each other as I slowly sink down onto him, relishing in the burn of him stretching me out to accommodate his size. I cry out the moment he is balls deep inside me.

"Kacey," I breathe out.

"Shut the fuck up and bounce up and down on my cock," he growls. I brace my hands on the tiled wall behind him as I do just that. This isn't slow or sweet, this is me needing to use him as an escape. He leans his head forward and captures my nipple in his mouth, swirling his tongue around the hardened peak as I cry out.

"Fuck, yes, Kacey. I'm gonna come." He bands his good arm around my waist and takes over thrusting inside me. "Kacey!" I scream as I come. He pulls his cock free mid orgasm so I can squirt all over his cock.

"Put it back in now!" he snaps. I fumble to grab his cock and put it back inside me thanks to the aftershocks tearing through me. Kacey doesn't give a fuck that I am boneless in his hold, he continues to fuck me, forcing me up and down on his cock. "One more, baby. Come one more time for me."

"Just like that, fuck, Kacey, don't stop," I moan. I manage to regain control of my body and meet his thrusts, slamming down hard onto his waiting cock chasing my release.

"Fuck, baby, I'm gonna come. I need you to come with me." His words spur me on. I grind down on his cock, riding him like a crazed animal. I come so fucking hard I swear I nearly black out. Kacey comes deep inside me with my name on his lips. I flop forward as tremors wrack through my body. He cuddles me against his chest as his cock continues to twitch inside me.

After Kacey and I got cleaned up, I help him into a pair of sleep pants and curl up beside him, but sleep still evades me as I stare up at the ceiling. My phone vibrates on the tables beside me. I untangle myself from Kacey and quietly slip out of bed to check my phone.

ROYAL

You up?

ME

Yeah, you good?

ROYAL

No, I need you, Sin.

Without hesitation I quietly creep out of my room and make my way downstairs. The clock on the wall reads three in the morning. I follow the dim light from the kitchen and frown when I find it empty, but I spot two shadows out back on the patio. I slip out the back door quietly and make my way over to them. I drop down on the other side of Chaos and lean my head on his shoulder. He still wears the same clothes that are covered in Havoc's blood. Royal reaches over and passes me an open bottle of Whiskey. I grab it and take a deep pull, relishing the burn as the alcohol slides down my throat. The three of us sit here passing the whiskey around without uttering a word. When that bottle is empty, Royal magically makes another appear.

When the darkness begins to fade and we see the sun cresting on the horizon, emotions begin to swirl inside me as reality comes crashing down around me. Havoc is gone. This isn't some movie where he will suddenly come strolling around the corner shouting *'gotcha!'* We will never see him smile, crack a joke or scare the piss out of his brother, but what

I will miss most is his presence. He was always our rock, silent and lurking in the shadows but always there.

"He's gone," Chaos rasps out. Royal wraps his arm around Chaos's shoulders as I rest my head against him. He shakes with silent tears and within seconds, Royal and I are both sharing in his grief and crying along with him. "He was the better one, he should be here, not me."

"Don't do that, man. Havoc would never want that and you know it," Royal scolds him gently.

"I can't do this shit without him. It's always been him and me, from the day we were born, he's always been there. He's always fucking been there..." His sentence trails off as tears grab a hold of him.

"We will never know the immense pain you are suffering through right now, but we loved Havoc like a brother, you know that. Royal and I will be by your side every step of the way. We got you, always." I hope he hears the truth in my words because I mean it. Whatever he needs we will be there.

"My mom can't even look at me." I wrap my arm around his waist and lean into him further. "All night she has been trying to call my dad but he's ignoring her calls. When she isn't calling dad she's sniffing Havoc's clothes and calling out his name like he is just going to magically fucking appear! He is never coming back," he screams out, then breaks downs again.

"Let it out. Get it all out now, because come morning, you are going to quit crying and hold your mother through this. When she finally leaves and we are alone, *we* will hold you while you break."

The sound of the back door opening draws my attention. Through the haze of my tears I see Kacey and Erika coming toward us, with blankets and cups of coffee. Erika wraps blankets around each of us while Kacey hands us each a cup of steamy goodness. The three of us exchange a look as Erika sits down beside Royal and Kacey claims the spot beside me. We each share a small smile as we fill our cups with the remainder of the whiskey. The five of us stay out here watching the sunrise.

"My mom used to tell me that you can make a wish as the sun rises, but this wish must be said out loud so the sun can hear you." I look over at Erika to find Royal looking at her in surprise. She never speaks about her parents much, so any tiny detail she shares I know my cousin cherishes.

"I wish Havoc ever lasting peace in the afterlife," Kacey says solemnly.

"I wish for everyone to be able to overcome this tragedy," Erika utters quietly.

"I wish for vengeance," Royal grits out.

"I wish for the motherfucker who did this to burn eternally in hell," I growl.

Chaos scoffs and shakes his head drawing all of our gazes to him. "We call ourselves the *Memento Mori*–the bringers of death, right?" He snorts and doesn't give us a chance to answer him. "We were supposed to be better than death. We evaded that bitch for years but now, that cunt took the one person who fucking meant everything to me. Ripped my soul right the fuck out of my body! Without Havoc, I am nothing but an empty shell. I don't wish for shit, instead I am going to make my brother a promise. I vow to wipe Quintin's bloodline from existence and I also vow to destroy the entire Dominico bloodline, Lailani included."

"Chaos–" Royal tries but he isn't hearing any of it.

"Yesterday, after the bodies of our soldiers were cleared away, I know you had Marco and Benny leave his Ace of Diamonds atop each of the bodies. That is the last time anyone will ever use that card, do you hear?" Royal and I both hum our agreement. "That fucking card is retired. It was his and no one will ever take that away from him, do you hear me?"

"You have our word," Royal answers.

"No one will ever use his calling card," I agree.

"Chaos, your mother needs you." We all turn to find Uncle Bishop standing there with Uncle King beside him. Chaos sighs and nods before pushing to his feet and walking away with his head down. My heart aches for my cousin. I would give anything to take away his pain.

Chapter Twenty-Six

KACEY

Koby and Knight chose to return Havoc to New York, where they will have a service for their son, then cremate him. Chaos pushed them for this because he wants his brother's ashes put into some jewelry so he can keep him with him at all times. I love the idea. I wish my parents had done something like that for Marcus. I admit, the flight here was over quicker than I would have liked. Amelia changed my dressing this morning and was shocked to learn that it was her fucking uncle who shot me!

I glare at the back of Vincent's head. The asshole shot me on purpose. I still haven't told Chanel it was her father who managed to take out Halil and in the process shoot me! Honestly, with everything that is going on, it seems kind of pathetic to whine over a bullet wound when they are about to lay their cousin to rest. We drive down a long road that leads us through a large gate. Three houses line either side of the road but we continue past them and head up to the main house at the back. Vin brings the car to a stop behind King and Allison's. Everyone climbs out and begins to head inside. Unlike everyone else who just walks inside, Vin, Gage and I grab our bags from the backs of the vehicles.

"Don't ever lose that." I cut my gaze to Vin as I fall into step beside him and Gage.

"Lose what?" I ask.

"Your humility. Never allow this life to change you as a person because it will try to. These kids grew up being fed with a gold spoon. We allowed them to be spoiled, but Gage and I didn't grow up in this life and neither of us will allow anyone to clean up after us, carry our bags or do our fucking dishes." I'm seriously humbled by the fact that Vincent is taking the time to even speak to me, but the most surprising fact is that he is speaking about me being a part of this family.

"You want to make it in this Murdoch world, you need to man the fuck up and not allow anyone to fuck with you, not even your future father-in-law." I choke on my spit. Vincent glares at Gage who just smiles and leads the way inside the massive house. I try to look around but Vincent nudges me forward in my injured shoulder. I grunt but refuse to the give the fucker the satisfaction of groaning in pain. We come around the corner into a large living room. I spot Chanel in the corner with Royal and Chaos, I stand here on the outskirts, feeling out of place.

I look around the room and marvel at the fact that I am in the Murdoch Mafia's home!

Many agents have tried to infiltrate their organization but none have been successful and yet, here I am standing in their living room, grieving with their family. I wish with all my heart that I was invited here under different circumstances, because in the short time I knew Havoc Murdoch, I could tell he was a solid guy and would have laid down his life for any of his family members.

"Koby?" Bishop calls to her as he enters the room from what looks like the kitchen.

"Yeah?" she answers without taking her gaze off the windows that overlook the backyard.

"Knight refuses to leave Havoc alone for his last night, so he is on his way here with your son." Koby snaps her gaze to her brother-in-law in stunned silence. "Havoc will remain here with the family for his final night before being transported to the church in the morning." Tears slowly trek down her cheeks. Carlina and Kiara both wrap their arms around her and hold her close.

By the time the hearse arrives, I've had the pleasure of meeting Rook and Gage's daughters. The three of them are so different from their older cousins. Unlike Chanel, these girls want to lead a normal life and have nothing to do with the family business.

"They're at the gate," Bishop announces. We all make our way out front and the sight that greets us has me stumbling over my own feet. Men line either side of the road from the gates all the way to the edge of the patio that we currently stand on. The hearse slowly makes its way toward us. As it passes by the men each of them bow their heads and place a closed fist over their hearts in show of respect for Havoc. The sight alone has gooseflesh breaking out over my skin.

Before the hearse can come to a stop, Royal, Chaos, Chanel, Rook and Bishop make their way to the edge of the drive. Once the vehicle stops the driver doesn't get out, but Knight does. He refuses to leave his son, even for a minute. He hasn't left Havoc's side since the night he arrived at Royal's. This will be the first time Koby has been able to see her son since then. All her sister in laws are gathered around her as her husband goes to the back of the vehicle where we can see a black coffin through the windows.

Knight opens the door, places a hand on his son's casket

and sobs. Rook breaks away from the others and goes to his twin. The moment Rook is within reach, Knight turns to him and pulls him in for a hug. The sound of his pained cries has the women around us crying along with him and a quick glance around at the others, they all have tears in their eyes.

"I fucking got you, do you hear me? I am right here, brother, and will hold you through this," Rook grinds out through his own tears.

"That's my fucking son in there," Knight sobs as he sags in his brother's hold. Bishop turns to Koby and nods. She pulls away from the girls and slowly makes her way down the stairs. Before she heads for her husband, she stops in front of Chaos. He stands tall and keeps his gaze focused above her head. Koby holds her hand out. Chaos frowns as he looks down. It takes him a second before he hesitantly reaches out and allows his mother to lead him toward his father. She pats Rook on the back. He untangles himself and steps back allowing Koby to claim his spot in front of her husband.

She grips Knight's hand in her own and pulls both her son and husband in for a three-way hug, while the rest of us stand here silently watching. It's so fucking hard not to get caught up in your feelings right now.

"Let's bring our boy home for the... last time," Koby manages to force out. Knight nods his head and steps back. Royal, Sin, Rook and Bishop rush forward to grip onto the handles on either side of Havoc's black casket that is decorated with wreaths of black and red flowers Koby and Knight each grab a handle at the back and carry their son. The six of them walk silently carrying the casket inside, the rest of us following after them. When we enter the living room, I see Clare and another man standing beside a frame that the casket will rest on. They place the casket on the stand, everyone but Chaos steps back. He begins to undo the screws to remove the lid. Royal tries to reach for him but Knight places his hand on his nephew's chest to hold him back. The moment the last screw comes loose, Chaos stands there silently for a moment as tears begin to gather in his eyes.

"You need to let him go, Son," Knight says softly, drawing Chaos's gaze to him.

"How do I do that, Dad? He wasn't just a person, he was *my* fucking person." Chaos's legs give out. Before he can hit the ground, Chanel and Royal are there to hold him up on either side.

"He will always be your person, Son." Knight's tone is thick with emotion. Bishop steps forward with King at his side. They each grip a side of the lid. Chaos tenses in his cousin's hold as he waits with bated breath to see his brother. Koby creeps up beside her husband and grips his arm for support. The moment the brothers remove the lid and step back, Koby screams and drops to her knees. Knight is right beside her, holding her as she claws at his arms, screaming for her son to get up and cursing God for taking her baby from her. I'll admit, there isn't a single dry fucking eye in this room. I watch as Erika pulls London in close. Clare, Anya and Allison have pulled their own children in closer.

"Let me go," Chaos says in a tone void of all emotion. Royal and Chanel release him so he can go to his brother, my heart warming at the sight of Royal drawing my girl into his side and holding her close. Without words he is offering her his strength and telling her he will be the rock that will carry her and Chaos through this pain. Chaos grips the edge of the casket and stares down at his brother.

Havoc isn't dressed in a suit like most would assume. He wears a black tee and jeans like he always did. The wound on his neck is cleaned and stitched, but to the naked eye you wouldn't be able to spot it because the Jack of Spades covers it–Chaos's calling card.

"You were supposed to be by my side, my ride or die." The

emotion in Chaos's voice is felt by everyone. "I'm so fucking sorry I failed you, Hav." He bows his head as he weeps quietly for his brother. "You loved me your whole life and now, I will miss you for the rest of mine big brother."

I wrap my good arm around my girl and draw her into my side as we stand back and watch Havoc's casket get lowered into the church floor where he will be taken to be cremated. Knight and Koby tried to convince Chaos not to watch the cremation happen. But he ignored them and jumped on top of his brother's casket and refused to leave him until the last minute.

We walk quietly out of the church. I head for our car but Chanel grips my hand and leads me around the side of the church. "Where are we going?" I ask.

"You'll see." Just as we near the back of the church, she comes to a stop and turns to face me. The look on her face has me stiffening.

"Chanel, what the fuck is going on?"

"You have given everything up for me and my family. I know you did it for us, so I am giving you one last chance."

"A chance for what?" I snap.

"A normal life without me." I snap my arm out, grip her throat and pull her to me as I bend so we are eye to eye.

"There is no me without you. Got that?" A devilish smirk graces her stunning face.

"Good answer, Loki." I roll my eyes. She continues to fucking call me Loki because according to her, he was a master bullshitter and the name fits me. "Follow me," she says as she yanks free of my hold. I follow her around the corner only to stumble to a stop.

"What the fuck?" I breathe out at the sight of my parents and little brother standing there with four guards standing watch. Chanel turns sideways to keep them and me in her gaze.

"The danger to them is now gone. I brought them here for you to say goodbye or if you should choose... you can leave with them." Now I get what she meant, she is offering me an out from this life. I close the space between us and kiss her. I show her without words that she is my endgame and I'm not going anywhere. I break the kiss, resting my forehead against hers, we're both breathless and panting.

"You will always be my first choice, Sin. I will choose us every time." Her eyes turn hazy. I pull away from her and face my family. The resentment I see in my parents' eyes stings but I weather it. Ash just looks pissed that he isn't the center of attention. I realize now after spending time with Chanel's family, that my own never cared about me or Marcus, they just cared about the son who was going to be famous and make enough money to fund their early retirement.

"What is the meaning of all of this, Kacey?" my mother snaps.

"You into some trouble aren't ya, boy?" Dad quips, while keeping his gaze on my sling.

"You know, everything I have done is to try to please the both of you, to make you proud of me." Dad splutters but I push on. "Marcus once told me that he could never live up to the expectations you both placed on him. I thought he was talking out of his ass. Turns out, he was right."

"What the hell are you talking about, Kacey?" Dad snaps.

"Marcus turned to drugs because of the pressure you both placed on him. I became an agent because it's what *you* wanted. Newsflash, Dad, I failed at that shit and now I'm dating the daughter of one of the most wanted men in America." My dad's eyes blaze with disgust, while my mom gasps and clasps her imaginary pearls. "I found a family, a place I finally belong. With the people I spent my life trying to put behind bars. After today, you will never see me again." Mom opens her mouth to argue but I push on. "Before you pass judgment on Chanel and her family, know this. It is because of her that you three are still alive. I hope Marcus finds peace in the afterlife because he sure as fuck didn't have it here on earth with you two." The look of indignation on their faces pisses me off. How they can stand there and act like they are innocent and had nothing to do with how their oldest son's life ended is disgraceful.

"You can't turn your back on family, we are all that you have!" Dad shouts, not caring who is around to hear him.

"Correction." At the sound of Royal's voice I spin around to find him, Vincent, Bishop, Erika and Chanel standing behind me with angry glares pointed at my family. "You were all that he had. He has a new family, and unlike the one he was born into, this one won't turn their backs on him." Fucking hell, hearing that shit come from Royal has a sense of belonging blooming inside me. Sin reaches for my hand and leads me away from my parents and their shouts for me to come back.

"What's gonna happen to them?" I ask once the five of us are in the safety of the car. Bishop drives while Vin sits shotgun and Sin takes the middle seat between Royal and me.

"They will be compensated for their time and then put on the first plane to wherever the fuck it is they want to go. They will never be able to contact you, but if you should choose to make contact with them, then you can." Unsure of what to say, I just nod my head and agree with what Chanel has said.

"How long are you going to wait before you tell Chaos?" Bishop asks, I frown and cut a glance to Royal as he runs a hand through his hair.

"I don't know," he answers honestly.

"He needs to know. You and I both know he is going to go after the Dominico family and there isn't a fucking thing we can do to stop him," Chanel adds.

"We may not be able to stop him but we are the *Memento Mori* and we do everything together. If he is going to war against the Dominico's, then we are all at fucking war!" Chanel beams at her cousin and hums her agreement. Vincent and Bishop both sigh knowing there is nothing they can do to stop their children.

"You best tell him you have the love of his brother's life locked up in your basement before he declares war on both of you." At Bishop's words my jaw unhinges.

"You have Lailani Dominico locked in your basement?" I rasp out. Chanel and Royal exchange a loaded look before my girl looks at me and bats her lashes.

"So, what's it gonna cost me to get you to keep that bit of information to yourself until we find the right time to tell Chaos?"

"Answer fucking wisely, shithead," Vincent warns, earning a chuckle from the other two males.

"Let me guess, if I don't answer correctly, you'll shoot me again?" Chanel gasps and Vincent visibly flinches.

"You shot my boyfriend?" she shouts so fucking loud Bishop swerves the car and curses under his breath.

"I missed, it's not a big deal," he lies.

"You never fucking miss, Dad!" I slouch back into my seat with a smile on my face, listening to these two bicker. I hope she rips her father a new asshole. Serves the fucker right.

Chapter Twenty-Seven

CHANEL

I lay flat on my stomach and position myself so the butt of my rifle is against my shoulder and press my eye to the scope. "In position," I say through the coms.

"All set here," comes from Royal.

"Overwatch in position in the east," Benny says.

"I got you, Kacey," comes from Ro.

"A bullet in his ass wouldn't hurt," Xav says. I chuckle but don't reply.

"Fuck you, asshole," Kacey says through clenched teeth. He stands against his car in the empty warehouse parking lot. Ever since we got back to Miami two weeks ago, Leonie and Owen have been blowing up his phone for a meet and debrief. I told him to ignore it because he doesn't owe those bastards a fucking thing. They left him out to hang after the shootout with the Albanians. The feds took no responsibility for it. To the world, Kacey is an escaped convict. I had hoped that given his history with the bureau that they would at least try to clear his name, but no. They plastered his face all over the news and put him up on the FBI's most wanted list!

"I got eyes on an unmarked car pulling in," Royal says. I go on high alert as I watch the unmarked car pull up next to Kacey. He looks like a fucking snack in his tight white shirt, dark wash jeans and Ray Ban sunglasses. His hair is a tousled blond mess but fuck, my man makes that look work. His hair is a mess because I was yanking on the strands of it half an hour ago as he fucked me in the rest room of the cafe a couple blocks away.

"Get set," I say through the coms as Owen and Leonie step out of the car. Benny, Xavier, Romeo, Royal and I are stationed on the roof tops surrounding Kacey. I know without a doubt that they are going to try and get Kacey to come in so they can pin everything on him and get him to take the wrap for their fuck up.

"Kacey," Owen says in greeting.

"Get to the point, being out in the open isn't good for me as you can imagine," Kacey bites back.

"You knew the risks," Leonie states as if that makes everything okay. This bitch put him up to going undercover one last time and never once thought to have a contingency plan.

"You knew I would be ambushed and didn't have a special ops team to pull me out," my man snaps.

"Judging from the state of the scene you had your own team," the bitch clips out.

"If I didn't, I would be dead right now or plastered across all media outlets so the Albanians could force our hand to negotiate a deal with the US government." The thought of him being tortured has my trigger finger itching to shoot the bitch. As if he has a direct line to my thoughts, his gaze flicks to me and he gives a subtle shake of his head.

"What would you have had us do? Our hands were tied, Kacey. This was supposed to be a simple ambush–"

He cuts the bitch off. "Where the fuck was the special ops team?" When the cunt doesn't answer he pushes on. "There was never a fucking team standing by, was there?" Again neither of them answer. "I would bet good money that you both hoped I would be killed so you could pin this whole thing on me. Now here is why I think that Quintin had shit on the both of you."

"Kacey, how could you think—"

"Shut the fuck up, Owen," Kace clips out. "I have some good friends who are pretty fucking amazing at recovering deleted data. You see, Benny took the hard drive from Quintin's office." I watch both the cunts stiffen and begin to fidget. "My friends were able to recover the data from the hard drive and reverse the encryption. You could imagine my shock when I found a file on the pair of you."

"That is federal property!" the bitch snaps.

"Oh, Leonie. Calm down, no one will ever know that you fucked your way to the top, provided you clear my fucking name!" Kacey roars.

"You've shacked up with the local mob. How are you any different than us?" Owen snaps back.

"I didn't just shack up with them, I am one of them now, and unless you want them to show up on your doorstep, I suggest you do as I ask." I sigh at the predictably of them when they both pull their guns and point them at Kacey.

"Put your hands behind your head, you're under arrest," Leonie shouts.

Kacey flicks his gaze to me. "Baby?" I flick the laser on my scope and aim right at the bitches head. Seconds later, four more lasers join mine and the pair of them begin to spin around in circles pointing their guns in every direction trying to find us, they never will. "You have three seconds to lower your weapons. I suggest you do it because my girl doesn't like it when my life is threatened. She tends to get a bit trigger happy." The sarcasm in his voice is thick. Owen is the first to lower his gun and raise his hands in the air.

"What the hell are you doing, he can't kill us!" Leonie screams at her partner.

"He can't, but they sure as fuck can. They were his special ops team. Did you see the carnage they left in their wake? I don't plan to be the next body with a fucking card atop of it!" Owen shouts back at her.

"Sin, give her a nudge," Royal orders. I oblige and shoot the ground right next to her foot. She screams and jumps so fucking high I can't hold the laughter that bubbles out of me.

"Ten bucks says she shit herself," Romeo wheezes out through fits of laughter.

"Loki, she has three seconds to drop the gun or I drop her." Kace smiles up at me and nods.

"You have three seconds, Leonie. My girl doesn't miss." The bitch grits her teeth and holsters her gun, then closes the space between her and Kacey. I shift so my laser is pointed at her head.

"Leo!" Owen warns but she ignores him.

"Kacey!" I grit out as the bitch leans in close to him, jealousy is something I am working on and I'll admit I am failing miserably at it. I can't stand any bitch getting close to him.

"Kace, unless you want her brain matter splattered on you, take a step back before my cousin's jealousy gets the better of her." The humor is thick in Royal's tone.

"Baby–"

The bitch cuts Kacey off. "Oh my God, are they listening in?"

"My girl has issues with me going off on my own," he says with a shrug. Leonie reaches out and snatches the earpiece from Kacey, ignoring his protests and places it on her own.

"Chanel Murelo, I presume," she says cockily.

"You assume right," I snarl.

"Why don't you come out here where I can see you and finally put a face to the name?" The others remain silent. I stand keeping my rifle aimed at her but I shift so the scope is aimed in the center of her chest where she can see.

"I'm right here bitch."

Her eyes crinkle at the corners as she stares down at the laser aimed at her chest. She tries to squint to get a better look at me but she won't see shit, thanks to the sun at my back.

"You know I will be coming after you. You have information that I can't allow to get out."

"You can try," I snarl. "You have two weeks to clear Kacey's name or I go to the congress woman Lynelle and tell her you have been fucking her husband and that little Louis that is currently being babysat at your apartment off main is her husband's bastard." Her eyes widen.

"You fucking—"

Kacey cuts off her tirade. "You finish that fucking sentence and you will have the *Memento Mori* and the Bloodhound coming after you and your son." He snatches the earpiece back from her. "Clear my fucking name, Leo, and you have my word no harm will come to your son. Fuck around and find out what happens."

Later that night Royal, Kacey, Erika and I meet Chaos at the tattoo shop where we all got our matching tattoos. I come to a stop in front of Chaos and study him. He looks like he hasn't slept in days. He's dropped out of UNLV and given up his dream of going pro in the NFL.

"You good?" I ask. He slowly lifts his gaze to mine.

"No, I'm not, but I will be when I finish what I started." Royal comes to stand beside me, his fresh ink on display. He and I got Havoc's calling cards tattooed on us but we also had the tattooist add some of Havoc's ashes in ours so he could be with us always. Royal got Hav's card tattooed on the other side of his neck. I got mine on the other side of my ribs. Chaos chose to get his brother's name across his shoulder blades with angel wings. Like us, he has Havoc's ashes in his. He wears his ring and necklace with some of Havoc's ashes in it every day and night, never taking them off.

"What are you up to?" Royal asks.

"I have a plan. I found everyone they love." His eyes darken, I see the devil in his gaze as he looks at us. "I am going to destroy them one by one, starting with that bitch."

"What do you plan to do with her?" I shoot Royal a look telling him that he needs to come clean, the bitch he speaks of is locked in our basement and it is only a matter of time before Chaos finds her.

"I plan to make them all bleed while she watches and then kill her. Once she is dealt with, I am going after Quintin's only living family member. I am going to wipe their bloodline from this fucking earth."

"How do you plan to get close enough to them?" I ask.

"I'm going make her think I'm Havoc. I plan to use the love she felt for my brother and break her emotionally before I finally kill her." Well fuck me, that shit is morbid as fuck.

"When we get home, I have to show you something," Royal says, then walks away. I feel like a weight is being lifted off me knowing he is going to finally come clean.

The moment we get home, Erika heads inside to check on London who remained at home with her tutor. The little shit refuses to go to school, so until Royal and Erika can convince her that school is good, she is being tutored at home. Chaos and Kacey follow us around the back. Royal opens the basement door and leads the way down. I've never brought Kacey down here before, so I know the sight of our little torture chamber is going to shock him. Before we round the corner, Royal stops and turns to face Chaos.

"Keep an open mind," is all he says before stepping aside and allowing Chaos to pass by. I make a snap decision to leave Chaos be and quickly lead Kacey back out the way we came. He says nothing as I lead him upstairs to our room. I know I'm a coward but I couldn't bring myself to stand there and see the look in Chaos's eyes when he comes face to face with the girl who broke his brother's heart and forced a divide between the two of them.

"You okay?" Kacey asks as I close our bedroom door. I slowly turn, face him and sigh.

"Do you think I'm a pussy for not staying down there?" His face softens as he comes forward and cups my face between his hands. He got rid of his sling two days ago. I know the wound still causes him pain but he never lets on. My dad is an asshole for shooting him!

"I fucking love the way you say pussy."

I roll my eyes and try to keep the smile off my face but fail. "I'm being serious."

"So am I," he deadpans.

"Would you stop thinking about sex for five fucking minutes?" I try to sound stern, but I can't mistake the breathy tone of my own voice.

"You say the stupidest things. How the fuck can I keep my mind out of the gutter when I have a literal porn star standing in front of me." This man, my God, he knows how to boost a woman's confidence, not that I was ever self-conscious, but if I was, Kacey would snap me out of it right quick.

"Kacey," I whine.

"Fine. I'll answer your question, but then I want you in the shower and bent over ready to take my cock." My breath hitches and a pulse begins to thrum between my thighs and butterflies begin to swirl in my belly as the anticipation builds inside me. "Answer me, Chanel."

"Y-yes." His eyes darken and fill with lust. I fight the groan from breaking free inside me.

"No, I don't think you are a pussy. I think you made the right call to allow him time to process what he is about to see. He didn't need us all crowding around him like some side show act. Now, get your fucking ass in the shower." Like a slave to its master, I practically run to the bathroom and strip my clothes off, not giving a fuck where they land. Shivers race down my spine as I turn the shower on and set it to a mild temperature, the pulse between my legs beginning to ramp up.

I keep my gaze ahead as I hear him enter the bathroom, the sexual tension thick in the air. My breaths are coming out in short rapid pants. I went years without feeling a man inside me —granted, Kacey is the only man I have ever had inside me— but now, I don't think I could go a day without the feeling of him filling me up and stretching me out. A draft hits my naked back, sending a shiver down my spine but not from the cold, my body is coiled with need. The instant I feel him pressed against my back, I melt into him and moan. His hands come around the front of me and cup my tits. They feel so full and heavy.

"Fuck, I love you." His words have me melting further into him. I feel his hard cock pressed against the swell of my ass. I tilt my head back and look up at him.

"I love you too." He pinches my nipples, drawing a sharp intake of breath from me, then seizes the opportunity and claims my mouth. The moment the taste of him hits my senses, my body takes on a mind of his own and I push my ass into him. He growls his approval.

He breaks the kiss. "You want my cock, baby?"

"Fuck, yes," I pant.

"Hands on the wall, ass out." I move at the speed of light

to obey him, needing this more than I need my next breath. He massages the globes of my ass before landing a swift smack to my right cheek. "You made me so fucking hard for you today getting all jealous." I moan when he lands another slap to my other cheek. Sue me, I have a kink for being spanked and my man knows it. "Is my pussy wet and ready for me, baby?" he asks as delivers another two hits to each of my cheeks.

"Yes, I'm fucking soaked for you," I cry out.

"I'll be the judge of that." He drops to his knees behind me, parts my cheeks and buries his face in my pussy, drawing a sharp cry from me. He sucks and licks at my clit, working me up into a frenzy. Right as I'm on the cusp of coming all over his face, he pulls back, climbs to his feet and lines his cock up with my entrance. Kacey doesn't ease inside me, he thrusts in one hard thrust that has us both crying out.

"Oh fuck."

"Take that cock like a good girl," he growls as he grips my hips and thrusts so fucking hard inside me I end up flat against the wall with my cheek pressed against the tiles. "Take that fucking cock, baby. I want to feel you strangling my dick."

"Fuck me like that, Loki. Make me come, please," I scream. He tangles his hand in my hair, yanks my head back so he can kiss me, but his pace never wavers. My orgasm tears through me without warning. I break the kiss screaming out my release. He wraps his free arm around my waist to keep me upright. He continues to fuck me hard, chasing his own release. I love watching him come. The moment his eyes meet mine, he roars my name as he comes deep inside my tight little cunt. We stay like this, panting and trying to catch our breath, then he places a soft kiss on my lips.

"You were made for me," he whispers. I open my mouth to answer him but the words die in my throat the moment we hear a gunshot ring out.

Epilogue

CHAOS

"Keep an open mind," Royal says with a stern look on his face. I say nothing as I brush past him and move around the corner. I expected to find Ricardo or one of his sons chained to a chair, but the sight of Lailani chained to the far wall has me slamming to a halt. Her big brown eyes widen at the sight of me. Her brown curly hair is cut short and looks like a tangled mess. She slowly stands, the chain on her ankle prevents her from getting anywhere near me.

Her gaze travels up and down my body, but they freeze on my neck. That's when it hits me, she's looking at Havoc's calling card. The anger that has been churning inside me for weeks resurfaces. My mouth waters for her blood to coat my hands. I want to fucking slit her throat and bathe in it. Her demise is going to be the greatest revenge I have ever known, but I won't kill her... yet. I want her to bear witness to each of her brothers dying by my hands, I'll save her father for last. I am going to make each of them suffer. They are going to feel the wrath of Chaos.

"Havoc?" The sound of her voice calls the demons inside me, a red haze takes over me as I slowly make my way toward her. The closer I get, the more tense she becomes. She keeps backing away from me until she is flush against the wall with nowhere to fucking run. I crowd her space, placing a hand either side of her head. Her chest rises and falls with quick succession.

"What's wrong, baby, you never used to fear me," I taunt. I can see it in her eyes that she isn't so sure of who I am anymore. If there was one person in this world that should have been able to tell us apart, it's her.

"Chaos," she breathes my name out like I'm the devil. I narrow my eyes and snarl at the bitch.

"You goddamn fucking right it's me," I grit out through clenched teeth.

"Where's Havoc?" She darts her gaze past me to try to find my twin. The notion that he isn't at my six burns like a fucking bitch, taking a white-hot iron to my heart would hurt less than knowing my brother isn't behind me. I grip her hair and yank forward.

"Uncuff her, now!" I seethe. Royal comes forward and unclasps the cuff around her ankle. I drag the bitch by her hair up the stairs and out the door. The moon is bright and high in the sky. I drag her to the tree line and shove her to her fucking knees. She starts to sob and shake, knowing that her life is about to end. I feel Royal close in behind me, he says nothing but remains close for support—not that I need it. I pull my gun from my waistband allowing it to hang loosely in my grasp at my side.

"Where is Havoc?" she chokes out as she lifts her tear-stained face to me. The sight of her doe eyes and the innocent look on her face disgusts me. How the fuck could I let this bitch come between me and my brother? She nearly destroyed us. *I* nearly allowed her to.

"You know he loved you?" She sucks in a sharp intake of air. "He was head over heels in love with you. I knew something was up with him back at UNLV. When he met you, he started blowing me off, skipping training and meet ups with Royal and Sin. So, one night, I followed him." Her eyes widen.

"You tricked me on purpose?" she whispers.

I smile darkly down at her. "Damn fucking right I did. I wanted to show my brother that your pussy wasn't anything special."

"Fuck you," she snaps.

"I thought he would get over you after catching us fucking. Turns out, he never did. He helped me get rid of Ricco Vargas for you. He killed the son of a cunt and dropped his body in the ocean. He would have done anything for you!" I shout.

"You fucking tricked me! He never told me he had a twin," she screams back.

"You should have known the difference between us!" I counter.

"I fucking hate you."

Lifting my gun, I point it at her head. "The feeling is mutual." I cock the trigger ready to end the cunts' worthless life.

"Where is he? He needs to know before you do this," she pleads. Pain blooms in my chest, I feel the burning sensation of his loss coursing through my veins. Losing a sibling is hard but he wasn't just a sibling, he was my womb mate, my day fucking one. Havoc and I were ride or die till the bitter fucking end!

"He's fucking gone!" I scream. "Your cunt of a father took him from me."

"No, no, no he can't be," she begins to ramble in a panicked state.

"He can't save you now," I snarl. Her brown eyes snap to

mine. At one point in my life, I thought I loved this conniving bitch. I know she never felt the same about me. She was always in love with Havoc. He was it for her, which is why I am going to make her pay for the fucking pain she caused the most important person in my life.

"It's not me I'm worried about," she whispers brokenly.

"Who the fuck are you worried about? A selfish cunt like you cares for no one except yourself. My brother was proof of that!" I push in a cold tone, her bottom lip begins to tremble and she shakes her head. Narrowing my eyes, I step forward looming above her. Trembles begin to tear through her, I relish in the sight of having a Dominico on their knees before me. I wanted to save her for last but the need for one of those cunts blood to coat my hands overpowers me.

"If he finds out, he will kill him, Chaos!" she cries. I feel Royal come up beside me.

"Kill who?" Royal presses. Lailani keeps her gaze on me, she implores me with a look to try understand. Truth is, I don't give a fuck what she has to say. Nothing that comes out of her lying mouth will change my mind on killing her.

"I had to keep it a secret after he cut me off..." Sobs claw out of her.

"Answer him, bitch, or I swear to God I will end you now," I seethe.

"Kill me but for the love of God please save him from my father." I crinkle my brow. What the fuck is this bitch on about?

"Save who?" Royal pushes.

Her gaze bores into mine. "Your nephew." I stumble backward and smack into Royal, my gun beginning to shake as I stare down at her, trying to gauge if she is lying. There is no fucking way Havoc had a kid and didn't tell me, right?

"You're full of shit, I know for a fact Havoc hasn't seen you—"

She cuts Royal off. "In one year, nine months. I didn't find out I was pregnant until three weeks after I last slept with Havoc, which was two weeks after he found me with Chaos. We got drunk and it was our way of saying goodbye. I only found out I was pregnant when my father brought me home to marry me off to Ricco."

"You're a fucking liar!" I shout.

"I swear to God I'm not. Kill me but please just save my son from my father. He doesn't know Havoc is his father, that's the only reason my dad hasn't hurt him. Chaos, why do you think I agreed to marry Halil?" She doesn't give me a chance to answer. "If I didn't do it, he would hurt my son."

"Havoc... has a one-year-old son," I mutter. Lani nods her head. I struggle to come to terms with what she is saying. This bitch is a liar and I know without a doubt she would have used this baby to get my brother back. "Prove it," I snarl as I step forward and press the barrel of the gun between her eyes. Her eyes dart around as if she is thinking of a way to either prove she is telling the truth or trying to come up with a better lie.

Her brows raise as she snaps her gaze back to me. She lifts her hand and yanks her necklace from her neck and holds it out to me. I frown down at the fucking sphere shaped looking thing with disdain.

"Use your phone's torch and shine it on it. It has a picture of him in there." I snatch the fucking necklace and grab the phone Royal holds out to me, turning the torch on. "It's a wear Felicity, they hold pictures of your loved ones but to the naked eye you won't see it until up close." I shoot her a glare before handing my gun to Royal. I shine the torch on the thing and bring it to my eye, it takes a minute for my eye to focus, the moment they do, my heart stills.

Scruffy brown hair and bright green eyes stare back at me. He has the same button nose and cupid's bow as Havoc. I'm frozen in place as pain explodes inside me. I toss the phone to Royal then snatch my gun back off him.

"What's his name?" I say in a deadly calm tone.

She darts her tongue out to moisten her lips. "To my father and the rest of my family he has the last name Dominico," I growl.

"What is his fucking name?" I roar.

"His name is... Ryat and he is a year old."

"Whose last name does he have on his birth certificate?" I wait with bated breath for her to answer. If his last name is what I think it is, then a war is about to ensue and the entirety of the Murdoch Mafia and the *Memento Mori* will reign hell on those sons of bitches. I will take everything from them, slaughtering anyone they hold near and dear before taking over their territory and claiming it as mine. Once I have succeeded in that, then I will go after Quintin's last living family member and destroy his bloodline.

Her gaze bores into mine. "Havoc's... His name is Ryat Murdoch." Without thought, I lift my gun and fire.

The Jack of Spades has been laid, they marked for the coming Chaos where I will make sure Havoc reigns on their family.

Pre Order In Havoc lies Chaos

THANK YOU

Don't hate me!
I know this book was rough and the feels you must be in after that loss but trust me! I swear I will mend your heart and put you back together again, that's a lie. I'm going to shatter your heart all over again before fixing it and hoping you will still love me. Chanel is one of my all time fav FMC and I fucking love her book so much! She is one badass and fucking takes no shit from anyone.
I love Royal, Chanel, Havoc and Chaos so much but please bear with me because this series will not go how you think it will. There will be situations where you will doubt me and want to cause bodily harm but trust the process and I swear it will be worth it.

Chaos's book– In Havoc Lays Chaos is next.

Again, thank you so much for taking a chance and reading this book. It means more than you will ever know. If you could leave a review on **Amazon, Goodreads *or* Bookbub** I would be ever so grateful.

Ruined By The Rook

<u>Murdoch Mafia Novella</u>

Stalemate

<u>Memento Mori Series</u>

Reign Of Royal

Broken By Sin

In Havoc Lays Chaos

<u>Fairytales With A Twist</u>

Condemned Beast

Sports Romance

<u>Playing For Keeps</u>

Offside

Touchdown

End Game

Hail Mary

Blindside

RH Sports

Hate Us Like You Mean It

Love Me Like You Mean It

Acknowledgments

Marcus, you set a challenge for me to write another 12 books for a year and here I am trying to smash that goal because we all know I am a sore loser. If I don't win, there will be no happy endings for you for many, many months, my friend! My demon spawn, I fucking love you both so much but dear God, you both do my head in when you fight. Always remember that no matter what happens in life, that you two will always have each other. Mummy loves you both more than you will ever comprehend.

My sissy, girl this one's for you because you remind me so much of Sin. You are a badass in your own right and honest to God, I fucking love you so much!

Also, I have to give my dad a shout out because you are the baddest motherfucker I know! Thank you for everything you do and have done for me, Mark and the kids. Boss, I wouldn't be where I am or who I am today without you. I love you so fucking much, old boy!

Thank you to my alpha and beta girls for all your hard work with this book and Royal, you ladies have no idea how much I adore and love each of you. These books would not be what they are without each of you xxxx

My Army: Alicia, Amber, Angel, Ash, Barb, Charlotte, Cyndi, Christina, Debbie, Jasmine, Jen, Kahanna, Katelyn, Kylie, Lakshmi, Lora, Lyndsey, Rebecca, Rizzo, Sarmi, Sonya, Terri and Tess. Thank you ladies so fucking much for being the best freaking team an author could ask for. Without all of you I

wouldn't be here and your support and constant love of each
of these characters means more than you will ever know xxx
Jaye-fucking-Pratt, thank you! That's all you're getting
because your ego is big enough without me saying some nice
shit about you, if you wan to sook call my kids they will boost
your ego!
My Dirty Dark Delicious Queens, I fucking love you all.
Thank you so much for being the best fucking hype squad and
supporting me this year through my crazy ass release schedule
and believing in me to hit this crazy as fuck goal!
My street team. Thank you so much for everything you do and
all the shares as well as pimping out each of these books all
over the socials. You ladies are amazing! Thank you for sticking
by me and loving each of these men and women the way
you do.
My editor, Lizz, you are the bomb.com and no one can tell me
otherwise. Thank you for always fitting me in and helping me
perfect these books. None of these would be what they are
without you. Thank you, my friend.
Leah Maree, what more can I say aside from I bow down to
you, Guru. You are the most fantastic human I have ever met.
You, my dark little soul, are amazing and I fucking love you.
Thank you for all the teasers and these amazing as fuck covers.
I couldn't do any of this without ya, babe.
Last but not least, you, my amazing readers, you mean
everything to me! Without you none of this would be possible.
Thank you for your continued support and reading my books.
It still stuns me to get messages from you telling me you love
my books. I really am living my dream and that's thanks to you.
Sam

About the Author

Samantha Barrett is a dark romance, PNR author who loves to write out-of-the-box stories. She is originally from the land of the long white cloud, New Zealand. She is totally fluking her way through this whole author gig, if she isn't writing you can find her kicking back with her kids and husband with a bag of chips and a glass of wine in her hand.

Sam loves Twilight and is a TWIHARD proudly.